UNTIL THE DAWN

Until the Dawn

To Teddy – king of the bar artists. Thanks for the

Alec Clayton

drawing.

Alec Clayton
1/20/01

Copyright © 2000 by Alec Clayton.

ISBN #:   Softcover   0-7388-3153-0

All rights reserved. No part of this book may be reproduced or transmitted in any form or by any means, electronic or mechanical, including photocopying, recording, or by any information storage and retrieval system, without permission in writing from the copyright owner.

This is a work of fiction. Names, characters, places and incidents either are the product of the author's imagination or are used fictitiously, and any resemblance to any actual persons, living or dead, events, or locales is entirely coincidental.

To order additional copies of this book, contact:
Xlibris Corporation
1-888-7-XLIBRIS
www.Xlibris.com
Orders@Xlibris.com

CONTENTS

Acknowledgements 9

1982 SoHo 11

Tupelo, Mississippi 1919 16

1982 The New Cedars Bar Manhattan, New York 21

1920 Magazine Street, Tupelo 24

Broome Street Gallery 31

Tupelo 34

SoHo Spring of 1982 45

1940s Tupelo 51

Willis Heights 61

Spring, 1982 79

Tupelo 82

The War Years 92

New Beginnings 105

1960 Tupelo 109

Labor Day Weekend 116

Spring of 1961 Tupelo 160

The sixties 172

1982 182

Mary Walker Bayou 190

Red Warner's Journal 197

Epilogue 233

Teddy m Haggarty
01-20-2001
Tacoma

DEDICATION

For my son Noel, with pride.

In memory of Bill, 1978-1995.

Rita + I called Noel Rockmore "our wayward son"

Jazz Bones muval dedicated to Noel Rockmore

"I'm a twin & it's my birthday"

"Did you see the article I wrote on Jazz Bones?"

ACKNOWLEDGEMENTS

For her tremendous work editing the manuscript in its many permutations, and for her brilliant cover art, I am indebted to my wife, Gabi Clayton.

For their encouragement and helpful editorial comments, I want to thank Larry Johnson, Catherine Dawdy, Pam Patterson, Tracey Thornton, Steve Schalchlin, Linda Dahlstrom, Michael Sugar, Valerie Peralta and Noel Clayton.

1982
SoHo

Painting can be an evil mistress. She can love you tender and she can love you raunchy, and she can rip your guts apart.

When you put that last stroke on your canvas and you know you've done it right, and you step back to look at what you've done, a deep sigh comes all the way up from your loins and you say "Yes! Yes, by God, I did it."

But it can also be like a cramp in the pit of your stomach that wrenches your intestines and won't let go; because to make a painting you have to reach deep down inside and pull it out, and when it doesn't come it's like the dry heaves. And the loneliness of it! The loneliness is unbearable. You're all alone in a huge loft and you're slinging paint with concentration so intense it's exhausting, and when you finally set your paint bucket down and step back to see what you've done there is not a soul to share that moment with, be it ecstasy or be it loathing; because you've experienced a rape or a battle or the most tender of caresses, and it was all between you and that goddamn canvas; and suddenly you get this memory flash from back when you were in art school and your professors ripped your work apart, and you look at your painting and you can't even see it. You haven't the slightest idea whether it's art or crap. So you grab the freight elevator down to the street and you walk to the corner bar and get gloriously drunk.

* * *

Red Warner wrote those words. He wrote them in that bold scrawl of his. He wrote them in his journal not long after his final exhibition and that now-famous party that ended with a scream and a mad rush of fleeing bodies, and Red Warner slumped on the floor in a pool of blood like the day's washing from a slaughterhouse.

He also wrote in that hallucinatory journal:

> After that I went berserk, raving around town with Cassie at my heels trying valiantly to hold me back.
>
> Time now expands and contracts. Memory and dreams and imaginings all become twisted like taffy in the hands of a madman. I'm sitting in a green aluminum boat on the bayou, recuperating. A dirty bandage. Warm beer, the taste of bile in my mouth. Confused memories. Brother Barnes in his black suit worn silver at the elbows, and wearing a white shirt and skinny black tie that cuts into his puffy, red neck like wire on a post, shouting, "Oh you vile generation of fornicators and blasphemers!" And I'm racing around the loft, swinging a butcher knife, and blood is gushing like gooey cadmium red squeezed from a tube, and the ceiling beams are swelling as if pumped with helium and they're swirling and swirling in a slow motion pool of crimson and black.
>
> My comings and goings are like debris in a tornado, all whirling and blowing and converging like the eye of the storm in a single moment and a single place. And Redneck Red Warner is the "I" of the

storm when some two hundred or so idiots crowd into my loft. Whores and pimps off the avenue and leather boys from the West Side bars and a slew of artsy hangers-on, and some dame named Dianna wearing black lace undies and spike heels and nothing else. Couples of both sexes groping each other. Air dense with the smell of marijuana and cigarette smoke. Something snaps in my mind again, and again and again, and suddenly I'm standing on top of a table in the kitchen area, shouting words from the Book of Job in the *Bible*—words that I never remember reading. I'm standing in the pulpit, calling them sinners to repentance, shouting with a righteous rhythm and providing the A-mens my own self.

If in bed I say,
A-men!
When shall I arise?
I am filled with restlessness . . .
Filled with it, filled with it!

I am filled with restlessness until the dawn. My days are swifter than a weaver's shuttle; they come to an end without hope. Remember that my life—My life, sweet Jesus—it is like the wind; I shall not see happiness again.

I jump off the table and grab a butcher knife from the counter and start weaving through the crowd, swinging the blade like a sword and screaming, "Scabs on humanity! Your days are numbered. Fornicators and liars, sucking off my fame and my talent."

I rip my shirt off and fling it away.

The idiots applaud. They started ripping their own shirts. Tattered garments in the air.

"I rend my garments!" I scream, "I'm a weird, wacko, washed up fool who can't even put his queer shoulder to the wheel (borrowing from Ginsberg). I used to be a simple country boy from Mississippi, but my pecker got me in a mess of trouble."

...And I raised the knife high over my head and shouted...

* * *

I slammed the journal pages shut. I could not read the next sentence. I did not have to read any more to find out the next chapter in Red Warner's story, because I was there with him. One way or another I'd been with him all along.

I knew him when he was a kid, before he took the name Red, back when he was plain ol' Travis Earl Warner. We grew up together. We were close. I was with him from the first time he played hooky back in Church Street Elementary School until he graduated from Tupelo High and went off to study art at the Memphis Art Academy. But I was not with him when he was the only witness in a murder case and had to give testimony that would send one or another friend to prison, and I was not with him when he fled Tupelo in shame. Later, when he became famous, I followed him from a distance, keeping up with his shenanigans through the art magazines and the stylish gossip rags. Finally, when he vanished after that last show and everyone was wondering whether he was dead or alive, I took it upon myself to find him. I spent the last few years putting the pieces together, talking to Mama Marybelle, trying to figure out what turned Travis Earl into Red Warner, trying to figure out what made him freak out the way he did, and trying to figure out if he was still among the living (which I never really doubted) and if so, where he might have gone.

To tell his story right, I need to tell it the way I told it to Jimmy on that long drive from New York to Tupelo. I've got to start back before Travis and I were even born. I've got to tell about his grandfather, Rudy Sullivan and his mother, Marybelle, and the Warner family who more or less adopted Marybelle when she was carrying Travis in her womb.

TUPELO, MISSISSIPPI
1919

In the fall of 1919 Rudy Sullivan walked into the imposing lobby of the Warner Bank. Smack in the middle of the lobby there was a fishpond, skirted by tropical plants. A dozen goldfish swam lazily in that pond. Rudy sidled up to the pond, his red, lumpy hands crushing the shapeless hat that he held against the crotch of his overalls. He dipped his hat in the water and wrung it out, then used the wet hat as a rag to wipe his sweaty brow, pushing aside the unruly strands of red hair that were sticking to his eyebrows. A bank teller pointed him out with a curt nod of her head, and said something to the customer who was standing at her window, a plump young woman with a severe hairdo. The young woman turned to look at Rudy. She shook her head and contorted her face into an expression that said, What's this world coming to? She stuffed her money into her purse, snapped it shut, and huffed to the door.

Rudy Sullivan recognized her. She was the new teacher at Tupelo High, where he worked as custodian. Mabel Cook by name. She directed the school choir and was a stickler for penmanship and insisted students address her as Mrs., even though she was an old maid. When not teaching, she spent her time playing piano for Calvary Baptist Church or teaching private music lessons in the parlor of her little house on the hill across the street from the old diner.

"Afternoon, Ma'am," Rudy drawled.

She swept past him and flung open the outside door. Nearby, another door stood partly ajar. The name inscribed on its brass plate was: Charles Warner, President. Rudy approached Charles Warner's office with a sideways gait and leaned around to peek in. Seeing that the office was empty, he sat down on a lushly padded wooden chair with an elaborately carved back and claw feet. He sat forward on the edge of the seat, his demolished hat clamped between his knees.

"Excuse me, sir," a lady said, "is there something we can help you with?"

"No Ma'am. I'm waitin' to see the coach, uh . . . Mr. Warner."

"I'm sorry, but he is not here right now. Could someone else help you?"

"Oh no Ma'am. I got to see Mr. Charlie. I don't mind waitin'."

Charles Warner was a legendary figure in north Mississippi, and Rudy Sullivan had seen the legend take shape. He had been in the stands at Tupelo High the year before the war broke out when Charlie had scored three touchdowns against Fulton. He had stood on the curb in front of the Rexall Drugs at the end of that war when Charlie had marched down Main Street in his uniform, with tears glistening in his eyes and medals sparkling on his chest, confetti flying, and people weeping. Charlie had been awarded the Purple Heart and the big one, the Medal of Honor, and he limped, because he had taken one in the leg.

Charlie's father had died at an early age. Charlie was in Europe at the time and did not receive the news until the war was over and he was on his way home to be greeted by Tupelo with a hero's welcome. Privately he was welcomed home by his wife, Becky, their daughter Becky, and his two-year old son, Chuck, whom he had never seen. Almost immediately he had to take over the responsibility of running a bank that had been held together by mostly luck since his father passed away. Charlie stuffed his uniform into a trunk, dug a suit out of mothballs and walked into the respectability and fortune that was his rightful due as heir to an old and worthy family, and as Tupelo's most illustrious son.

Rudy Sullivan's world was far removed from Charlie Warner's, even if the little shack where Rudy lived in East Tupelo was only a thirty-minute walk from the Warner Bank. His shotgun shack was perched on a rise in the middle of a field that was flooded half the year, in that godforsaken bottomland that splays out between the fairgrounds and the red clay cliffs east of town.

Some of the guys who hung out with Rudy in the cafe down on East Main had been known to make some pretty nasty remarks about the Warners, and about anybody else who had more than five bucks for that matter, calling them money grubbing and tight fisted. Having never been the kind of guy who liked to argue a point unless he had to, and not really caring too much one way or another, Rudy always let such comments slide. But back at home he'd talk about it to Nora Lee, saying things like, "Some folks are downright spiteful. They's folks that hate old Charlie just 'cause they ain't got nothing and he got just about everything. But I figure God's got His purpose in making some folks rich and others poor, and if anybody deserves to have it made, I reckon that'd be Charlie Warner. 'Sides, didn't he ask me to help him move in when he bought the Simpson house, and didn't he pay me right good? And when he built the ballpark for the kids and asked people to donate their help, didn't I work 'til after dark three days running without ever asking for a red cent? I say one hand washes the other. That's what I say."

The afternoon sun cast violet shadows across the Warner Bank lobby. Rudy watched the shadows crawl over the edge of the fishpond, creating cool spots into which the goldfish settled. After a while he heard the uneven clump of Charlie Warner's approaching steps. When he stood up to intercept him, a secretary scurried to place herself between them. She said, "This gentleman has been waiting to see you, Mr. . . ."

"Hey Rudy. How's the missus?" Charlie broke in, signaling the secretary to get back to her desk.

Rudy said, "We'uz all just fine, Coach... uh, Mister..."

"You wanted to see me?"

"Yassuh, I uh..."

"Well come on in. Have a seat."

Charlie directed Rudy to a chair next to the mahogany desk. The office was rich in manly browns. A profusion of photographs covered the wall: family photographs, his high school class picture, shots of Charlie and Ed Hooper and some other man proudly hefting strings of speckled trout on a pier in Gulfport.

"What can I do for you, Rudy?" Charlie asked.

"Well Coach, it seems I done gone and got my Nora Lee in a family way."

"That's wonderful, Rudy."

"Yassuh. Sure is. But this ain't the first time. She done lost two younguns and she's mighty sceered this time. Doc Littlejohn told her she best not try birthin' at home again, and... well, to tell the truth, I cain't afford to put her in the hospital."

"Don't you worry, Rudy. We'll work something out."

Rudy stood up. He said, "I ain't gonna take no charity, Coach. What I thought was, maybe I can do some work for you. I know you got that big house on Magazine Street. Must be a tol'able 'mount of work needed around a house that big."

Charlie knew good and well that Rudy's health was not good, and that it was all he could do to hold down his job at the school and try to keep that miserable little dirt farm of his from killing him. "I'll tell you what, Rudy," he said, "I can't think of much that's needed by way of building or yard work—maybe come spring—but there's a powerful lot of cleaning and what-not needed inside. Now the way I see it, it'll be a few good months before Nora Lee gets too far along to tend house, and we need a good housekeeper. If she could help

Becky with the ironing and house cleaning, we could pay her a decent wage. Then after she has the baby and is back on her feet we can take out of her pay, say five dollars a week. That way it won't be charity, not really. I'll pay the doctor and Nora Lee's wages'll take care of it, and you'll never miss the money. Besides, Becky could really use the help."

Rudy sat back down and muttered, "That's awful good of you, but that's . . . that's nigger work." Immediately he jumped back to his feet, and in a rush of apology said, "Shucks, I shouldn't a said that. Nawsuh, I didn't mean it a'tol. It's mighty kind of you. Nora Lee'll be glad to work for your missus. I'll tell her right away. We'll be beholden to ya."

1982
THE NEW CEDARS BAR
MANHATTAN, NEW YORK

The New Cedars Bar was dark inside. A deeply scarred mahogany bar that looked somewhat like a whale washed onto shore dominated the narrow room. Diffracted afternoon light slanted through dusty windows that opened onto Broome Street, casting a parallelogram net of yellow on the hands of chess players who nursed their beers while plotting their next moves. A stream of dust motes floated from there to the corner booth where Randall Jarrett, the art critic, lounged in his black suit, watching the men at the bar. They were an intimate group, argumentative and familiar. They arranged themselves casually on their bar stools in a triad, like a Renaissance composition, with the burly redhead in the center. He was wearing paint-splattered overalls and a plaid shirt with a frayed collar. He sat loosely on his stool, and his heavy body lurched when he laughed—which he did often and loudly. Everyone in the New Cedars Bar turned at the sound of his booming laugh.

He swiveled around and hefted his beer mug as if proposing a toast, and announced, "I'm for an art that ejaculates!"

Randall Jarret smiled to himself with a smile that said here he goes again.

A group of out-of-towners who had drifted in carrying packages from a nearby boutique stopped and looked at each other, questioning their choice of bars.

Red Warner bellowed, "I'm for anarchistic art! I'm for an artist who turns down galleries. I'm for an artist who vanishes, only to reappear ten years later as a fisherman living in the wilderness. I'm for Goya's madness and van Gogh's ear and Rothko's suicide! I'm for confrontational desperational art!"

Randall Jarrett shook his head, wondering where he had heard it before, that repeated phrase, "I am for an art, I am for an art." It was something he should know. Red Warner was quoting somebody, but Jarrett couldn't figure out whom.

A big grin played across Red Warner's face. Blue eyes alive like lasers, red-rimmed and swollen, he scanned his audience, recognizing the art critic in the corner. Good. With any luck his aphorisms would be quoted in Wednesday's paper. It had been a long time since his name had been in print, and he needed any publicity he could get—especially now, with his show scheduled to open in two weeks and his career on the downturn.

Red Warner had come to New York from a little town down south. He had come to town, and he had made it. Made it big. His paintings were on the cover of *Art News* and *Art Forum*. He showed up in gossip columns and was considered a must on the guest lists of anyone who was anyone. He was, for a while, the darling of the art world; famous for his outrageous way of talking, a hybrid of Beat Era speed rapping and Southern revivalist preaching, for his legendary debauchery, and, of course, for those harshly dramatic abstract paintings that made viewers so deliciously uneasy. But at the height of his career his work fell out of fashion. Critics said he was undisciplined and accused him of repeating himself—as if every other artist in New York didn't do the same, as if the market and the gallery system and those self-same critics didn't demand it of them.

His dealer, Leo Garner, threatened to drop him if his next show was not a success, and he had been painting with a vengeance for the past month, determined to shock the art world with a new, more powerful Red Warner. He had been living on speed and booze and coffee and cigarettes, going without sleep until he dropped, stopping his frenzied work only long enough to stagger down to the New Cedars Bar to make an occasional appearance.

The chess players and the art critic and Red's fellow artists at the bar all swam in a haze of tears before his burning, booze-bleary eyes. He said, "I am for an art that destroys itself through its own excesses. Down with namby-pamby, non-committal art. Down with no-hand-of-the-artist art. Down with . . ."

What? Red Warner had never before been at a loss for words. Years before he had created and perfected a public persona that he called the Redneck Dean Moriarty, an alter ego patterned after Kerouac's character from *On The Road*, with a heavy dose of Southern black and revivalist preacher lingo. This character was never at a loss for words. He could spew forth an endless tidal wave of poetry, with never a pause to let his thoughts catch up.

So how could he end his dangling sentence? He thought quickly and said, "Down with this beer," and swigged the liquid down in a series of great gulps. Then he pushed himself off the bar stool and walked out of the bar and across Broome Street. Everyone in the bar watched him step onto the loading dock and unlock the freight elevator and disappear into his loft, where he had been working on a new series of paintings. Word was this new work would either be the most revolutionary thing since de Kooning's *Woman I* or the pitiful, dying gasp of a no-talent painter who had made it big on sheer bravado. Most bets were on the latter, partly out of envy.

1920
Magazine Street, Tupelo

Across from the Warner house a foot path ran between the Casey's and Doc Littlejohn's, through a short stretch of woods and over the railroad tracks. The path led to a horseshoe-shaped street lined with ramshackle Negro shacks. If a stranger followed that path, he would be surprised when it opened into the Negro community, which was hidden like a clearing in a forest. Hidden from sight and out of time, it remained a vestigial community. The people who lived there called it the Alley. Probably older residents could recall that the Alley had come into being when the elite of Tupelo's pioneering families built their homes and situated their servants in easy proximity. Many of the homes in the Alley were homes without men, or they were homes in which the men were too old or too crippled or too defeated to work. Most of the women worked as maids in the homes of white women who lived in stately old homes shaded by oak and magnolia on nearby Church Street and Magazine Street and Green Street.

The white women who lived in the big houses where these Negro women worked were fond of saying that their maids were like members of the family. Most of the big houses had a spare room off the kitchen and, at special times such as a wedding or family reunion, the maids would work late and stay over in the spare room.

Charlie and Becky Warner had never hired a full-time maid, but when they threw parties, which was at least once a month, a Negro woman named Christine walked over from the Alley to clean up. After Nora Lee went to work for Charlie and Becky, both Nora Lee and Christine were brought in on special occasions. Often Becky insisted that Nora Lee stay over in the spare room. Nora Lee's health was not good. The Warners fretted over her.

Early mornings found the Negroes walking in twos and threes down the path between Casey's and Doc Littlejohn's. Doc Littlejohn would stand outside and greet them as they passed, inquiring about their health and about their families and, since they were all patients of his, he would often hand them drug samples given to him by the salesman from Memphis.

After greeting Doc Littlejohn, the women would part with lackadaisical waves and walk to their various white ladies' homes, where they would enter through the kitchen doors.

Rudy Sullivan would pull his old Dodge pickup to the curb in front of the Warner house and let Nora Lee out. He always got out himself and walked around to open the door for her, and she always sat with her hands in her lap while he did this. At first, Nora Lee waited until she saw that all the Negro maids going into adjacent houses were inside, but after a few weeks she started getting out as soon as they arrived, because she came to know the other women and looked forward to the few moments every morning in which they exchanged gossip about their employers.

In the teachers' lounge at the high school, Mabel Cook said, "Doesn't that Charlie Warner beat all! Who else but Charlie would think to hire a white nigger?"

One morning after Nora Lee had been working for the Warners for a few months, and was well past her due date, she was standing on the curb talking to Luella, who worked for Mrs. Long, and Jocelyn, who worked for old man Culpepper, when suddenly her water broke. She gasped and grabbed herself, and the two women looked down, then they shouted, "Miz Warner! Miz Warner! Come quick!"

Becky Warner rushed out and shoved Nora Lee into her car and drove her to the hospital. She called the school and left a message for Rudy, who was in the middle of some plumbing work and could not leave, and she called Charlie, who left the bank and rushed to the hospital.

The baby did not come until late that night. She was a beautiful little girl, and loud. Her coloring was that of a week-old infant, with none of the redness that is common with newborns. A fine film of red hair covered her head. It was this combination of red hair and an almost olive complexion that made her such a strikingly beautiful child.

Nora Lee convalesced in the room off the Warner's kitchen. For the first few weeks it seemed she would never regain her strength and be able to handle normal household duties; Becky and Christine tended her every need, and bathed and changed the baby. If Nora Lee had not breast fed the baby she would have had absolutely nothing to do, because Becky and Christine wouldn't let her lift a finger.

Rudy, intimidated by all the women, stayed away.

When the baby, named Marybelle, learned to crawl, it was in the Warner kitchen, prodded by four-year old Chuck, who teased her with a rattle, gradually moving it away as she reached for it until she had no choice but to crawl after it.

As soon as she was able to, Nora Lee went back home to Rudy, but she kept on working as the Warners' maid. Rudy drove her into town from East Tupelo six days a week. She brought baby Marybelle with her, of course. As usual, Rudy dropped her off at the curb every morning, where she stood on the sidewalk, Marybelle on her hip, gossiping with Luella and Jocelyn.

At work, Nora Lee was not so much a maid as a helpmate. Becky Warner would sit at the table with her and shuck corn and shell peas, while Marybelle played with a rattle and a rag doll on a quilt on the kitchen floor. Little Chuck brought toys down from his room for the baby to play with, but she paid little attention to them. Whenever the women had to leave Marybelle alone, they would say, "Chuck, you watch the baby now. Don't let her put anything in her mouth." And except for the few times he gave in to urges to pull her hair or tease her by taking away her rattle, he was a reliable baby sitter.

Nora Lee would say, "Lawdee, Miz Warner..."

"Becky."

"Yessum, Becky. (She never could get used to addressing her employer with such familiarity.) "These kids are gonna grow up not knowing who is whose mom."

Everybody seemed happy except for Rudy, who complained that Marybelle would grow up expecting to lead the good life like Becky Warner, and would be sorely let down. Mabel Cook, who had no reason to express an opinion on the subject but did anyway, agreed with Rudy, but for reasons of her own. "It's not healthy," she declared at her Thursday afternoon bridge club, "If we all treated our domestic help the way Becky Warner does, pretty soon there'd be no class distinctions at all. Now wouldn't that be a fine kettle of fish."

The Warners took the Memphis *Commercial Appeal* and Becky saved the Sunday edition for Nora Lee, who read the society pages avidly. She would talk to Becky about ladies whose pictures constantly turned up in the Memphis paper, gushing over them as if they were personal friends; and she would show the pictures to Marybelle, who would try to crumble the pages and cram them in her mouth. "She's going to grow up to be a newspaper woman," Charlie liked to say. "Time she's three she'll have printers' ink in her blood."

Chuck taught her to walk, with the patience that only a child can have with another child—patience that would occasionally give way to sudden temper tantrums, moments of surrender to an unreasonable desire to hit the baby or pinch her, just to make her cry. Of course he never did such things when an adult was watching. He was a good baby sitter, but not perfect.

When Marybelle grew old enough to play in the yard without constant adult supervision, Chuck was her guardian and playmate. When she grew older still and displayed an inquisitive nature, he taught her the facts of life as he understood them.

"When I grow up," she said, "I'm going to marry you."

"You can't marry me, silly. I'm your brother. You can't marry your brother."

"Why not?"

"You just can't."

Shortly thereafter he got his facts straightened out, and he announced to her, "You don't have a brother, silly. You're just the maid's girl." That made her cry.

He reversed his stance again when she entered first grade at Church Street Primary. He introduced her to his friends as his little sister. She had grown into a stunning little girl who was almost a head taller than most of her classmates and looked far too mature for her age. With the complexion of a brunette and that glowing red hair, she was radiant, so much so that she won the blue ribbon in her age division in the Little Miss TVA Pageant. Each little girl in the pageant was escorted on stage by an older boy. Chuck escorted Marybelle, and people in the audience said they looked like sweethearts, and that Marybelle's poise was a cute counterpoint to Chuck's clumsy little swagger. He was going through growth spurts in those years. One year he would shoot up like a beanstalk and be all gangly, uncoordinated legs and arms all out of proportion to his little trunk; the next year he would fatten out and be as chubby as could be. The year of the pageant was one of his fat years.

He avoided Marybelle during those years, and when he could not avoid her, he either tormented her or ignored her. Charlie and Becky apologized for him to Nora Lee and assured her that Chuck would grow out of it, which he did, of course.

Shortly before the Depression, Charlie Warner bought a chain of movie houses, not so much as an investment, he jokingly told Becky, but because he wanted to close down the theater in Saltillo, which was losing money, and confiscate the equipment to show home movies. He also invested in a meat packing plant, because he had met a man "who makes the best damn sausage you ever put in your mouth." There were other investments, too, all made for similar reasons; all small companies that for various reasons were not hurt by the Depression.

Rudy Sullivan was not so fortunate. In the first year after the crash, the school board decided that a hired janitor was an unnecessary expense. The teachers could take care of his chores. Mr. Preston told Rudy on a Friday that his services would no longer be needed. The following Monday morning Rudy showed up for work as usual. When he was gently reminded that he no longer worked for the school, he said, "I know that, Mr. Preston, but what else am I 'posed to do? If I don't work I'll just wind up gettin' drunk."

"But . . . but you can't simply . . . "

Rudy interrupted. "You ever been down't the fairgrounds of a morning? 'Course not. If you did, I tell you what you'd see. You'd see 'bout twenty 'r thirty men lollin' around wid nothing in this world to do. Waitin' for a truck to come by and a man to holler out, 'Need a couple of men to work!' But them trucks don't hardly ever come by, and when they do they don't never want but one 'r two men. The rest of 'em just sits. Sooner 'r later they gets into a crap game and somebody breaks out a bottle of shine. Mr. Preston, them men is starving. They wives and chilluns is starving. And it just gets worse and worse. Nawsuh, I ain't gonna do that. I'll be here every day to work, and if you cain't pay me, I'll be here anyhow."

They lived on Nora Lee's wages. Charlie and Becky gave her a raise, hoping that would help out, and Becky gave her leftovers to take home for supper, and hand-me-down clothes.

Once Nora Lee went home, beaming, to show Rudy her new clothes. "Look here, honey," she said, "I've got a yellow sundress, practically store-bought, and a Sunday meeting dress and . . ."

"Where did you get 'em?"

"Miz Warner give 'em to me."

"Well that's nice, honey, but we don't need to be taking no charity. What I think you best do is just take 'em and give 'em to one of them colored women down't the Alley. They need 'em more'n you do. You don't need no fancy dresses. If you did, I'd buy 'em for you."

Becky Warner was surely surprised a few days later when she saw Jocelyn coming from old man Culpepper's house, wearing the yellow sundress she had given to Nora Lee.

At the school where Rudy worked, some of the teachers, appreciating his willingness to work without pay, decided to pitch in and start a fund for him. They kept it up for a few months, but times were rough for everyone, and the Rudy Sullivan fund grew slim in a hurry.

"He spends it all on whiskey anyway," Mabel Cook told the math teacher. "Now don't get me wrong, I believe in Christian charity same as anyone. Lord knows I never failed to give my tithe, and I never accepted remuneration for playing organ at church, even though Brother Barnes offered it, bless his heart. But giving money to a man like Rudy Sullivan is no more than throwing pearls before swine."

"He spends every red cent on whiskey," the math teacher agreed. "Besides, as long as his wife works for Becky Warner, they are well off."

"Probably better off than either of us."

It wasn't long before Rudy started hanging out with the men down by the fairgrounds, shooting craps. He also got hooked up with a bootlegger in East Tupelo, making deliveries, and made enough money that way to keep himself from feeling completely useless. And he started drinking. A lot.

BROOME STREET GALLERY

The exhibition of new paintings by Red Warner at the Broome Street Gallery was a disaster. The opening could not have been worse. It would have been better if they had laughed at him or expressed outright revulsion, but no—they were politely non-committal. Hoards of hangers-on milled around the gallery, drinking the free wine and rolling their eyes at his paintings as if they were being asked to accept sideshow posters as serious art (which, actually, they would have accepted more readily). Then the reviews came out. The reviews were not politely non-committal. They were vicious. It was as if each reviewer in New York were the only one who had been able to see Red Warner for the charlatan he had been all along, and their judgment was finally vindicated. Randall Jarrett, typically, had written two years earlier: "In a sea of salmon, each swimming madly to reach the spawning ground of the latest 'in thing' in contemporary art, Red Warner placidly swims in his own current, securely locked into the mainstream of art history and confident of his very personal vision." After the Broome Street show he wrote: "In a frenzy of desperation, Red Warner has raped the history of art, trying to prove once again that he is on top of the avant-garde heap, but proving only what this reviewer has suspected all along—that his rise to fame is a sideshow act, all bluster and devoid of soul."

The reviewers expected their readers to have short memories, which they did.

For the artist there were days and nights of drunkenness. Red Warner had finally, at last, gone totally berserk. And a party in his loft, a party peopled by people he despised, and him entertaining them all with his outlandish impersonation of a hell-fire-and-brimstone preacher. Then the air closed in and the atmosphere changed. The hairline that separates a laugh from a scream was crossed, and nobody could say when it happened.

We've all seen it. We've seen it when an overly playful uncle teases a little child, throwing him high in the air or dunking him in the pool, and the child laughs at first, but that laugh changes to a scream; and the uncle doesn't want to admit that he's gone too far, so he keeps it up, trying to make light of it, and no one knows whether to stop it or not and the child keeps screaming and a moment arrives when everyone realizes that maybe—just maybe—the uncle may hold the child's head under water a moment too long, may throw him too high in the air, and the sound of brittle bones breaking or the horrible resonance of a dying gurgle simmers in everyone's imagination.

That moment came and went; yet party revelers kept on laughing—uneasily. And the lunatic artist kept on doing his preacher imitation. But the text of his sermon became harsh and his allusions to the tortures of the damned were no longer funny. Then he grabbed a butcher knife off a table and started swinging it wildly in the air. There was blood, a spurt of blood that splattered across a woman's face, and the artist fell to the floor like some wild creature brought down by a hunter's arrow, and there were screams and a mad rush for the door, and within seconds there was silence and emptiness. Only Red Warner remained, doubled up in his own blood, a dark and beautiful woman slumped over him.

Some said the woman was his patron and his lover, some said she was a hooker who had wandered in. Somebody even said that she was Red Warner's sister, but nobody knew for sure. Nobody knew her name. There were rumors enough in the days that followed, but even eyewitness accounts that matched in detail were soon dismissed as tales told by drunkards, too absurd to be believed.

Red Warner was never again seen in New York.

Tupelo

In 1936 a tornado ripped through Tupelo, destroying many of the beautiful old homes on Church Street and taking many lives. Damage could not be assessed for weeks. People injured in the storm were rushed off to hospitals in other towns. Loved ones were lost in the confusion, and in some cases weeks passed before hospitalized family members could be located. Rudy Sullivan vanished the night of the storm and was not located until two weeks later, when Charlie tracked him down at the Baptist Hospital in Memphis. A leg, trapped under debris, had been amputated.

Even death and destruction do not cause all routine to cease. Marybelle went about her business, learning the ropes at her new job at the Esquire, a clothing store where she had worked after school and weekends up until she graduated from Tupelo High and where she now worked full time in the junior fashion department. Charlie Warner, of course, still ran the bank, and his wife still took in what seemed to be every stray soul in town, that huge house of theirs being something like a boarding house and community center. Chuck had gone to Tulane University, where he was pursuing a general business degree. His sister, Becky had also gone off to college. (When she left home Charlie said, "Finally, we won't have to explain every time which Becky we're talking about," and Becky retorted, "Thanks a lot, Daddy. It's nice to know all my leaving means is you won't get me and Mama confused anymore." Their banter was all in jest, and the matter of the confusion of names would soon become moot anyway, after everyone started called the older Becky Mother Warner.)

UNTIL THE DAWN

Chuck was in New Orleans. He listened to news of the tornado on a radio in the Kappa Alpha fraternity house at Tulane. Sitting next to him on the couch in the frat house dayroom was a pretty girl from Memphis who danced like the wind at fraternity parties. A short girl, standing five feet tall in heels, Janet Holliman wore glasses and walked with an exaggerated sway from large hips and a long waist. Her legs were short and beautifully proportioned, her waist so tiny that Chuck could reach his hands all the way around and touch fingers where they teased her belly button. But in the fraternity house there was no reaching of hands around waists; the housemother, who always chaperoned the boys when they had female guests, prohibited any display of affection.

Janet studied painting and drawing. Her professors said she had a lot of talent for a girl. Her faculty advisor suggested that she switch to Elementary Education as a major and take Art as a minor, because there simply were no opportunities in art for women. She understood and harbored no resentment. She was going to marry Chuck Warner anyway, and devote her life to raising his children—nine boys, he said, a baseball team. Janet figured her paints would go into storage until after the kids were grown, and then she could dig them out and astound everyone with her talent.

It wasn't long before Chuck took her home to meet his parents. He also took her out to the Sullivan house to meet Marybelle, whom he introduced as "a kind of a sister."

"Janet and I are going to be married after graduation," he said, as if graduation were imminent, when in fact it was two years away.

Marybelle congratulated them. If her tone was cool, neither Chuck nor Janet seemed to notice.

The wedding took place in February of thirty-nine. A freak ice storm hit Tupelo that week. Ice weighed down telephone lines and broke them. Fires broke out, and it was almost impossible to extinguish them. Firemen's hands froze to their water hoses. The Lee County Hospital was overrun with frostbite victims. The huge oak tree in front of Calvary Baptist split down the middle on the day of the wedding. The senior class from Tupelo High volunteered to escort wedding guests up the slippery walk to the church. Inside, Mabel Cook played the organ and sang "Deep Purple."

At the end Chuck and Janet kissed, and to the delight of the wedding guests, Chuck said, in imitation of Woody Woodpecker, "Da-da-da-dat dat's all folks." And they rushed arm-in-arm up the aisle and out onto the portico and down the slippery steps and down the walkway to the street where Louis Hutchinson's beatup old Hudson waited like an armored tank at the curb to whisk them off to the reception in the Warner house.

Everybody gathered there. Chuck and his friends took off their jackets and loosened their ties. Janet and her bridesmaids went upstairs to change out of their wedding dresses in a guest bedroom. Janet changed into a corduroy skirt and pullover sweater, and she sat on the edge of the bed, then fell back in a swoon, momentarily giving into exhaustion. "You okay, honey?" Becky asked.

"Yes. I just need a moment. All the tension, all the . . . oh, I don't know."

"Yeah, I know. It's pre-nuptial jitters kicking in too late."

"Probably." Janet exhaled deeply and rubbed her hands together in a washing motion. She let loose a little shudder and said, "I'm excited and happy and scared, Becky. Now I'm here in his world. I don't know these people. I don't know what's expected of me."

"Oh, you'll be fine, Janet. Don't you worry. And you'll find that Chuck's friends up here are great. They'll come to love you in no time, just like we have, me and Mama and Daddy."

"Oh I know. Ya'll are great. I noticed your parents downstairs when we were coming in. Your dad was laughing and talking with some other men, and your mother was bringing a big tray of chicken into the dining room, and they both looked so happy, so contented and self-satisfied, and I thought: boy, that's gonna be me and Chuck twenty years from now."

"That's right."

"Yes, I know. But I'm still scared. This is my wedding night, Becky. What if when we . . . you know, do it. What if we're not good together?"

"Oh, I wouldn't worry about that."

"I don't know. Sometimes I think I should have given in when he wanted me to. He said . . ." She cleared her throat and dropped into a deep voice, mimicking Chuck, "You wouldn't buy a car without test driving it, yet you enter into a lifetime commitment with a spouse without finding out if you're sexually compatible. Maybe he was right."

"You'll be great together, I just know it." Then Becky giggled maliciously and whispered, "Don't you dare tell anyone, but me and Bobby have been test driving for a couple of months now."

Janet squealed, "Ooh, that's delicious. But tell me, have you decided to buy the car yet?"

"I think maybe we'll take a two year lease on it, until we finish college at least."

Later, after they came downstairs to join the crowd, Becky danced with Chuck, while Janet huddled with a group of excited young ladies by the dining room table, showing off her rings and hugging everyone. Chuck asked where Marybelle was.

"I don't think she came," his sister answered.

"Why not?"

"Well, I'm not sure she was invited."

"Damn." He glanced around the crowded living room as if expecting to see her there anyway. Instead, he saw a coordinated blur of movement like a military maneuver. A group of his friends, all former teammates in football and basketball, were closing in on him from four different directions. It was an old game they had played many times before, going back to when they were all classmates at Milam Junior High. They called it houseball, and it was basically football played without rules, inside, running around the house, leaping furniture. The Warner house was a perfect place to play because it was so large. The big room they called the everyday living room opened onto a screen porch on the side of the house, which in turned opened onto a wrap-around porch that was wide enough for kids to ride bicycles. They could run out onto the porch off the everyday living room, circle around to the front door, into the living room, through the dining room and kitchen, cut through Charlie's den and run back into the everyday living room. Enroute, they could slide under the huge dining room table, leap two couches and take a side route if they wanted that included a great slide down the length of the hallway. Of course, now that they were all grown men they were too damned strong to play such a game. It was too dangerous, too dangerous for anyone who happened to get in their way, especially too dangerous in a wedding reception crowd. But they were rambunctious boys at heart and wouldn't let a little danger get in the way of their fun.

Chuck saw Bradley Smith and Louis Hutchinson closing in on him, and he knew that whatever they were up to, it was more ominous than houseball. They were out to get him.

"Oh shit," he said, "I'm in for it now. The guys are up to something and I'm it."

His sister, Becky scooted to the safety of the dining room, where she stood with the other girls, laughing. Janet said, "What's going on?"

"Just watch," Becky said. "They do this all the time. It's a little game they play. I think they call it destroy the house and everyone in it."

Louis Hutchinson, a hulk of a man who had played center for the Golden Wave, shouted, "Now!"

Four men rushed toward Chuck. Louis reached him first,

arms spread to clasp him in a bear hug. Chuck ducked away from Louis and spun around, sidestepping Bradley Smith. He knocked over a chair and ran into the hall.

Guests screamed with laughter, hugging the safety of the walls as the four men chased Chuck around the house. Leaping couches and chairs, skirting around tables, grabbing people to use as shields, darting into the family room, Chuck taunted his buddies for being so slow and clumsy. Becky (his mother) shouted, "Stop it! You're going to destroy the house."

Becky (his sister) shouted, "Go, Chuck!"

Janet cried, "Chuck! Chuck! Chuck!"

Finally Chuck tripped and fell across a footstool, and Louis Hutchinson's two hundred and fifty pounds crashed on top of him. Bradley and the others jumped on, and they forced him into the bathroom.

Charlie laughed and said, "Damn those boys. I don't think they'll ever grow up."

The guests all shuffled their feet and nudged one another, facing the closed bathroom door, waiting. Scuffling noises and loud cursing from Chuck, and laughter from the others, came from behind the door.

"Hold him still."

"Watch that leg."

"There! Got him."

"Watch out! He's slippery as an eel."

Then the noise subsided, and after a few minutes they all came out, arm in arm, laughing. Chuck's face was flushed. His tie had been pulled loose and his shirt was untucked. He left the men and went over to pull Janet away from the women and lead her out to the side porch, the only uncrowded spot he could find. She said, "What are you doing, honey? It's freezing out here."

"But we've got our love to keep us warm."

"Cute. Real cute. What was all that ruckus about, anyway?"

"Nothing. Just the guys trying to razz me. Hey, are you ready to sneak out of here?"

She said, "You bet," huddled close to his chest, with her head bent backward to look up at him. Had her glasses not been fogged, he could have seen her eyes twinkle.

They managed to sneak out of the house without being detected, they thought, and they trudged over icy sidewalks to the Texaco station four blocks away.

"Why are we walking?" Janet asked.

"We can't use my car. The guys will follow us. I've got another car waiting at Andy's Texaco."

She slipped on the icy sidewalk and he grabbed her. "Is it really worth all this?" she asked. "We're going to be too cold to do anything." His arms were around her and they were practically running, shivering, sliding and clasping each other.

"It's worth it," he panted. "Believe me, it's worth it. You don't know those guys. They'd follow us to Timbuktu just to razz me on my wedding night. When Louis got married—it was July and hot as Hades—we found out what room they were staying in at the hotel for their honeymoon, and we snuck in during the reception and put bubble gum in the fans and glued the windows shut. It was so hot they couldn't even sleep, much less consummate their vows, so they went out to Tombigbee—his wife told this later—and they did it in the lake."

They reached the station and got the keys to the waiting car from John Coe. Then they drove to the hotel, where Chuck canceled their reservations and gave the clerk ten dollars and instructions to tell anyone who asked about them that they had gone to the summerhouse at Pickwick. "And I'll bet you another ten," he told the clerk, "that Louis Hutchinson will drive all the way to Pickwick, and probably kill his damn fool self trying to negotiate those icy roads. And I'll scalp you if anybody finds out where we are."

Then they drove to the Alamo Plaza Motel.

Not one to waste time, Janet Holliman, now Warner,

stripped out of her dress the moment they got inside. She stood naked in front of her new husband, hands on hips, those curvaceous little legs spread in a defiant attitude, taunting, "This is what we've been waiting for, Mister Warner. Now what are *you* waiting for?"

"Don't you think maybe we ought to turn out the lights first?"

"Why honey, I swear to goodness, I do think you're embarrassed."

"No I'm not. It's just... uh, I'm still cold."

"Like you said, honey, we've got our love to keep us warm. Besides, they got the heat blasting in here. It's not cold."

He hesitated. She said, "You *are* shy. I can't believe it."

"No I'm not. It's just that..."

"You are too. My goodness, you're turning red as a beet."

"Am not."

"Are too."

"Naw, it's just that... It's just that—well..."

"Well what?" She looked down at the bulge in his woolen pants and said, "I seeee something."

"Aw hell. All right. But you've got to understand. The guys did something that... Aw, what the heck."

He stripped, and the two of them stood five feet apart, gaping at each another. Her mouth opened as if a scream were going to explode from her throat. Instead, laughter poured out. Then he started laughing. Squared off like boxers readying themselves for the first punch, they laughed at the great red protuberance that stood erect like a buoy bobbing in the bay.

When she stopped laughing long enough to ask him about it, he said, "That's what was going on when the guys carried me to the bathroom. Louis and Bradley held me down and John Lewis painted my dick red. I think it's... Oh, I don't know.

Some kind of paint or something. Oh God, I hope it's not enamel. I just pray it'll will come off."

"It had better, or something else ain't going to come off."

So, for the second time on his wedding night, Chuck Warner retired to the bathroom, where ministrations to his member took place. The soap went to work, latheringly, slipperingly, laughteringly.

"Hey, not so hard!"

"I'm just trying to help. Whoops! I slipped."

"More soap."

"More soap! Are you kidding?"

"Here. Ooooh, oh my."

"Nothing's happening. At least not with the paint." She was rubbing up and down furiously with a washrag.

"Keep that up and it's not going to matter if we get the damned red off or not."

She giggled, "Maybe if I used steel wool."

"Oh no, God in heaven! Not that."

Janet fell to the floor laughing, tears wetting her cheeks. "Cold cream," she said. "Maybe cold cream will do the trick."

"Do you have any?"

"Yes, in my purse."

"Okay, let's try that." He watched her stand up and walk away, the sway of her naked hips so enticing, that perfectly round bottom so pretty, so pert, so proudly promising of pleasures that at the moment seemed never to be.

Sitting on the edge of the bed, she started rummaging through her purse. He said, "I think it's beginning to crack. It's drying up like parched dirt. Ow. I can feel it pulling against the skin."

"Well, if it falls off, we can keep it in a drawer as a memento. We can . . ." breaking into uncontrollable laughter, "frame it. Frame it and . . . ooh, ha ha ha, put it on the wall next to our marriage license."

Finding the cold cream, she came back to him and started

rubbing it on him. Soon the red color spread onto his thighs, and their hands were covered with it, and they were rolling on the cold, white tile floor of the bathroom in room number twenty three of the Alamo Plaza Motel, with splotches of red like puddles of plasma spreading to floor and arms and legs and faces where tears of laughter ran, as outside the renewed ice storm pelted the window like shots from a thousand b-b guns at eleven thirty on a night so quiet that any movement outside of private homes was an event.

At a quarter to twelve, Louis Hutchinson and Bradley Smith drove up to the Texaco station in Louis's old Nash sedan. They were alone, except for a passenger in the back seat, because Louis's wife had gone home early and he had stayed to have a few more drinks with the boys—quite a few more. The passenger in the back was Marybelle Sullivan. She was hugging herself inside her imitation fur coat. She had decided to attend the reception party, invitation or no invitation, and had caught a cab to the house on Magazine Street only to arrive as the last guests were leaving. Louis and Bradley offered her a ride.

"Are you sure you want out at the Texaco?" Louis asked. "I mean, it's late and it's cold. What if you get stranded?"

Bradley said, "Yeah. We'd be glad to take you home. A pretty thing like you, shucks, we'll take you anywhere you want to go."

The car radio was tuned to radio station WELO; hillbilly music screeched through static, a scratchy voice that could barely be recognized as Hank Williams singing "Hey good lookin', what you got cookin'. Howzabout cookin' somethin' up with me." Bradley put his hand on Marybelle's leg.

"Cut it out," she demanded.

"Aw come on, baby. Don't be shy. We know how it is. You been saving your love all these years for old Chucky boy. Now old Chucky boy's done took."

She shoved the door open and jumped out, running to

the welcoming flame of the gas heater inside the glass-enclosed station, where John Coe bounced from foot to foot and rubbed his hands together, the reflected light of the heater giving his face the appearance of a jack-o'-lantern.

Screeching tires and skidding on the icy pavement, Louis said, "I know exactly where Chuck and his bride are, I bet'cha."

Bradley said, "Shee-it, I'uz only funnin' her. And she goes running in there to that Coe character. She's in real trouble now."

"If I know Chuck, he's done set it up to look like he went somewhere far off, like Pickwick. Bet'cha anything they're at the Alamo Plaza. I know Chuck. That's 'zactly what he'd do."

"What we gonna do if they are there?"

"I don't know. You got any ideas?"

"Maybe we ought to just drop it. Hell, the red paint on his pecker was enough. Can you imagine what she did when she saw it?"

SoHo
Spring of 1982

The gallery was crowded. I heard that it had been constantly crowded since Red Warner's mysterious disappearance. Interest in his work had become infectious. There was a constant flow of gawkers in and out of the Broome Street Gallery. They came in, gave the work cursory glances, and talked to one another in excited tones; or they came in, looked at the paintings in befuddlement, and walked out shaking their heads.

The main exhibition gallery was a deep rectangle. Six of Red Warner's latest paintings hung there, each one measuring seventy-two by ninety-eight inches, loosely stapled to unframed stretcher bars. At the back of the gallery was a small alcove where works on paper from the permanent collection were exhibited. A mirrored door opened into Leo Garner's office. Ajar, the door provided a full view of the gallery from inside the office and from the gallery looking in a view of Leo himself seated with legs crossed and a magazine open on his lap. He was not reading the magazine. He was looking out into the gallery. He was looking at me. Leo Garner was wondering about me. I could see it in his expression, in the way he pretended to not look. He was wondering if I was as rich as I looked. Did I spend my money on art? Was I gay? Well, I'm just guessing that he was wondering that, but I've been in enough French Quarter bars and played enough glancing games to recognize it when I see it. The position I was in put me in an advantage that would have been fun if I had wanted to take the time to play the game. I could tease him;

lead him on, both as a prospective buyer and as a prospective lover. Ooh, it was delicious to think about it. I thought about walking right out, only to come back the next day after he'd had time to worry himself silly about me and finally wipe me out of his mind. But the massive presence of Red Warner's paintings stopped me from playing any silly games. Suddenly it was, to borrow a Red Warner expression, just me and those goddamn, awe-full paintings, locked in a jazz duet. The people milling around the gallery dissolved. Awareness of Leo Garner vanished. I was mesmerized and really, really disturbed by paintings that seemed too massive and too intense for the gallery walls. They were like a sudden splash of cold water. I didn't like them at all, at least not at first. Maybe it was because I had come to expect a certain look in a Red Warner painting, and that look wasn't there. But as I stood there, they began to work on me. Oh boy, did they work on me!

Across the street, the bartender at the New Cedars Bar was polishing the mahogany bar top. I could see him through the windows. Momentarily my vision split, creating a slow motion, split screen movie in my eyes. Through the gallery window was the industrial gray of the street with the faded red facade of the New Cedars across the street. Framed behind the front window of the bar was the bartender, posing as if for a painting, slightly distorted by haze and windowpane dirt as if a picture under glass smeared with a clear gel. But Red Warner's paintings were in this picture too, bright spots of intruding swirls of color.

I saw a 1968 Volvo maneuver for a parking space next to the bar in the no loading zone in front of the building where Red Warner's loft had been. A woman got out of the car, granting the bartender a momentary glimpse of sensuous legs under a denim skirt, legs like you'd expect to see on a very tall woman, which was deceptive, as the woman was actually petite. Even from across the street and through two windows, I could see the way he looked at her legs. She glanced into her rearview mirror and brushed her hair with her hand. When she slammed the car door there was a momentary flash of red, a reflection from a Red Warner painting, or maybe from the front of the bar. The woman's hair was like brushed fur, dark, with a patina of gray. With cat-like grace she crossed the street and entered the bar.

I refocused on the paintings with a feeling like I get when I watch an old musical, one I've seen a dozen times before. Something about that woman reminded me of a movie star from the forties. Seeing her made me feel like I was back home. Maybe she reminded me of someone from long ago. Anyway, I returned my attention to the paintings, and they were no longer disturbing.

Then an old van pulled up across the street and double-parked next to the Volvo. I caught sight of it with a sideways glance out the door, one small section of my mind playing with observing the street action while the rest of my mind remained mesmerized by Red Warner's paintings. The driver of the van got out, popped a plug of chewing tobacco into his mouth, and leaned back against his truck, waiting and watching. Inside the bar, the woman with steely hair abruptly stood up, dropped a bill on the table and hurried out.

The last thing I caught out of the corner of my eye before I finally approached the door to Leo's office was a blurred picture of the woman and the man standing by their vehicles. Since Leo's door was partway open, I stuck my head in as I knocked, and said, "Excuse me."

"Yes? Can I help you?"

"Perhaps. If you don't mind, I would like to ask you some questions about the show."

"Sure. Come on in." Leo pulled a vacant chair next to his own and patted the seat in invitation.

I said, "Could you tell me how much these paintings sell for?"

"Thirty thousand," Leo said.

"A piece?"

"Yep. And I'll tell you something: that's cheap. Prices on Red Warners are going to skyrocket."

"Why is that?"

"Because he's vanished. Poof! Disappeared."

"Yes, I know all about that, but . . ."

"Yeah, well if he's dead or something, or if he doesn't ever make any more paintings, then . . . well, we're talking about a possible bonanza investment here. Everybody knows artists are worth more dead than alive, and an artist who has vanished mysteriously is worth even more."

"Oh, I see. Do you mind my asking these questions?" Of course he didn't mind. He loved it.

"Nope. That's what I'm here for. Fire away."

"Okay. There's just one other thing that I'm curious about. If somebody bought these paintings and then the artist shows up, maybe ten years later, would he get his share of the money?"

"Who? Red? Sure he would. Red Warner may have acted like a buffoon, but he was no dummy. He had a sharp lawyer handling his business, and man that lawyer was on the phone to me the minute Red's disappearance was announced. His part of the money will be placed in an account to be held until either he claims it or he's pronounced dead. If that happens, his mother down in Mississippi gets it all—with interest."

I lit another cigarette. I held it with fingers extended and arched, and blew little doughnut puffs of smoke into the room, resuming my little cat-and-mouse game. "Okay," I said, "I'll take them. All of them. I'll have a cashier's check in your hands within the hour, and I'll have my secretary contact you to arrange for shipment to my warehouse in New Orleans."

Leo was dumbstruck. I deftly fingered one of my smoke rings and twirled it like a lariat. I said, "There's one other thing. If Red Warner is still alive, I'm going to find him."

Leo Garner still didn't know who I was. He wouldn't know

until he saw my name on the cashiers check. When I walked out, he'd be left wondering if he had really sold all those paintings, or if it had all been some kind of weird joke. Of course I had been buying paintings from him for years, but an associate always took care of it.

I left the gallery and walked across the street to have a drink at the New Cedars.

The men in the bar were speculating about the steely haired woman. She had let the trucker into Red Warner's loft and had supervised as he loaded rolled-up canvases and cardboard boxes into the van. One of the men said, "I'll bet'cha she's the one—the woman that was with him at the party."

"Did'ja ever see her with him?"

"Not in here, nah. But I saw her go in and out of the loft often enough."

"Jesus, she's sexy. Wonder who she is."

"Who knows?"

The woman and the van driver finished loading the van and drove away in their respective vehicles, the van following the Volvo. I swigged down a bourbon and Coke and headed back to my room at the Hilton. Jimmy was there, waiting on me. He was wearing a blue robe and was sprawled out on the bed, propped on pillows, a half empty drink on the bedside table. Jimmy was a marvelous architect who was among the first to start bringing back art deco ornamentation, a kind of pre-post modernist. We had been together for two years. "It's about time you showed up," he said.

I ignored him. Plopped down on the bed and reached for a bulky envelope and spilled its contents onto the bed. They were clippings from newspaper and magazine articles, all about Red Warner, everything from a one-inch tidbit in a gossip column to a five-page, full-color layout. There were also a bunch of newspaper clippings from the Tupelo (Mississippi) *Daily Journal* from the early 1960s, sports write-ups, all touting the accomplishments of a ferocious defensive lineman named Travis Earl Warner who had led the Big Eight Conference in unassisted tackles two years in a row.

I lit a cigarette. Jimmy said, "Must you smoke so much?"

I continued to ignore him, as I'm afraid I had been doing more and more lately. Obsessively I studied the pictures for the longest time, shuffling them around, comparing photos. Finally I said, "There's not a single clear shot of his face. I wonder if I will recognize him when I see him."

I had already, by then, decided that I had to go back to Tupelo.

1940s
Tupelo

A face as familiar to Marybelle as the face of Chuck or Rudy or any of the kids from town she had grown up with was the face of Arman Roulin, a Frenchmen who had grown up a century before her time in the South of France. He lived in the town of Arles. The son of the town postman, Arman Roulin was sixteen years old in the year 1888 when his neighbor, the artist van Gogh, asked him to pose for a portrait. In one of the portraits van Gogh painted that year, Armand looks a brooding boy. Pained eyes stare out of an angular face with clinched jaws. A thin mustache sets off a fleshy, sensitive mouth. A blue hat sits on his head. He is a handsome enough youth, but there is something menacing in his look. Marybelle Sullivan had seen that portrait of Armand as reproduced in a book that adorned the Warner's coffee table. From early childhood she had enjoyed studying the paintings in the book, and the portrait of Armand had been her favorite.

On Chuck's wedding night she ran smack into the face of Armand, partially shielded by the upturned collar of a woolen overcoat. Brown hair brushed across a wide brow in imitation of the rakish dip of the blue hat in the painting. The glow from a gas heater reflected red in heavy-lidded eyes. Under a broken Roman nose, a smear of grease looked like a thin mustache over pouty lips.

She had rushed into the gas station without looking up, looking instead at the pavement in front of her feet. Gray globs of sand on the frozen pavement left tracings of earlier traffic. Bursting into the station, she stopped short in front of John Coe, a copy of the van Gogh painting. An amber light reflected on his face. It blinked once, twice. She stood motionless, dripping. A small moat formed under the hem of her coat. He looked at her; neither spoke. Blink, blink, blink, an amber glow on his ruddy face. At last she said, "Ca-cooold." Shivering.

"Sure is," he replied.

The station sat on a corner in marbled loneliness. John and Marybelle stood behind plate glass; reflected lights from a myriad of sources (the heater, the blinking sign outside, a neon sign on the corner, moonlight reflected on ice) made them look like figures on a stage. She peered around the interior of the little station, as if searching for something. He asked, "Can I help you with something?"

"No thank you. I uuuhm..."

She eyed the Coca-Cola cooler and shuddered. Her gaze finally focused on a steaming coffee pot behind a cluttered desk. "I'm kind of stuck," she said, "I was at a party, Chuck Warner's wedding party. Maybe you know him."

"Who doesn't?"

"Yes. Well, I sort of got myself stuck."

"If you want to hang around here 'till Andy gets back, I can give you a ride home."

"Oh no, I couldn't let you do that. I mean, well, I don't know if I should. I don't know you."

He smiled with one side of his mouth and lit a cigarette, offering her one. She shook her head. "My name is John," he said. "I wouldn't hurt you or anything, lady. Maybe I ain't one of your fancy society boys like Chuck Warner, but I wouldn't try nothing. I just figured if you needed help, I'd offer. That's all. Wouldn't want to see a pretty lady like yourself in any trouble."

She said, "I didn't mean to imply that you aren't a gentleman, but it isn't proper for an unescorted lady to let a stranger take her home. Not this time of night. People would . . . you know."

"It doesn't matter to me, Miss . . . uh . . ."

"Sullivan. Marybelle Sullivan."

"Miss Sullivan. Pleased to meet you. To tell the truth, I do know who you are. It's not like we live in Memphis or Chicago. Hang around Tupelo very long and you get to know everybody."

He knew who she was all right. Among young men of a certain age, Marybelle was Tupelo's equivalent of a movie star, a pin-up dream walking. And her walk was famous. There had been times when John Coe had stood on the corner a block below the Esquire and watched her walk to work wearing those tight skirts she always wore. There had been times he had gone to work half an hour early just to be there when she passed by, and he wasn't the only man on that corner.

"You can't hang out here forever. We close up when Andy gets back. What are you going to do then?

"I'm not sure. Probably someone I know will come by."

"Sure." He started laughing, and she laughed with him. Sure, somebody would come by after midnight with the streets covered with ice and the temperature hovering around six degrees.

"I guess maybe I ought to accept your offer after all," she said.

"How did you happen to get stranded?"

"To tell the truth," she lied, "I never should have accepted Chuck's invitation. I really didn't belong there at all." (She mixed generous portions of truth into her lie.) "I'm not a friend of theirs, don't even belong among the same people. My mother is, or was, their maid. Chuck invited me out of spite. You see, we were childhood sweethearts. I don't know why I'm telling you this, you being a stranger and all."

She stopped her rush of words for a moment and shuddered, still cold. Then she said, "Oh, I ought to be ashamed of myself.

I was getting all fired up to tell you just about the biggest lie I ever told. I was going to tell you that Chuck Warner was in love with me, and that it was me he really wanted to marry, but he had to marry this society girl because of the family name. That's a lie. It was me in love with him—why am I telling you this?—in love with him and mooning over him and imagining I was some kind of Cinderella. If he really had loved me he would have married me. Me being dirt poor wouldn't matter. The Warner's aren't uppity like that, not at all."

John poured them each a cup of coffee. Handing Marybelle a steaming cup, which she grasped with both hands, he said, "You do go on, don't you?"

"Yes, I guess I do. I don't know what's come over me. I don't usually prattle like this."

"That's all right. I enjoy it. You sound like music."

They talked for well over an hour, until Andy finally arrived to close the station. Then John Coe took Marybelle home.

When they drove up to the Sullivan house they saw that Rudy and Nora Lee were waiting up. John hopped out of his truck and rushed around to open Marybelle's door with a sweeping, exaggerated bow.

"Thank you, kind sir," she said.

"You're welcome."

"Good night."

"G'night."

Rudy greeted her with scattergun questions: "Do you know what time it is? Where have you been? Who'uz that man that brung you home?"

"I was at Chuck's wedding reception, Daddy. You know that. No, I don't know what time it is, but I'm sure you're gonna tell me, and the man who brought me home was John Coe. He works at the Texaco station and . . ."

"I know who John Coe is," Rudy interrupted. "He's bad news."

"He's a gentleman. That's all I know. He treated me kindly and behaved like a perfect gentleman."

"Sure he did. Just like his old man. I seen his old man in action. He'uz a ladies' man, that's for sure. Treats women like queens—slick as snot—'till he gets what he wants. That's the way them Coes are, the whole lot of 'em."

"What do you mean, the whole lot of 'em? His daddy's gone and he doesn't have any brothers or sisters. It's just John and his mama."

"Well now, sounds like you got his whole history. I'm warning you, honey. He ain't the gentleman he seems."

Nora Lee butted in to ask about the party: "Who was there? What did they wear? Did little Becky wear that darling blue dress?"

Marybelle said, "I don't know, Mama. It's late. I'm tired. I've got to go to bed."

The next day a Western Union messenger arrived with a telegram from John Coe. The telegram said, "For warmth of heart on a cold night."

A few days later he called and asked for a date for the following Saturday night. She could hear loud noises in the background, a cacophony of voices and something that sounded like hard wood sharply striking. She said she would be glad to go out with him. His reply was muffled by background noises.

"I can't hear you," she shouted into the phone.

He shouted back, "I said I'll pick you up at seven."

Hanging up, he turned to replace the pool cue he had been fondling while talking to her. Then, running his fingers along the rack like a boy running a stick along a picket fence, he stepped over to the bar and shouted to a friend, "Let's blow this joint. Maybe we can find some action over in Shakerag."

They got into the truck, John and one of his cronies, and drove to Shakerag and parked in front of Lulu's Cafe.

They could have bought their booze at Lulu's, but John said, "You can't trust nigger bootleggers. They's liable as not to mix rubbing alcohol with the real stuff."

Shakerag is black. Black from dirt, black from fear, black in the night because there are no streetlights, and black in the day because a cloud of factory soot hangs overhead. Cops never entered Shakerag, not back then, not unless some of the white men who went there for booze and gambling got into trouble, and that hardly ever happened, because the Negroes were afraid to cause trouble with the whites, and the white cops figured it wasn't any business of theirs if niggers got drunk and beat each other to death.

The whole state of Mississippi was dry then, but prohibition wasn't enforced in Shakerag. Lulu's Cafe featured greasy-spoon cuisine for blacks at the tables, and poker for whites in a small room behind the kitchen. Whites bought their booze at a drive-in window and drank out of paper bags; Negroes ordered theirs inside from Lulu, a woman out of a painting by Renoir, only with creamy brown skin instead of flushed pink. Lulu had wide hips and arms like a lumberjack. Few whites ever entered her cafe, especially not through the front.

John and his buddy got out of the truck. He stuffed the bottle of Old Crow under his belt and pulled his coat tightly across it. They walked slowly, glancing surreptitiously up and down the wet street. There was little to see but distorted shadows, as there were no streetlights. Quickly they entered Lulu's. Customers stopped their conversations to watch the white men walk through. Lulu stood at the end of the counter and followed them with her eyes. A striking woman with ochre skin, her rust hair had been straightened with an iron. A too-tight white dress covered her meaty figure, a pink apron with white lace riding her round belly. John winked at her as he walked into the kitchen, and he gave the cook a hearty wave as he passed through, going to the poker room.

Joshua Culpepper was there, along with two men John did not know. One of them introduced himself as Billy and the other as Sandy from St. Louie. They were playing five-card draw, nothing wild. John sat down. "I got twenty bucks," he said. "That ought to last me at least two hands, lessen I get on a winning streak. But then, that's 'zactly what I aim to do. I'm fixing to take you boys to the cleaners. Ain't gonna be nothing left in your pockets but lint."

Turning to address the white-haired Negro who stood patiently with his back against a wall, he said, "Bring me a bottle of Coke and a glass, boy. One for my buddy too."

"Yassuh," the man mumbled, hurrying to fetch the set-up.

Sandy from St. Louis dealt the cards. He dealt John a pair of kings. John discarded a deuce, a six and a seven, and drew three jacks. There were twenty-five dollars in the pot. Culpepper bet another five.

"Shit!" John barked, "I don't know why I got into this dumb game anyway. I got better things to do than play poker in a nigger dive."

"You're welcome to leave," Culpepper said. "Didn't nobody invite you no how."

"Where's that boy with my Coke? Shit, I might as well drink the booze straight. Damn bootlegger probably watered it down anyway." He turned up the bottle and took a large swig, spilling some down his chin. Then the old Negro brought his Coke. John poured it into the glass halfway, and filled the rest with whiskey.

Culpepper said, "Are you going to jerk off all night, or are you going to play cards?"

"Don't get your bowels in an uproar. I'm playing. Is it my bet?"

"Yeah."

He took another big swig of his drink, and spilled even more. A regular brown lake was taking shape on the white tablecloth.

"Jesus, man," Culpepper complained, "my grandmother is slow, but she's ninety years old."

"Awright, awright. What the hell, I might's well bet it all and get this crappy game over with." He tossed the rest of his money on the table.

"Good," Culpepper said. "I'll call you. Read 'em and weep, boys." He snapped the cards one at a time: ace, ace, ace. Sandy from St. Louis whistled. John let them all marvel a moment at Culpepper's three aces, then he laid down a full house and scooped up his winnings. Culpepper was livid. The man from St. Louis, if he really was from St. Louis, laughed. He congratulated John for playing Culpepper (and himself) right into his hands.

Two hours later John pulled out of the game with winnings of over two hundred dollars. The cafe was almost empty when he walked out. His buddy, who had not said a word all evening, following him like a lap dog. Two chocolate brown women and an old man were sitting at the counter. Lulu was counting up the night's take. She quickly shut the cash drawer when John approached her.

"Don't be so jumpy, woman," he said. "I ain't gonna rob you. I got my poker winnings in my pocket. Won big. Yes indeed. Look. Come here." He motioned with a twitch of his head, and she leaned across the counter. He whispered, "Are you running whores out of this joint?"

"Might be," she said, inclining her head in the direction of the only two women there. "'Pends on who's asking."

"I ain't interested in them fat brown jungle bunnies. A good-looking yallar woman like yourself is more to my liking. What'cha say, Lulu, you interested in this wad of cash that's burning a hole in my pocket?"

"Not me, white boy." She pulled away and straightened herself proudly.

Stung at her rejection, he sneered, "Whassa matter, you uppity nigger whore? You think you too damn high and mighty for white meat?"

"I think you best leave now, Suh."

He slammed his now-empty bottle against the counter top and bristled like a cat in a back-alley fight. Amazingly, the bottle didn't break. Lulu reached under the counter. He could see her heavy arms tense as she grabbed something solid. Probably a weapon of some sort she had stashed under the counter. Backing off, he hissed, "You better watch your ass, woman. One of these days I'm liable to run across you somewhere 'sides Shakerag."

"Let's get out of here," his buddy said, grabbing his arm and pulling him toward the door. John went with him, patting the bulge of his wallet and laughing. Back in the truck he said, "Imagine that colored gal talking to me like that. Imagine that. Hell, I wouldn't touch her. You'll never catch this old boy screwing no nigger."

* * *

Saturday night he took Marybelle out. They ate at Mike's Restaurant and went to see a musical at the Lyric. The next day he drove her out to Saltillo, across the narrow wooden bridge where he told her he had once caught a ten pound bass on a doughball-baited hook tied to a piece of catgut that he looped around his finger—"I was fishing for bream, wasn't more'n ten years old, and that old lunker grabbed the bait; nearly took my finger off, but I caught him"—and on up an incredibly steep hill to the old house where he lived with his mother.

"My John was always a sensitive boy," his mother told her. "He acts real tough most times, but that's so as people won't think he's sissified, which he ain't. Don't let him fool you. He's like a old hound dog that growls and growls and then'll up and lick your face all over."

He told her he was reading *The Man Nobody Knows*, a best seller at the time, a book that presented Jesus as a Rotarian and salesman and the favorite dinner guest in Jerusalem.

"I'm learning how to sell myself," John told her, "learning how to talk to people so they'll never guess I'm an uneducated country boy. I'm gonna take some night classes over at Itawamba Junior College too. I don't plan to be no grease monkey forever."

She thought about John fishing for bream with doughball bait, the image of tiny bream nibbling at the bait, wearing it down, mouths too small to take the hook, analogized the voices that assailed her: voices of reason and warning, Nora Lee's voice gushing over the society column in the *Commercial Appeal*, a voice of hope for a better life for her daughter; Rudy's voice warning: "Sure, he seems like a perfect gentleman now. He wants you. He wants to be the man you want. But let him get you, let him think that you belong to him, and he'll be a different person, just you wait and see." Even the tiny voice of the girl she had once been made itself heard, reminding her of dreams that would vanish if she kept fooling around with this man from the wrong side of the tracks, but another voice said, "What dreams? What foolish dreams! Grow up, little girl."

The thing that worried her most about John Coe was the fear that his tough act (the toughness everyone else saw) was not a cover for the sensitive man underneath, but rather that the sensitive man she saw was a cover for the tough hombre underneath.

Their courtship progressed too quickly for her to sort out any of those warnings and worries—John's obvious infatuation with her was like the big bass that scared away the pesky little, nibbling bream.

Since she had never truthfully looked at her love for Chuck, she never considered the possibility that she was rushing away from that rather than into something else.

WILLIS HEIGHTS

Marybelle Sullivan and John Coe were married by a justice of the peace in a chapel in the justice's home. They rented a one-bedroom, furnished cottage in Willis Heights, across the street from the war memorial. Their wedding bed was old. It sagged in the middle and the mattress felt as if it were stuffed with straw. The springs squawked and John made harsh, guttural sounds when he lowered his weight onto her like retribution for sin.

Later, a mocking bird sang in the back yard, and John's hands gripped her shoulders and shook her. "Wake up, Marybelle."

"What? Oh, I must have dozed off."

"Dozed off! You slept all night. It's morning."

"Morning? What time is it?" She pulled the sheet over her nakedness.

"It's eight o'clock."

"Eight o'clock! Oh no. I've got to get up. I'm late." She clutched the sheet under her chin and dragged it with her as she scrambled out of bed and rushed toward the bathroom. He grabbed a trailing corner of sheet and held tight, laughing as it pulled loose. Naked, she scurried into the bathroom. John pulled himself to a sitting position against the metal headboard, locked fingers behind his neck, a satisfied grin on his face as his eyes followed his wife's bouncy butt. Then he rubbed his jaw, enjoying the raspy, manly feel of his beard, rolled his neck to loosen the kinks and pulled himself out of the bed. The mirror over the dresser reflected a body with broad shoulders and

61

hard muscles. As he slipped his feet into bedroom slippers he grabbed another glance into the mirror and flexed his shoulder muscles. He shuffled into the bathroom where Marybelle now stood in front of the sink with a towel wrapped around her hips. He stepped up behind her and reached under the towel to grab a hunk of flesh. Bending forward, he nuzzled the back of her neck with his chin. "Hey, quit it," she complained. "You're like sandpaper."

"Sorry, babe." He dented the soft flesh of her buttocks with one hand while reaching around to fondle her breast with the other.

"Not now," she said, smiling at his reflection in the mirror. "I'm late already."

Anyway, she was still sore from the night before. Her initiation into sex had been fun, but rougher than expected.

"Now just what do you reckon you're late for, honey pie," he crooned.

"For work. I do have a job, you know." She pushed his hand away.

His voice was sneering and syrupy, a voice she had never heard before. "Why honey pie, you don't have to work no mo'. You got a man to take care of you."

"Yeah, yeah, sure. Hey, this play-acting and the smarmy voice and all would be funny another time, but I really am late, and in case there's the slightest bit of seriousness behind this stuff, you should know that I enjoy working. Besides, working at the station, you can't make enough money for both of us. I've got my car payments and . . . "

He interrupted, his syrupy drawl obliterating her words. "Now what kind of man would I be if I couldn't support my woman proper, without her having to work? Naw, honey, you ain't working no mo'. Your place is here in the house."

Squeezing past him and hurrying into the bedroom to slip into a dress, she said, "We'll talk about it another time. Right now I've got to go."

His voice changed. The syrup melted. He growled, "I said you ain't going to work."

"But of course I'm going to work. The very idea, thinking I'd quit my job just because I'm married now."

He mimicked her. "The very idear. The very idear. But of course you ain't neither going to work. Ain't no woman supposed to work outside the home. You get that straight right now."

"You're being silly, John Coe. This is the middle of the twentieth century. You don't have to keep your woman chained to the stove to prove you're a man." She picked up her purse and dug into it for keys to the old Plymouth she'd bought only a week earlier. "I'm expected at the Esquire. We'll talk later."

There had been a hard look on his face such as she'd not seen before, but as she paused at the door waiting for him to apologize or at least wish her a good day, she saw the hardness begin to melt a bit. "I shouldn't a talked like that," he mumbled, looking not at her face but down at the hardwood floor. "Thing is, I reckon I'm just not used to being married, but you know guys say a man's gotta establish his authority right off the bat and I guess, you know, I'm just trying to figure out how to do it."

Marybelle, who all her life had displayed an uncanny ability to think of sassy rejoinders under stress, and who usually sassed back at the most inappropriate moments, said, "Well shit man, maybe we can find you an instruction manual, maybe something like How to Subjugate the Little Woman in Ten Easy Lessons."

He slapped her. It was vicious and unexpected. Her cheek turned red and she fell back against the flower-print loveseat that was propped up by bricks where a leg was missing. Her Cocker Spaniel puppy, which had been quietly watching, started puppydog yapping.

John Coe shouted, "Don't nobody talk to me like that. And get this: You ain't working. Period! And as for your high-falutin' ideas about dressing fancy and spending your own money on makeup and fancy hairdos, you can forget it. I expect you to stay home, and when you do go out, I want you to wear plain dresses that fall straight from the shoulders where cain't no man see the shape of your body. I know how you used to go sashaying 'round town, making all the men hot and bothered just a looking at you. I know how all the boys used to hang their tongues out when they seen ya. But no more, baby. No more."

As he ranted, Marybelle pulled herself up from the loveseat and smoothed her dress with her hands, and her mind collected itself, distancing herself from what was happening. She stepped past him, right out the door, saucily dashing her hips like redundant exclamation points.

"Hey! I'm talking to you."

She wheeled around in the dusty front yard like a soldier executing a sharp about face. "Mister Coe," she spat, "that was a marriage license we signed yesterday, not a purchase order. Unless you change your tune in an all-fired hurry, you can take that license, all neatly rolled up the way it is with the little pink ribbon tied around it, and you can dip it in that can of axle grease down at the station and get it well lubricated, and you can shove it up your ass. I'll be at my mother's house after work. If you decide to act like the gentleman I thought I married, you may call on me." Her voice was controlled, but her hands were shaking. She huffed off to the curb, little balls of dust sending signals with each step.

He stood in the doorway, hopping on one foot, trying to pull up his pants. Watching her drive away, he muttered, "The little slut. The little slut."

He ran out into the yard, stuffing his shirt into his pants and tugging on his belt, and shouted at the disappearing car, "I didn't mean it, honey. Marybelle! Come back!"

Marybelle drove two blocks then pulled over to the curb to have a good cry. She let it out in a sudden torrent, and then, as quickly as her tears had gushed out, her crying jag was over. She wiped her eyes with a handkerchief, took a few deep breaths, and drove to the Esquire.

John still stood impotently alone in the front yard of their pathetic little house, their honeymoon cottage. He looked at the houses on either side to see if anyone was watching. Inside the house, water put into a kettle earlier to boil built up under pressure that could only escape in a desperate and unheeded cry of steam. Across West Main at the war memorial, a cannon stood guard, aimed at the Coe house.

After work Marybelle drove out to her folk's. "I thought getting married was supposed to make me happy," she said. "If I'd known it was going to make me feel so lousy, I never would have done it."

"Well honey, that's sorta the way it is," Nora Lee said.

Rudy said, "It'll be awright, honey. You just gotta stick it out." The old man was full of advice. He was sitting on a broken cane chair, his wooden leg propped on an old nail keg. The nails had long ago rusted into a heap like tangled barbed wire. Next to it was the old ottoman, its fake leather cover as dull as mud. Marybelle had slept on it when she was five years old. Now she slapped it a couple of times to brush off at least some of the dirt, and sat down.

Rudy played the old game of identifying cars as they passed on East Main Street, speaking as if to the trees, "Here comes a one-eyed Jack. Bet that's Jake Hollis's Oldsmobile."

Marybelle said, "It's like he thinks once he married me he owns me."

Rudy said, "Uh mmm. Well I warned you, didn't I? Remember that first night John brought you home after Chuck Warner's wedding. I told you then he'd change his tune once he got his clutches into you."

Marybelle shuffled her feet and said nothing. Rudy continued, "Look here, honey, I maybe shouldn't a said I told you so, but the fact is you're married and there's certain obligations and you gotta meet each other halfway and all. But if he ain't willing to give in, then you've got to 'cause he's the man."

Changing the subject without a pause, he mused, "Old Jake's been driving around one-eyed since kingdom come. Now here comes a Studebaker. That'll be old Gus Bertrand."

Nora Lee said, "You made your bed, Marybelle. Now you've got to sleep on it."

"But why? Who says it's got to be that way?"

"The good Lord says it," said Rudy. "That's who. The good book says that the man is lord of his castle and the woman's 'posed to serve him all her born days."

"You can't mean that, Daddy."

"Well I do. I ain't saying you s'posed to let him slap you around or nothing like that or that you ain't got a right to stand up for what's yours, but when it comes down to where one of you've gotta give in, it's gotta be the woman that does the giving. It may not seem right, but that's the way it is."

Marybelle looked into the distance as if expecting that somewhere out across the desolate bottomlands or somewhere over the precipitous clay bluff to the east an answer to her dilemma would come. It certainly wasn't coming from her parents. She didn't tell Rudy that it had already come to slapping.

Rudy said, "Here comes a Chivvy pickup. Naw 'taint, it's a Dodge. I seen it before, but I cain't recollect whose it is. Hey, he's turning up the drive."

Marybelle swiftly swiveled on the ottoman in a childish reflex gesture as if she could hide by simply turning her back. "Oh my God! It's John. What am I going to say to him?"

John came bearing flowers and apologies. Like a child who has made a terrible mistake, he was sweet and lumbering in his attempts to make amends. Marybelle was afraid of what she had seen in his eyes, of what she had heard in that growling, sneering voice so unlike the sweetness in the voice of the man who had courted her so swiftly. How could someone she thought she knew and loved become a frightful stranger? And yet, here he was, as sweet as ever. Reluctantly and fearfully, she went home with him. And they talked about it. John talked about his temper, about how sorry he was. She told him that she understood that she had wounded his pride. She just hadn't thought, she explained, about how important it must be to him to be able to support her on his own. They talked and they talked, and they each gave in on little things, each proud of their ability to compromise, to listen to each other.

Together they tried, and each tried separately to adjust their expectations to a reality that neither of them could have guessed. Perhaps their marriage was not as comfortable as Chuck and Janet's. It certainly wasn't as romantic as the images she had taken from books and movies and nurtured in a secret part of her heart. But it was a marriage, probably better than many. At first.

When eventually those moments came, as they did more and more often, when the immensity of married life seemed forever beyond their abilities to cope, John sought solace in the pool hall in Saltillo and in Lulu's Cafe in Shakerag. Failing to win at poker in the back room, he started hanging out in the cafe with the Negroes. He told them jokes they'd heard a jillion times, and they politely laughed. He sat close to Lulu at the counter and looked down her cleavage.

Marybelle turned to her mother for companionship.

"We've really tried," she said, "at least I have, and . . . yes, I think he has too—in his way. But I don't know if we can ever be happy together. I quit my job because he wants me home all the time. Cleaning, cleaning, all the time cleaning. No matter how sparkling the house is, he's never satisfied. He expects everything to be perfect, but of course he doesn't think anything of tracking mud in and scattering his stuff all over. He's taken up smoking a pipe. Thinks the smelly thing makes him look dignified. And if the ashtrays aren't washed when he gets home, he gets furious."

"Well honey, when a man works hard all day he has a right to expect a clean house to come home to. I don't know what you're fussin' about. When you was a girl I worked all day cleaning Miz Warner's house, then had to come home and clean this one and make supper for your daddy. Now't I got the job down't the mill, I work even harder, and I still got to cook for your daddy and do the ironing and whatnot. I got to do everything now 'cause of his bum leg, but you don't hear me complaining none, do you? Naw. You young folks just don't seem to have no spunk about you."

Marybelle looked to the red clay bluff, which was slashed away from the roadbed like a novel without any end, and she shook her head.

Rudy was listening to Mr. Roosevelt on the radio, Mr. Roosevelt talking about the Germans, Mr. Roosevelt talking war. The excitement of it sent a quiver up Rudy's ghost leg.

"I haven't been feeling well lately," Marybelle told her mother on one of her frequent visits. It was early June and she had been feeling vaguely sick for days. Nora Lee said, "I told you, you younguns ain't got no spunk about you."

"Maybe I'll go see Doc Littlejohn. Maybe I need vitamins or something."

Doc Littlejohn said, "There's not a thing wrong with you, Marybelle." It was a week later.

"Then why do I feel so lousy?"

"Why that's natural as can be. You're going to have a baby. Oh, it'll be a fine, healthy baby. I know it will."

John Coe's pride was evident. He told anybody that would listen, "John Coe's rifle don't shoot no blanks. Nosirree." His pride even overflowed to his work. When people drove into Andy's for a fill up, he would rush around with arms waving in dramatic gestures, checking the oil and washing the windshields with vaudevillian histrionics, putting on one heck of a show. Andy said, "Look at that boy strut his stuff. He puts me in mind of that nigger drum major at Carver High."

At home John would place his hands tenderly on Marybelle's stomach and say, "How you doing in there, Junior?" His feelings of tenderness, joy and pride were temporary, however, a reaction to the novelty of her condition. Seeing her belly grow, and then seeing, with amazement, the baby kick in her belly—that touched him. But seeing her big and slow day after dreary day grew old, old, old. It was not long before he quit placing his hands tenderly on her stomach. Instead, he glared at that monstrosity as if daring the baby to come out and show himself.

He spent fewer and fewer nights at home, and nothing she did pleased him. When he came home late and kissed her roughly, the whiskey odor on his breath nauseated her; she turned her face away, which made him resentful. More than once she had to rush to the bathroom in the middle of their sex.

He started complaining about her frequent visits with Rudy and Nora Lee. "No wonder you cain't ever get nothing done around here. You spend so much time visiting your folks that you don't have time for anything else."

Then she turned to Chuck and Janet for solace, which infuriated him. He didn't like Chuck Warner and didn't trust him. Besides, he knew that Marybelle had once upon a time fancied herself in love with Chuck. To even imagine that his wife, who was now five months heavy with child, could be having an affair, or even thinking about having an affair with Chuck Warner, who was happily in love with his new bride, was too far fetched for even John Coe; but John Coe could not bear the thought of his wife having anything in her life that was not directly related to him. He knew, or found out, every time she left the house in Willis Heights. He fixed her wagon on that score by taking the wheels off her old Plymouth so it sat like some kind of pregnant monolith on concrete blocks, a visual counterpoint to the Civil War cannon that guarded their cottage from across the street.

* * *

1941 was ending in a whisper. Autumn leaves had not turned golden, but had dried a sickly brown, withered and dropped. There had been no brisk days, only cold ones. Even the Golden Wave football team had a dismal season.

When the year was young Marybelle had been vibrant and exciting. She had worn smart new fashions beautifully colored to set off the fire in her hair, hair like burnished flax that bounced when she walked past downtown stores with shoulders thrown back haughtily. A young woman only recently out of school with a promising career in a new and fast-growing business, she had been pampered by her boss, who, despite being married, had more than once hinted at a romantic interest in her. She found his infatuation with her, if that's what it was, to be flattering, even though she would never let it go beyond innocent flirtation. Her boss was Ray Prichard. Marybelle had known him in school—not personally, because he had been three grades ahead of her—but she had certainly been aware of him. He had been class president and had been voted most likely to succeed. He was a handsome man who always dressed impeccably.

But wearing smart new fashions and bouncing down the street had been a recent yesterday. Now she was dowdy and defeated. The fire was ash that no longer even smoldered. Marriage to John Coe had done more than put out the fire; it had taken away the matches. She sat on a chair in the front room of a nondescript and colorless house and stared at the bleak grayness of the war memorial across the street. Random puddles lay like ink blots on the street. The sky was a shroud.

UNTIL THE DAWN

Marybelle could have been wondering where her husband was, or she could have been dreaming of romantic adventures in a brighter world or recalling childhood joys or wondering what to get Rudy for Christmas. But the shroud of night was on her face and her eyes focused on nothing. Her husband was in town at the movies. He was watching *Citizen Kane* at the Lyric.

He slouched in his seat with feet propped on the back of the seat in front of him, munched popcorn and tossed the kernels at silhouetted heads five rows in front, guffawing into cupped hands when his victims turned to see who was pelting them. Propped on the empty seat next to him was a quart bottle of bootleg whiskey in a paper bag. By the end of the movie the bottle was empty.

He shuffled out and slouched on the corner, hunkered down inside his heavy coat. Holiday tinsel glittered dully overhead. He watched the white folks leaving the movie house for a while, and then ambled around to the side where the Negroes exited. They left in huddled, chattering masses that split left and right like a marching band fanning in formation. The Alley was nearby to the right, and most of those who were walking headed that way in a group. The ones who lived in Shakerag headed toward the church parking lot where their cars were. One Negro woman left the theater alone. John saw her cut across the street to the courthouse. It was Lulu. He followed her. She cater-cornered the courthouse lawn and veered off toward the church. A glittering mist hovered in the glow of streetlights like the sparkle of metallic icicles on Christmas trees. This unearthly light fell on Lulu's body. John could see her form undisguised by the old sweater and white dress she wore, rounded and succulent like something juicy in the farmers market. Rich ochre skin like the beckoning glow of reflected fire on worn wood of a winter's night. The stark contrast in the black night of white jersey clinging to the brown woman. White like the white of white silk panties stretched across the moving moons

71

of muscular buttocks. Virginal white. A white to be defiled. "Hot damn!" he said out loud, as he squeezed the Swiss Army knife in his pocket and started running across the street.

The old church offered cover of heavy shrubbery. There he caught up with her and pushed the blade of the knife gently against her back. He reached around her neck and held her tightly with his body shoved close to hers, holding the blade firmly. He felt her body stiffen. He spoke hoarsely and urgently, "Turn around, nigger. Slowly."

When she saw his face her eyes widened like two moons. The knife was now pressed into her belly, and he was holding her left arm. He said, "I told you I'd catch up to you one of these days when wadn't nobody around to protect you. You be still now and go along wid' me. You just might enjoy it."

Carefully, using his left hand, while his right still pressed the blade to her belly, he unbuttoned her sweater, then the dress, the same stained, white dress with the dainty pink collar she always wore in the cafe.

"Please le'me go, Suh. I'z beggin' you please le'go."

"Shut yo' trap, bitch!"

The blade inched upward, leaving a fine white line against her brown skin like a hairline crack in baked mud. The point caught under her bra and cut it.

"Please Suh. Least not here." Her voice trembled and he could feel her flesh quiver beneath the point of the knife. Bearing down and twisting the blade, he reached with his free hand and jerked away her bra. Her skin was like old, soft leather worn smooth. A muscle in her stomach began to jump spasmodically. He cupped her breast in one hand and felt the nipple harden—from the bitter night air, from panic, from a sudden adrenaline surge.

"You getting excited, ain't ya," he said. "I told you you'd like it."

A Ford coupe drove by. In it were teenagers with their windows rolled down, despite the cold. Their car radio was blasting Gene Autry singing "Rudolph the Red Nosed Reindeer."

John shoved Lulu into the shrubbery. "Get out of sight," he demanded. She tripped and rolled on the ground, and was up and running before he could grab her again. He lurched for her and crashed against the bushes. A hanging branch slashed his face. Flailing at the bushes and cursing loudly, he stumbled into the stone wall of the church. By the time he got to his feet Lulu was gone, running across the open lawn, clutching her tattered sweater across her chest. The Ford turned a corner just as she burst free of the bushes. Luckily for John, none of the boys in the car saw her—not that they would have done anything about it.

John Coe knew she would never report the attack. He walked to his truck and drove home.

Marybelle had been sitting in front of the window for hours. The glass was fogged and the cannon across the street was no longer visible. Time had died. Every once in a while a car had slushed past, appearing suddenly in shrouded light and passing in a momentary blur, with headlights searching, and just as suddenly leaving the night undisturbed in its private death. Many little eternities had passed since the last car had slushed by. She pushed herself off the chair and shuffled to the bookcase in slippers that made sweeping sounds on the hardwood floor. She wore a shapeless housecoat the color of the night.

Picking a book off the shelf without reading the title on the spine, she went to bed. That was where she was when John got home, stretched out on the bed with the book flat on her chest. The first thing she noticed was the long scratch on his cheek.

"What happened to your face," was her greeting to him. The innocent and obvious and innocuous question, "What happened to your face" was a slap to his manhood. It was as if she had said, "I've been fucking the next door neighbor while you were out. Had to find myself a man that could satisfy me."

He ran across the room in two gigantic leaps and grabbed her by the arm and jerked her off the bed and held her and slapped her over and over.

"What the hell's it to you?" he spat. "It's none of your goddamn business what happened to my face!"

"I just... I ju-just..."

"Shut up!"

"I'm sorry," she cried, but her weak apology went unheeded. Her head bounced side to side as the blows landed. Blood oozed from the corner of her lip. He clinched his fist and swung. His fist crashed into her face with a sickening thud and a rasping sound like wood splintering. She fell back against the bed, dangling like a broken puppet held partially erect by the one hand that still gripped her arm. Above her he hovered like a beast preparing to pounce, his disheveled hair falling across crazed eyes, hands trembling with controlled fury. The fingers that clawed into her arm let loose, and she plopped to the bed like a broken, used and thrown-away doll. There she lay, helpless, watching him remove his clothes. There she lay, broken, as he furiously ripped her gown apart. Yet from somewhere deep within a soul nurtured by Rudy Sullivan's independence and Nora Lee Sullivan's quiet strength, a spark of the old flame ignited, and seconds before he took her she stiffened.

He could use her and throw her away. He could rape her. He could hit her, bite her, rip her clothes to shreds, pull her hair and scratch her skin until it bled, but by God he could not and would not get one moment's satisfaction from it. No, she would not be a discarded rag doll after all, because she would not be soft and pliable like a doll; she would be as hard and unyielding as concrete.

When it was over he administered a parting blow: he kicked her in the stomach and said, "I hope I killed the brat.

Probably wadn't my baby nohow." And he got dressed and walked out again.

Everything was askew. Marybelle sprawled across the bed with one arm and one leg dangling slantwise. A chair was overturned. A picture teetered on the wall, dangling from one corner. She cried. Her tears were not bitter tears. She was not hysterical, but rather, her tears came long and dull, as long and as dull as the last few months of her life had been. Of course it was only in that moment that she realized how much of her had died since her wedding. She wondered if she could revive what had died within her, and said to herself, "Of course not. How could I?"

She pushed herself off the bed and keeled over to the closet where she snatched the first dress she could reach and got into it; lumbered to the wall by the front door and pulled a coat off the hook. Out the door, cold, early morning air slapped her cheeks. The hour was in that lost time that lurks somewhere between midnight and the first pre-dawn hint of light. The cannon slanted skyward and she saluted it with a cockeyed, mock salute, and began to walk.

Her feet dragged her toward Crosstown where the big arrow proudly proclaimed Tupelo the nation's first TVA city, past fields where she had long ago watched Chuck Warner play football with the Bradley kids. There were seven of them, six boys and a tomboy sister who could run and slam and tackle with the best of them. They made an unbeatable football team. Past the creek of confused memories that spilled into Blue Hole—or was Blue Hole that other swimming hole east of town? Which one was it where Louis Hutchinson had seen Chuck and two of the Bradley boys skinny-dipping and hid their clothes? Anyway, somewhere near Tupelo there was a place that was a popular spot for all the boys to go skinny dipping, and they called it Blue Hole because, as Chuck told it, the water was so cold it turned their balls blue. And what difference did it make that somewhere and sometime kids had enjoyed such innocent wickedness?

She left Main Street before reaching Crosstown, avoiding Andy's Texaco, wandered a few blocks, and then took Jackson back to Gloster by Danny's Diner. From Mabel Cook's house, elevated in a canopy of trees on a hill, Christmas tree lights blinked dully. Behind Mabel's house there was a sheer cliff where the hill had been sliced away to build a parking lot behind the Buick dealership on Gloster. Once, when she was in high school, Marybelle had left Danny's with a boy she had a crush on at the time. They snuck around through Mabel's side yard, climbed down the cliff, and smooched on the back seat of one of the used cars on the lot. It had been the most daring thing she had ever done.

She walked to the football field. Next to it was the swimming pool and behind it, protected and sealed off by a ten-foot high cyclone fence, was the playground behind Church Street Elementary. This quadrant of football field, pool, school and playground had been a dominant scene of her childhood. She lingered there and let the brittle December air nurse her wounds while memories flooded over her like the wash of water from the pool when Chuck and the other boys had cannonballed her and the other little kids who were wading in the shallows.

Climbing the slope to the fence, she meshed her swollen face into the wire as she had done as a little girl, staring wistfully at the pool, waiting for one of the older kids—one of Chuck's friends—to give her a dime so she could go swimming. As a little girl, Marybelle had walked the circumference of that pool in chest-high water near the bank, with Mother Warner holding her hand, while Chuck, strong and precocious, raced to the diving platform to pit his diving skills and daring against the older boys. As a high school senior he performed the most astounding feat Marybelle had ever witnessed, except maybe in a circus. He climbed up to the top of the diving platform and instead of going off the board, he jumped off the back, landed on the low springboard ten feet below, sprung high into the air, and cut a double front flip.

But on this freezing morning in the first hours after midnight there was no water in the pool. The lifeguard stands and platform stood like abandoned towers in an old fort. There was an ache in Marybelle's swollen limbs. Her cheek and jaw throbbed. The baby in her womb stirred as she gazed across the pool to the empty schoolyard.

In the fourth grade she had climbed that fence. It was near the end of school. Some of the boys were playing softball behind the school. One of them hit a fly to left field and it went sailing over the fence. A homer, smack into the swimming pool. The boy whose ball it was started crying. "My daddy'll spank for sure," he whimpered. "He said I'd better not lose that ball. I just got it." Marybelle walked over to them and said to the crying boy, "I'll get it for you," and she climbed the fence and retrieved the ball. Someone told, and the next day she was called to the principal's office and punished for climbing the fence. "But I was just trying to help," she cried. "Doesn't matter," the principal said. "You should have known better. We never go onto the swimming pool property. If you fell in and drowned your parents could sue the school, and we can't take a chance on anything like that happening."

Every day for the next week she was forced to sit in the principal's office during auditorium and for thirty minutes after school. There was an old grandfather clock in the principal's office. Hypnotized by the monotonous march of the pendulum ticking off minutes that crept by as the other kids cheered and laughed at end-of-school programs in the auditorium, she sat and sat and sat, stewing with impotent thoughts of the injustice of it all.

That was long ago. On this night, Marybelle walked around the football field, past the cemetery and the school. Her steps now traced a path so familiar that every hedge and shrub was an old friend. Each held a memory of hide-and-seek or of competing with the boys as they leapt hedges. She walked past the staid churches, First Baptist, and then Calvary Baptist, with those strange basement windows where as a child you could climb down and pretend to be in a cave or at the bottom of a well or in the dungeon of a Medieval castle; the old house on the corner of Church and Magazine where she got her first kiss, the Prater house where the old maid sisters had made lemonade for all the kids on the block. Finally she stood in front of the Warner house. How natural it would be to walk right into the screened-in side porch and enter the everyday living room through the side door that was never locked.

There were no lights on in the house. Chuck's new Packard sedan was parked in the drive. It was light blue, but looked a ghostly white under the streetlights. The one he had bought the year before had been black. Chuck bought a new car every year.

Spring, 1982

I told this tale to Jimmy on that long drive from New York to Tupelo. Jimmy did most of the driving. He also did most of the talking. At first. He tried to draw me into conversation, but I was deep in private thoughts. He wanted to know why I was so quiet, what had me so preoccupied, and why I was so goddamn obsessed with Red Warner.

Red Warner. How can I explain my obsession with Red Warner? He was unique in the history of art, the last of the agonized geniuses. There was a long history of the artist as outsider, the misunderstood genius whose angst can only be expressed in tortured images. It goes back to Michelangelo and his tortured vision of damnation. Rembrandt's revealing self-portraits. Goya. Van Gogh. Picasso's Guernica. Pollock and de Kooning. It ended with Andy Warhol. "At least Andy had the balls to mock himself and his whole fashion and celebrity obsessed generation," Red Warner had said in one of those famous tirades of his that were always quoted in the *New Yorker*. He said, "Nobody can see Andy's irony, and all the rest of these so-called artists today are a bunch of sniveling, effete wimps. They don't know that painting doesn't come from the eye and the hand; it comes from the gut and farther down. They don't know that the seat of art is a hard dick."

There may be a few painters now who are as ballsy as Red Warner, but for the most part there are no more artists; only media stars. Everybody's living Warhol's vision of being famous for fifteen minutes. We've got Post Modernism now, for godssake. Things like color and texture and composition take a back seat to narrative content. It's all cerebral, conceptual. Ideas.

And most of the ideas aren't even original. Today's so-called artists rip off ideas from earlier artists. They call it appropriation. In this sea of surfaces, Red Warner is an anachronism. He paints from his guts. He tortures the canvas, trying to force it to give voice to his private demons. So to me, Red Warner is like the essence of modern art, the whole of it as an historic continuum, right up until it veered off the track in the seventies.

But my obsession, as Jimmy called it, with Red Warner was much bigger than his art. I knew him back when he wasn't known as Red, but as Travis Earl Warner. We were neighbors. Grew up together. And I always looked up to him, dreamed of being like him. So many evenings we spent in his bedroom, the three of us: me and Travis and Cassie, propped on big pillows in the bay window that overlooked his backyard dreaming about some romantic future. They were both dreamers, especially Cassie, who wanted to be a dancer and dreamed of moving to New York and studying with Martha Graham. Only I never said anything about my dreams. I was ashamed to because I too wanted to be an artist, but I couldn't tell that to Travis who had all the talent while I had none. I envied him and worshipped him. I guess it was inevitable that I would eventually take up collecting, and that as soon as Red Warner became famous I would start acquiring his works.

Jimmy said, "I might as well tell you that I'm jealous of Red Warner. You never loved me the way you seem to love him."

"Guilty as charged," I said, making no excuses. Our relationship was solid enough that I could talk of loving another man—a ghost from childhood—without Jimmy feeling threatened. "But it's not romantic love, it's family love."

"You mean you're actually related?"

"Not by blood, but there was a family relationship between the three of us: me and Travis and Cassie. The two of them grew up as brother and sister, living in the same house and sharing an extended family, but they were not biologically related. And I lived next door and practically lived with them for eighteen years."

"Thank God. I was afraid you had been lovers. Like the first ever, you know, the one that imprints your heart and you're never able to forget."

I hesitated a moment too long, and he screamed in a kind of mock hysteria, "Oh no! He WAS your first!"

"Sort of," I said. "These things are always more complicated than that. There was a one-time sort of a thing. I wouldn't really call it my first experience. I don't know if you could really call it sex, but it was the event that marked my first acceptance of my sexual orientation. For Travis it was probably something different. I don't think he's gay, but he did have more than one same-sex experience that I know of, and I'll tell you what: I think it was devastating to him every time. Talk about your internalized homophobia. Think what it must have been like for him twenty to thirty years ago, a football hero whose father and grandfather had been war heroes."

But before I could get into all that I had to tell Jimmy about Marybelle and how she became a part of the Warner family. A lot of it I guessed at. Stuff I didn't even know when I was trying to explain it to Jimmy. Stuff I learned about later during those lazy summer days I spent with Travis down on the bayous.

TUPELO

Right after Chuck and Janet were married, Charlie Warner passed away. As his father before him had, Charlie died young from a massive coronary. Chuck and Janet, at his mother's request, moved into the big house on Magazine Street. Becky, who was not that old, became "Mother Warner," the prototypical grandmother. Her namesake, young Becky, Chuck's sister, was off at college. They turned Becky's room into yet another guest room. Mother Warner moved her belongings into one of the other guest rooms upstairs, and Chuck and Janet took over ownership of the house, at Mother Warner's insistence, and they moved into the master bedroom. The small bedroom next to theirs would soon be converted into a nursery, for Janet was expecting a child. They had found out only a week ago, and already Chuck was talking about buying little boy football outfits.

Everyone in the house was sound asleep. It was two o'clock on a bitter cold December morning. Outside, Marybelle stood for a long time, leaning against the new Packard. Finally she opened the back door of the car and climbed in. She stretched out on the plush seat and tucked her knees tightly to her chest, as tightly as she could with the baby in her stomach. She wrapped her coat snugly around herself and fell asleep.

Chuck discovered her there the next morning when he got into his car to go to work. He'd already opened the driver's side door to get in when he saw her in the back seat. He left the door ajar so as not to startle her with its closing and came around to get in the back with her. He sat down softly, putting his hands on the seat first, then slowly easing his weight down. He put one hand on her forehead and gently pushed her hair to the side. "Marybelle, wake up."

She jammed her hands between her knees and shuddered. "Good morning. Guess you didn't expect to find me here."

He could see a bruise on her face and redness from sleeping with her face buried into the seat. But she was smiling. He helped her out of the Packard and guided her with one arm around her back and the other on her elbow into the house, where Janet fixed breakfast for her. As Janet scrambled the eggs she kept looking back and forth from Marybelle to her husband.

"I don't know what in the world you're doing here," Chuck said, "but you'd better eat up and get yourself some decent rest." She nodded her head and looked up to him with her chin tucked like a child being reprimanded. He lifted the tucked chin and asked, "Want me to stay home and keep you company?"

"No. You've got to go to work."

"Well you know good and well that the bank can survive a day without me."

Janet piped in, "You go on, Chuck. I can take care of Marybelle."

"Okay," he said, "but you take good care of her."

He kissed Janet goodbye again, a soft kiss on the lips, and then kissed Marybelle's cheek. "I expect you to be here when I get home. Bye now."

"Bye. And . . . oh Chuck, thanks."

Janet was flustered. She understood that there was a powerful bond between her husband and this woman who had grown up with him, and even though for a short time after Marybelle married John Coe, she had visited almost every day. But Marybelle and Janet had never gotten to know one another intimately. Each had always felt in the other's presence somewhat like a reluctantly accepted in-law.

Janet said, "Do you want some coffee, honey? Or maybe you'd rather take a nap. You can use Becky's room. She's off at college, but I guess you knew that. There are clean towels if you want to take a bath. I can show you where they are. Ooh, that bruise looks bad." She inhaled deeply. "Maybe you'd like to talk."

"Yes," Marybelle said. "All of that. Coffee, and a nap and a bath and yes . . ." she giggled, meekly. "Yes, I think I do want to talk. Do you mind?"

"No, of course I don't mind. What happened?"

"He beat me. He beat me bad."

All Janet could do was console her. All she could do was hold her while she cried. Later, Marybelle showered and went into Becky's room for a nap. That was where she was when Chuck came home that afternoon. With hot toddy in hand, he tiptoed into the room and whispered, "You awake, Marybelle?"

"Yeah, I'm awake. Sort of." She pushed herself to a seated position and let him fluff the pillow behind her. He handed her the hot drink.

"Here, sip this. It'll make you feel better. Janet told me what happened. I called Sheriff Dobbs and he said he'd go out and talk to John if you want him too. Can't do much of anything unless you press charges, maybe not even then; the law tends to believe that a man's got a right to beat his wife if he wants to. But I don't think John'll give you any more trouble."

Later, in the kitchen, Mother Warner had come in to help Janet get supper ready while Chuck hovered about. Janet asked Chuck, "Do you think she will go back to him?"

"God, I hope not. No, not Marybelle . . . but you never know. I've heard that some women who get beaten by their husbands just go back for more, over and over, because as horrible as it is, they'd rather be beaten than be alone. I can't imagine Marybelle being like that, though. She's strong. She'll put up with a lot, but boy when she gets her back to the wall, you'd better watch out."

Marybelle had gone back to sleep. They could see her through the door that had been left open a crack. "How long should we let her stay here?" Janet asked.

"Forever, if that's what she needs. She's as much a sister to me as Becky, even closer in some ways."

They saw her smile in her sleep. "She's chasing rabbits," Janet said. "Did you see the way she smiled just then, like she dreamt a joke? We used to see dogs do that in their sleep and say they were chasing rabbits."

"Babies too. Babies do that."

"Yeah, I've seen 'em."

Mother Warner opened the door from the kitchen and said, "Supper's ready. Ya'll want to eat?"

"Yeah. Be right there" Turning to Chuck, she asked, "Do you think we ought to wake her?"

"Yeah, I think so."

It was a meat and potato supper, with beans and salad and corn bread. Marybelle skipped the meat. She dawdled with her food, sopping up the juice from the beans with her corn bread. Her jaw was swollen. The whole left side of her face was a deep purple bruise. She chewed the soggy corn bread slowly. They ate silently.

The sudden, jarring ring of the telephone ripped the silence. Chuck excused himself to answer it. "Hello. Yes, she's here. No, she can't come to the phone right now."

There was a pause in the conversation while he listened to the voice on the other end of the line, a pause in the chewing of food and the clatter of utensils and the breathing sounds and softly swishing feet that shuffled under the table and all the other little sounds that a moment earlier had comprised silence, as Janet and Marybelle and Mother Warner all strained to overhear Chuck's end of the telephone conversation. They heard him say, "No, you're dead wrong. You've got no right to speak to her, none whatsoever. And I don't want you calling here again. Do you understand?" He slammed the receiver down.

"That was him, wasn't it?" Marybelle asked, when Chuck shuffled back to the table.

"Yep. Don't you worry about it. He won't bother you as long as you're here."

A moment later the phone rang again. Again Chuck excused himself from the table and went to answer it. "Hello," he snapped. Silence lay on the line. "Hello," he repeated. "Who is this?"

Returning to the table to the unasked question, he said, "I don't know. They didn't say anything."

Marybelle said, "It was him."

"But why would he call and not say anything?"

"Maybe if I answered . . ." She pushed her chair from the table and mumbled, "Excuse me," and walked into the living room and stood by the window, facing out. Janet exchanged glances with Chuck and he nodded affirmation. She eased her chair back and went into the living room and gently laid her hands on Marybelle's stiff shoulders. Moved to a loud cry at the touch, Marybelle spun around, and the two women hugged each other as she let the sobs pour from her heart. They were inches from the telephone.

Marybelle jumped when the phone rang. Janet, still hugging her, could feel a shudder run down Marybelle's body like a tidal wave. Janet picked up the phone.

There was a short pause, and then she said, "Oh my God!" and quickly flung the receiver down.

"What was it, honey?" Chuck asked. "Was it him?"

"I . . . I guess so. It must have been."

"What did he say?"

"I can't repeat it. I've never heard language like that."

Marybelle said, "Maybe I should go somewhere else. He's gonna keep calling, just to harass us. Maybe I ought to leave."

"Leave? And go where? Back home? Back to that useless son of a bitch? Maybe to your folks? Hell, poor old Rudy couldn't handle it any better than we can. Besides, you said he thinks your place is with your husband, no matter what. He'd probably invite the bastard in with open arms."

"Chuck, do you have to use such language?" Mother Warner interrupted.

"Sorry, Mom."

Marybelle laughed, a stifled, bitter laugh. "You're wrong about Daddy, Chuck. Sure, he's got some old fashioned ideas about a woman knowing her place. Long as all John did was slap me once, Daddy figured I probably had it coming—figured he should have done it more himself when I was growing up. But this is different. Nobody can get away with hurting Daddy's little girl like John did. If he showed up out there, Daddy'd probably shoot him."

Chuck laughed, "Hey, maybe that's not a bad idea."

Janet said, "Chuck! Don't you talk like that."

Mother Warner said, "The man is simply frustrated because he knows he has lost. He lost his wife because she's too strong to stand for his beating her, and he'll never get her back because she has us to stand by her and we're stronger than he is. If we don't give him the satisfaction of getting mad he'll give up sooner or later. Just don't let him ruffle your feathers."

"Wise advise, Mother Warner."

"But it's not right that I should drag you all into my problems."

"Shucks, child, I've been involved in your problems since you were in diapers." Mother Warner's hackles were up.

The phone didn't ring again that night, but it rang often in the days to come. John Coe did everything he could to make their lives pure hell. He called the Warner house and set the phone by a radio to let whoever answered listen to whatever happened to be on the air at the time. He called and let the person who picked up the phone listen to cold silence. He called and cursed. He drove by the Warner house and threw rocks at the windows (never succeeding in breaking one, because the distance from the street to the house was too great). The harassment was relentless. Then on a Sunday morning early in December Chuck discovered that all four tires on his Packard were flat, cut with a knife, with stab wounds near the rims where they could not be patched. He was livid. He stomped the ground. He kicked the tires. He cursed with loud bellows, oblivious to the families walking up Magazine Street on their way to Calvary Baptist Church. "God damn you, John Coe!" he shouted. "Damn your worthless hide."

Old Doc Littlejohn snickered and said, "Never you mind, you young scamp," when his grandson, Sam asked what Mr. Warner was shouting. Joshua Culpepper, who was walking by with his wife and little Josh Junior, stepped off the sidewalk to see what all the commotion was about. Mrs. Culpepper clapped her hands over little Josh's ears and muttered, "Such language!" (as if she didn't hear it from her husband constantly).

"Whassa matter, Warner?" Culpepper asked. His wife walked ahead even faster, pushing little Josh in front of her.

"Son of a bitch slashed my tires."

"Geez, he really done a good job of it." He whistled with admiration. "Do you know who done it?"

"Yeah, I know, but I can't prove it."

"Hell man, you don't have to prove it. If you know who done it, just do the same to his. Who you think it was anyhow?"

"Your buddy down at Andy's. You know, John Coe."

"Naw man, it wadn't none of him. He wouldn't do nothing like that. Probably some shiftless nigger."

Culpepper ran to catch up with his family, and Chuck went back into the house.

John Coe made his last call to the Warner house that morning. He apologized to Chuck for all the trouble he had caused, denying any knowledge of the slashed tires, and begged Chuck to please let him speak to Marybelle. Chuck hesitated. You could see it on his face, the whole story of how he had been raised to be polite to everyone, to be forgiving and always give a guy a second chance, ingrained Christian charity fighting with a devilish desire to take John Coe by the throat and squeeze until his face turned purple. He said, "Oh, awright. Just a minute." Then covering the receiver with his hand he spoke to Marybelle. "He said he was sorry, and he said he'd never try to call you again, but that there was something real important he had to say. I don't trust him and I don't think you ought to talk to him, but it's your decision."

The whole family stood by expectantly as she put the receiver to her ear and said, "Yes? What do you want?" They watched her face. They saw the color change as if a syringe had been inserted and the blood drawn out. They saw her hands began to shake until she had to grasp the phone with both hands to hold it still. Janet put her hands over Marybelle's.

They heard her say, "Can't you take her? No, I can't. You know that... Well, I... No. No. I'm afraid to... But that's not... I'll think about it. Really I will. Give me time, John."

She sat the receiver in its cradle and sat herself down in Chuck's easy chair. Chuck and Janet and Mother Warner all hovered around her, waiting. Marybelle said, "About a week before we were married I adopted a little puppy, a rusty brown Cocker Spaniel named Ginger. Such a pretty little thing. John said she's sick. He said if I wanted her to live I'd better come get her. I told him I couldn't. I asked him to take her to the vet for me, and... and he said... His exact words were, 'She's your dog. She's gonna croak any minute if you don't get over here.'"

"It's a trick," Chuck said. "He's trying to lure you over there. What a cheap trick!"

"But what if Ginger really is dying?"

"Aw come on, honey. He's just trying to get you over there. Don't fall for it."

"Yes I know. You're right. At least he said he wouldn't bother me any more. No more calls. At least we have that to be thankful for."

"As if we can believe that," Chuck muttered.

But John Coe was true to his word. No more calls. The morning had gone. They had eaten a light lunch in blessed peace. The afternoon sun slanting through the living room windows gave warmth to the day. Already Christmas presents in bright wrappings were stacked under the tree. It was a huge tree in the Warner style, bedecked with popcorn strings and icicles and bespangled with homemade ornaments. A low flame danced in the fireplace. The sweet scent of burning pine floated in the room. Janet set the card table near the windows, and Marybelle brought in folding chairs; they prepared for a game of bridge. Chuck went into the next room to listen to the football game on the radio. The Giants game was being broadcast live from the Polo Grounds. While Chuck listened to the ball game and while the women played cards in the shadow of the Christmas tree, there came a knock on the door. Mother Warner answered it. Four-year-old Josh Culpepper stood at the door holding a package. "A man gi'me a nickel to bring this," he said.

It was just at that time when Chuck came back into the room to tell everyone they had interrupted the ball game with a special announcement. The Japanese had bombed Pearl Harbor. But before telling them the news he stopped to see whom the package was for.

The package was wrapped in shiny red paper with white ribbon. It was the size of a jewelry box or a watchcase. The attached card was addressed to Marybelle. "Listen to this," she said after opening the card, "The man is sicker than I thought. It says 'I love you dearly and hope you can find it in your heart to forgive me. Your faithful husband.' Can you believe it! After all he's done he thinks he can just say he's sorry and I'll come running back."

"The man is sick," Mother Warner said.

Marybelle tore the paper from the package and lifted the flap to the cardboard box inside. Ribbon hung like leftover tinsel from a party gone sour. She screamed! The box plopped onto the floor. They all hovered over the box that sat on the floor. A small metal tag attached to a chain hung out of the opened end. Inscribed on the tag was the name "Ginger."

The War Years

The year 1942 had just arrived. Travis and Cassie and I were in our mother's wombs preparing to come out into a world at war. Chuck joined the Army in January and was stationed in Texas, where he remained for the duration. John Coe was sent to Europe, where he was eventually to become part of the United States invasion force at Normandy. Other young men from Tupelo were sent to various parts of the globe to defend democracy, all having volunteered in a patriotic rush in the first few days after Pearl Harbor. "Goodbye Mama, I'm off to Yokohama," the young men sang, going off to war as they would rush into a gridiron battle. Among men in Tupelo still young enough to fight, only Ray Prichard remained, the victim of a congenital heart condition. Ray Prichard was the owner of the Esquire. He was still Marybelle's boss, and he was probably a little bit in love with her, or maybe he simply lusted after her. At any rate, he was married, and Marybelle never encouraged his occasional hints and tentative passes.

The first boy from Tupelo to get himself killed in the war was Charlie Speed. He died right before Travis was born. Chuck and Marybelle had known Charlie Speed. His name was a name, at least, that was familiar. A name among names, a number on the back of a purple and gold football jersey, a sprightly stride of brown pants and yellow sweater in the hall at Tupelo High, and later on campus at Ole Miss. He had played football with Chuck, had been a year or two ahead of him in school. Part of the gang. A face. A name that was known, a set of dog tags snagged on a ship's carcass somewhere in the Pacific Ocean. Charlie Speed: a name like so many names that nearly everyone could recall, but hardly anyone could put with a face or with any specific event. Charlie Speed: a name that appeared in the *Daily Journal* exactly nine times: five times in the sports section, once when he graduated from high school, once when he was accepted into the Ole Miss law school, once when he got married, and once when his dog tags were found adrift in the Pacific Ocean.

For a few days nearly everyone in Tupelo talked about Charlie Speed. Rudy said, "Charlie Speed. Wasn't he the boy that used to run the hot dog concession down't the fair?"

"Naw, that wasn't him," Andy said. "That was the Smith boy. The harelip. Remember?"

"Oh yeah. Oh, I remember. Charlie used to run the mile."

"Yeah. He come close to breaking the state record once."

"Damned if he didn't. And now he's dead. Ain't it a shame."

The girl Charlie Speed married was named Rhonda. She lived with an aunt in a brick house on Church Street near Calvary Baptist Church. Like Janet and Marybelle, she was pregnant. It was a time for bringing new life into the world.

Rhonda Speed was admitted to the maternity ward in the Lee County Hospital on Valentine's Day. Her aunt brought her to the hospital and held her hand during labor. Rhonda cried until they wheeled her into the delivery room and put her to sleep. The baby she gave birth to was a boy. She named him Charlie Speed Junior. After he was taken to the nursery and Rhonda was wheeled back into her room, she cried again, searching the ceiling as if in supplication to a God she could not find, and weeping until she finally fell asleep.

Marybelle was admitted to the maternity ward that same day. For a very short time she talked to Janet and Mother Warner between contractions. "I think he's about ready," she said. "That's my little Travis. He's not going to be the kind to wait around for anything."

"What makes you so sure it's going to be a boy?" Janet asked.

"I just know. A mother can always tell. Don't you know what yours is going to be?"

"Yes, a boy. It'd better be, or Chuck will murder me."

Suddenly Marybelle screamed, "Ieeee! Quick, get Doc Littlejohn. It's time. I know it's time."

Mother Warner rushed into the hallway and grabbed a nurse. "Get Doc Littlejohn. Quick! She's having her baby now."

Two orderlies ran in, along with the head nurse. Marybelle screamed. Janet grasped her hand and squeezed as hard as she could. Doc Littlejohn met them in the hall enroute to the delivery room, and very quickly it was all over. Soon Marybelle was back in her room, a tiny, red-faced baby on her breast. His hair was red like hers. That red hair was just about all of him that she could see, as his face was buried into her breast, his little mouth sucking voraciously. Marybelle muttered over and over in a joyful, tired, other-worldly voice, "Travis, oh my Travis, little Travis, oh my baby."

Half an hour later Doc Littlejohn came back with paperwork for the birth certificate. He asked for the father's name, as if he didn't know damned good and well who the father was, and Marybelle blurted out, "Chuck Warner." It was a tense moment. Everyone exchanged looks, trying to read one another's thoughts. Then Mother Warner said, "That's right. Chuck Warner is the father." The three women smiled at one another, pleased with their little deception and with the shared thought of what Chuck would think about it.

Doc Littlejohn said, "All right, if that's the way you want it." The way Marybelle told us years later, it had been little more than a matter of a wink and a nod and John and Marybelle Coe's son became Travis Earl Warner. Mabel Cook, who still had no business voicing an opinion but did so anyway, all over town, said, "I don't care what they claim. That kid is carrying John Coe's blood, and blood will out. Just mark my word and see if it ain't true. You can take a criminal's kid and let a saint raise him up and he's still gonna turn out to be a criminal." Mabel Cook's opinions, in a warped kind of way, epitomized the opinions of the community at large. She was a Greek chorus of one. And since children are often molded by other people's expectations of them, Travis Earl Warner came into this world bearing the cross of a busybody music teacher's damnation.

Six months later on a hot August night after midnight Janet went into labor. Her water broke on the way to the hospital, and they rushed her immediately to the delivery room, but she would not dilate. Her labor continued for twelve hours, twelve hours of excruciating pain.

Chuck arrived before the baby. He had been granted an emergency three-day pass and had averaged eighty miles per hour all the way from Houston. He arrived in time to pace the lobby for over an hour. Then, at last, the baby came. It was a girl.

The doctor, a young resident who was filling in for the vacationing Doc Littlejohn and who had only delivered one other baby, told Janet she should have her tubes tied. "This one almost killed you," he said. "Another one might."

She was groggy. Exhaustion hung over her like a rain-laden cloud. She said, "Whatever you say, Doctor. You're the doctor."

It was Chuck's last day at home before they got to take the baby home, where they placed her in a crib next to Travis, who was sucking his thumb. The twin cribs sat only a few inches apart. Travis reached his pudgy hand through the bar as if trying to touch the other baby. The grown-ups stood for a few moments, watching the infants. Then Janet went to her room to relax for a few minutes and try to see once again if she could make heads or tails of Faulkner's *The Sound and the Fury*. Mother Warner and Marybelle went to the kitchen to start working on a stew, and Chuck retired to his study, his private room where he always went to be alone with his thoughts.

It had been his father's study before. It was a dark room with tongue-and-groove, pine paneling shellacked to a high gloss. A bookshelf covered one wall. The furniture consisted of a pair of matching leather chairs, a file cabinet, and a roll-top desk aclutter with paper. On the wall facing the desk were a score of framed photographs of men and boys in football uniforms and baseball uniforms. There were plaques presented to Charley Warner in recognition of his unselfish service to the boys of Tupelo. There was a picture of Charley Warner standing under a basketball goal with Chuck, age six, sitting on his shoulders, dunking the ball into the net. There were also pictures of fishermen and hunters, family and friends, proudly displaying heavy strings of striped bass, a deer lashed upside-down to a pole propped on burly shoulders, trophies of all kinds. They were black and white photos in brown frames jammed together in random juxtaposition on the shellacked pine wall. The only spot of color was a small, glass-covered frame that held Charlie Warner's faded Medal of Honor.

That den, a legacy from Chuck's father, was a homey replica of his office at the bank, another legacy from his father. Into this den came Janet Warner, shuffling duck-like, in her fluffy slippers, clutching in her hands the pillow that she used as a cushion wherever she sat her tender bottom. Chuck patted his lap in invitation. She plopped the pillow in his lap and fluffed it, then gingerly eased her butt onto it. "Are you terribly disappointed?" she asked, "That it wasn't a boy?"

"Disappointed! How could I be disappointed? We have a beautiful baby."

"Yes, I know, but you wanted a son."

"Yeah, sure. But hey, the next one can be a boy, the next two or three."

"No they won't," she said. "There won't be any more." And she explained that the doctor had said she would have to have her tubes tied.

He looked at the pictures on the wall. He looked at his wife, whose expression was that of a parent who had been forced to back down on a promise to a child. He could see the shame in her eyes and he could see on the walls of his study the end of a legacy. With no male child, the Warner name would not be carried on. He squeezed her hand and said, "It's all right, baby. We have a daughter, a beautiful daughter who is going to grow up to be the spitting image of her mother. No man could be prouder."

They talked about the baby and her future. He said he wanted to name the baby Cassie, after his grandmother. She said that she hoped Cassie would learn to play the piano; he said he hoped she would dance like the wind, the way Janet had in college. She told him to be careful way out in Texas, and to write every day. He told her to follow doctor's orders, and he said as an after-thought coming from nowhere, "Maybe you ought to take up painting again. I remember that you were quite good, and it'll keep you busy."

She said, "I think taking care of Cassie will keep me busy enough."

They talked of many things, and before they knew it, it was time for him to leave. The one thing they had not discussed, because neither of them had ever considered the possibility, was that perhaps the young doctor was wrong.

So war was waged across the seas and back home babies were popping out all over the place, babies who were smothered with desperate love in homes without men. I was born that year too. I was a sickly child and a plaything for my older sister, who decided I made a much better doll than any old store-bought doll. Ours was a dull and lifeless household. Up the hill at five-fifty Magazine life was much more interesting. Marybelle started working for Ray Prichard at the Esquire again, and Janet did take up painting—again. She set up a studio in the room that had once been the maid's room, the room Marybelle practically grew up in.

Travis and Cassie grew into happy toddlers. Model children they were, perfect in every way, almost to the point of being eerie. Cassie, in particular, was so perfectly well behaved that they sometimes worried she would not be a normal child. There's something wrong with a child who never gets in trouble. Everybody knows that. But Janet and Marybelle thought she was simply adorable. Travis was more demonstrative. All boy is how Mother Warner described him. He managed to get himself in trouble often enough—always out of excessive exuberance, never out of meanness. When he did something wrong, he would punish himself by standing in a corner.

"Travis," his mother would say, "Why are you standing in the corner?"

"Cause I did something bad," he'd say. He'd never say what, but he'd punish himself quite severely. The kid came into this world with an oversize sense of remorse.

* * *

It was a summertime Sunday morning in the later years of the war. We were playing on the front porch. Cassie and I were stacking blocks near the steps; Travis was stretched out on his stomach in front of a large newsprint pad, drawing with crayons. Sunlight slanting through magnolia leaves painted bubbles of light on the porch. My mother and the Warner women, including Becky, who was home from college for the summer, were all lounging on the porch. They sat in reared-back chairs like old men, their feet resting on the porch rail.

During those years my mother spent a lot of time at the Warner house. She was lonely and had nothing much to do with herself. That was fine by me. It meant I got to play with

Travis and Cassie. I spent so much time with them that it seemed we all shared mothers. There was my mother, who seemed to blend into the shadows on the porch, and there were Travis and Cassie's mothers whom we all called "Mama Janet" and "Mama Marybelle." I don't remember why, or who started it. Mama Janet, for some reason I couldn't explain, looked to me like what a mother should look like: always neatly dressed, always smiling, and never still for a moment. She was always rubbing her forehead or the back of her neck. Mama Marybelle, on the other hand, didn't look at all like a mother. She looked like a movie star, or like a princess gracefully floating in dancing circles in a golden ballroom.

So anyway, all of these women were chattering away in a rather desultory way while Travis and Cassie and I played on the porch. Nearby, some older kids from the neighborhood were playing in the front yard: Sam Littlejohn, old Doc Littlejohn's grandson, Josh Culpepper, who was the oldest, and the Casey boys, all four of them. I think that even at that young age I disliked Josh Culpepper and was afraid of the Casey boys, all of them. I didn't much like fat and funny Sam Littlejohn either, although later, when me and Travis and the guys were older, we all developed a fondness for Sam, who was lovable and clumsy and the butt of everybody's jokes.

They were playing soldier. Josh was the drill instructor. He barked orders as he had seen it done in the movies, and the other kids all snapped, "Yes Sir!"

Marybelle said, "Look at the way those kids follow the Culpepper kid, like he's some kind of hero."

"Just 'cause he's the oldest," Janet said.

"You gotta keep an eye on that kid. He's got a mean streak in 'im, just like his old man."

"What were we talking about, anyway?"

"The war, naturally. What else?"

The feeling all over America was that it would be over soon. Hope intensified with every newscast. The Americans were advancing on the Germans. Russians were winning in the north. Hitler was sending his troops on suicide missions.

Janet said, "I read in the paper that it'll be over within the month."

"Maybe," Mother Warner said. "Maybe in Europe. But it won't be over in the Pacific until every last Jap is dead. They'll never give up."

It was a lazy conversation, interspersed with long silences as they watched passersby on Magazine Street. An oscillating fan, brought out to the porch and hooked up with an extension cord, stirred the ladies' hair. Marybelle rocked in her chair, nervously bumping the legs against the porch. Janet kept looking at her daughter—constantly amazed that such a pretty little girl could have come from her.

Old man Long drove by in his Plymouth and tooted his horn. Ray Prichard cruised by in his Cadillac. Samantha Jones, the widow woman who had raised her only child, Wallace, all alone in the old family house on Green Street, walked by with her two cats on a single leash. The cats were wearing little jackets that she had knit herself. "Morning ladies," she chirruped. "How ya'll doing this fine morning?"

"Just fine, Miz Jones," Mother Warner shouted. "Have you heard from Wallace lately?"

"Yessum, I sure have. I got a letter from him just last week. Said they're going to let him out of the hospital soon. He'll be coming home."

"That's wonderful, Miz Jones. I'm sure you just can't wait."

"No I cain't, but it's going to take a heap of getting used to, him being blind and all. Just don't seem right. But I reckon the good Lord's got His reasons."

"At least he's alive, Miz Jones. Be thankful for that."

"Yessum, I am thankful for that. Mighty thankful." She started on down the street. Josh Culpepper was hiding behind the garage door, next to the chinaberry tree. "Bang! Bang!" he shouted, pretending to shoot Mrs. Jones. Then he scooped up a handful of chinaberries and slung 'em at the cats.

"You boys behave yourselves, now," Mrs. Jones said as she daintily stepped across the jagged sheet of concrete where roots from an oak tree had ripped up the sidewalk.

About that time Josh's father showed up. He pulled his pickup truck to the curb and hollered out, "Mornin' ladies," tipping his Brooklyn Dodgers cap, a wet stump of cigar clamped between his teeth. "Ya'll seen my boy? He been over here?"

"Here I am, Pop." Josh's voice came from high in the dense foliage of the magnolia. He was quick. After being reprimanded by Mrs. Jones he had climbed high in the tree where his face could barely be seen amidst the shimmering leaves. We all looked up, the women and all us kids, and even Travis, who had been drawing so intently that he had not shown any interest in the big kids.

Mister Culpepper hollered, "Git down from there, boy, afore you break your darn fool neck."

"Younguns!" he snorted, addressing himself to the women. Then he pulled away from the curb and drove home.

Becky watched the car head down Magazine Street. "I can't stomach that man," she said.

Mother Warner admonished her. "Hush, girl. You ought to be ashamed."

"Well it's true. I can't. He gives me indigestion."

Mother Warner dismissed her with a flick of her wrist, as if shooing flies, and turned her attention to the boys in the yard who were getting louder. Josh had climbed down from the magnolia and was shouting orders: "Hit the dirt! Zero at five o'clock!" And the Casey boys were yelling, "Bang! Kapow! Rat-ta-tat-tat!" And poor little, chubby Sam Littlejohn couldn't seem to make up his mind which way to go. He would start in one direction, then turn, then turn again. The Casey boys were laughing at him. Marybelle said, "Poor Sam Littlejohn. He's always the butt of the joke."

Becky said, "Well I just wish they'd all go away. Why do they have to play in our yard? Don't they have yards of their own?"

"Becky!" Mother Warner exclaimed, "I don't know what's come over you. You don't seem to like anybody today."

"Aw, she's just being testy 'cause she hasn't heard from her boyfriend in over a week," Marybelle said.

Mother Warner said, "Waiting to hear from a soldier is no laughing matter." She said it with such a stern voice that nobody could say anything for a while. We thought it was a marvel how Mother Warner could scold grown-ups just like they were children.

After they were quiet for a while, Marybelle said, "I know it's strange, but I've been thinking about John lately. He's over there risking his life, and he's probably seen buddies get killed right in front of him. There's no telling what horrors he's seen. Maybe it's changed him."

"You're not thinking of making up with him!" Janet exclaimed.

"No, of course not."

"Thank God."

"No, I could never go back to him, not after what he did, but if he lives through this, the least I can do is let him see his son now and then. Travis is his son too. And . . . and he's really not such a bad man, despite what he did to me. He was . . . it must have been some kind of sickness. Some kind of rage just came over him. He couldn't help himself."

Her words were extracted from between clinched teeth. All of Magazine Street, as if waiting for her to formulate her thoughts, quieted. Even the rambunctious boys in the front yard hushed. They were crawling in the grass with sticks clamped between their teeth, make-believe bayonets. In a stage whisper, Josh Culpepper barked the hushed order,

"Sneak attack!" And they all rushed Sam Littlejohn, wrestling him to the ground and pretending to spear him with their bayonets.

Travis stopped drawing. In imitation of the other boys, he crawled stealthily to where we were working on our building-block castle. He looked like a lion cub practicing for the hunt. He stopped, chewed on a crayon, and looked at the grown-ups. He stared at his mother the way some people stare at radios, as if they are trying to conjure up the face of the announcer by force of will.

It was then that the letter arrived. Later, Marybelle talked about having a premonition.

The letter gave no details. It didn't tell the tale that was later told by a returning GI who had been with John Coe. This man said that John Coe was hated by the other men in his platoon. He said the men joked among themselves that when they got into battle it would be a toss-up who got to shoot him first, his own men or the Germans. He said the landing on Normandy Beach was bedlam, with screams and shouts and gunfire and men not knowing which way to go, but John Coe, he said, sauntered forward as if he owned the beach. With a cigarette dangling from one corner of his mouth and his helmet pitched forward at a rakish angle, his rifle slung uselessly across his back, he swaggered into the oncoming bullets. And a kid, a frightened kid from a ranch somewhere in Wyoming, went bananas. He started shooting in all directions, spinning around drunkenly and yelling like a cowboy in a brawl in a cowtown bar. A bullet from his rifle hit John Coe in the back of the head. It entered below the rim of the cocked-forward helmet and ripped his head like a watermelon dropped on the road.

The letter did not tell this tale. It merely said that the country regretted to inform Mrs. Coe that her husband had been killed in action.

Marybelle laughed hysterically. Tears glazed her cheeks and she did not stop crying and laughing until she choked. Mother Warner held her in her arms and rocked her, and Marybelle gasped between choked surges of hysterical laughter, "I'm glad he's dead. I'm glad he's dead. I know it's wrong, but I'm glad he's dead. Oh my God, forgive me, I'm glad he's dead."
    Travis started crying, and he swiped at our block castle with a roundhouse blow, and the blocks tumbled and clattered down the steps in a jumble of alphabet letters, and Josh Culpepper shouted, "Enemy fire! Hit the deck, men!"

New Beginnings

After the war, Chuck Warner came home to a wife who had only a short time before been a vivacious and exciting young coed, but who had taken on the look and personality of what she had consciously become: a housewife. She wore her hair in a sensible way and dressed in a sensible style and kept the house reasonably clean. She had gained about twenty pounds, and she had headaches, migraines that were a constant source of complaint. He also came home to a darling daughter and a couple of permanent houseguests: Marybelle and Travis.

It was in the first days after the war that the story of Chuck and Janet and Marybelle began to trickle to a close, like a stream that flows from a river into a winding bayou and finally trickles over soggy grass and is consumed by the earth; but from the wet earth bubbles forth fresh water that eventually becomes again a raging river. Thus did Travis's story begin.

He was a sweet kid who tried very hard to please the grown-ups around him: Papa Chuck, Mama Marybelle and Mama Janet (even I called them by those names). Often shy and conscience-stricken, he nevertheless had about him something devilishly playful and mischievous. He was also big and clumsy from the start, and had a way of breaking things. Yet he was always gentle with me. Growing up, I was never much good at wrestling or throwing or tackling or any of those boyish things that he did so well, despite his clumsiness. But he was patient with me and always took up for me and made sure I was included when the other kids wanted nothing to do with me. In a way, I guess you could say he babied me;

then everybody did. They either babied me or neglected me, especially my mother and my older sister, both of whom seemed to think I was some kind of doll to be fawned over and dressed up and fondled and tossed in the toy box when they were done. That's why I spent so much time at the Warner house, even after my mother quit going over there. Everybody was welcome at the Warner's, especially people who weren't necessarily wanted anywhere else. It had always been that way, even back when Travis's granddaddy was alive. As Mabel Cook was fond of saying, the Warners always took in strays.

Looking back now it seems that I somehow appropriated Travis's childhood, claimed his memories as my own, as if I had none to claim for myself. I even appropriated his childhood traumas. There were a couple of things that stand out. One of them was what happened when Travis tried his hand at shoplifting. He was about eight years old. The Casey boys, or maybe Josh Culpepper, put him up to it, dared him or somehow planted in him the seed of an idea that it was a thing he had to do to prove he was a real boy. He tried to shoplift a baseball from Page's Market, and Mr. Page caught him in the act. He snatched him up by the collar and dragged him into his office and called the cops. Little Travis, trying mightily not to cry, sat in that cubbyhole of an office awaiting the cops who were going to cart him off to jail. Of course they wouldn't put a little kid in jail for stealing a baseball, but when they arrived, the cops figured if they made him think they were going to he'd never try anything like that again. There were two of them, Bucky Norman, who was fat and sloppy and constantly fiddled with his clothes, stuffing his too-short shirttail back into his breeches and adjusting his tie and the like, and another one whose name I can't remember, a skinny cop with pale skin and freckles. Travis said they looked like Abbott and Costello.

With Travis seated on a box in the close space of Mr. Page's office, they strutted and postured and talked to one another about him as if he wasn't there, talking about whether or not they ought to run him in. The skinny one said, "This here's Chuck Warner's kid. I can't imagine Chuck Warner's kid doing anything so low as to steal."

"He ain't none of Chuck's," the fat one said. "Not really. His real daddy was John Coe."

"Well that explains it. John Coe weren't nuthin' but common. Like father, like son."

"Yep. Blood will out. That's what I always say, and it's right as rain."

That was when they noticed that he was crying. Sometimes there's no holding back the tears. That's when they told him that he could go home, after making him promise, of course, that he'd never again steal anything.

The other thing that stands out is the summer he befriended the black boy, Man. I don't know if Man was his real name. I don't know if anybody knew. But that's the only name he was ever known by. Man was a child of the Alley. Christine, the Warner maid, said he was a free spirit. "Sometimes he stay down't Preacher Johnson's. Sometimes at Brother Lubba's. But mostly Man keeps to his self. He don't answer to nobody."

Man had to be at least four years older than us, and he was the strongest boy I'd ever seen. To Travis he was some kind of hero, not only because of his strength and independence, but because of knowledge he had of things exotic to us, like spells and potions and playing the blues on a twelve-string guitar.

For one whole summer Travis pretty much abandoned his other friends for Man. Then one day near summer's end we were all playing in the Casey's back yard, the Casey boys and Sam Littlejohn, with Josh Culpepper nearby, whittling on a tree trunk. We saw Travis and Man crossing the railroad tracks. They waved to each other and Travis came on toward us, but Man stood still on the tracks. Josh took off walking their way and the Casey boys followed. It was a moment like in the movies when the sexy lady gets in her car and the camera lingers on the back of her head and you just know there's some guy hiding in the back seat. Sam and I stood still, watching. It was like those choreographed fight scenes in *West Side Story*, each participant timing his movement within the tableau. I watched. There were four simultaneous moves. Man eased back across the cinders into the edge of bushes. Josh placed himself in Travis's path and stood there punching the palm of his left hand with the balled-up fist of his right hand. The Casey boys shuffled crab-like closer and closer to Josh, and Sam ambled slowly in their direction. Josh insinuated himself in Travis's path. He got himself right up in Travis's face, poking his chest out. He said, "Well, well, well. Look at what we got here."

"Looks like a nigger lover to me," the oldest Casey boy said. He was scratching his butt.

Josh said, "Yep. Sure looks like a nigger lover to me."

There was some pushing and a lot of hollering, then all of a sudden Sam was in the middle of it and Travis slipped away and was running for home and Josh started punching on Sam and Sam was making like it was all a game, laughing and saying, "Aw come on, Josh. Cut it out." And for awhile the Casey boys joined in and they were all slapping at Sam, who kept laughing and saying, "Aw come on, cut it out," until they finally got bored and did cut it out.

Later, in the Warner house, Travis said to me, "Why didn't Man take up for me? What'd he have to hide like a sissy for? He could have beaten 'em all up. It would have been easy for him. He could have slung Josh Culpepper clean across the tracks. He could have knocked the Casey's heads together. I thought he liked me better than anybody and he didn't do a thing but hide in the bushes."

We were ten years old. We didn't know anything about black and white. We didn't know that lynchings have grown out of lesser incidents. But Man knew. He knew only too well.

1960
TUPELO

After a lifetime of trying desperately to grow up and thinking it would never happen, we were suddenly big shots—high school seniors. And now, thinking back over all the stupid things we did back then and remembering how terribly important the most trivial things were to us, I feel compelled to write something about what it was like to be a teenage boy in 1960, as if eighty percent of everyone in the world doesn't already know. We were animals, at least most of us were. Charlie Speed was the living embodiment of a popular, wisecracking, macho, girl-crazy adolescent of the time. He was handsome. He was first-string quarterback on the football team. He couldn't say three words without cursing. He could chug-a-lug a whole can of beer and crumple the can in one hand. And he bragged about making it with the most popular girl in school.

All the other guys tried to be just like Charlie, all that is but Sam Littlejohn. Sam was just a big, lovable guy that nobody took seriously. We all thought he was a little bit retarded. Oh yeah, Travis was different, too. He pretended to be tough and smart-alecky like all the other guys, but his heart was never in it. He wrestled constantly with the need to be liked and the need to be whatever it was that was truly him deep inside. The things that struck me most about Travis were that mop of dirty red hair that would never stay in place, and that aw-shucks grin of his, and his body. He had a body like a sculpture by Michelangelo. Another thing that I liked was his gentleness. As big and strong as he was, he would never fight. He even took a lot of teasing about being afraid of a good fight, although anybody with the sense God gave a billy goat should have known that Travis was never afraid.

I just wanted to touch him. So often I'd watch him do push-ups and sit-ups on his bedroom floor and chin himself on the doorframe, sweet sweat gleaming on that wonderfully muscular body of his, me sprawled across his bed, yakking about nothing in particular, watching him. On the floor of his room sat that ridiculous damned pink portable stereo with the detachable speakers. Invariably Elvis or Bo Diddly or Little Richard would be rocking out on that stereo, and Travis would time his exercises to the rocking beat of the music. Worn out for a moment from his exercises, he'd plop down on the bed next to me, innocently brushing a naked thigh against me, and where our bodies met I'd burn, trembling inside, afraid to move a muscle. His body was like a padded rock, simultaneously hard and soft, with rippling muscles, but not grotesque like those muscle men in the magazines.

So many times I would find myself accidentally touching him in places I shouldn't touch. He maneuvered himself in ways that caused the touch; yet I was sure, or almost sure (that tiny doubt drove me crazy), that he was totally unaware of what he was doing. How easy it would have been to caress that creamy smooth body! But I was horrified at the thought of how he might react. What made it worse was that Travis was actually tender, and even affectionate. For all his he-man posturing, he was not afraid to show affection. It wasn't like I was in love with him or anything. Well, maybe I was. But being affectionate was one thing; being gay was a little more dangerous.

It was a hot summer day and the end of summer vacation. We were cruising up and down Gloster, as usual, in Charlie Speed's red Impala. We pulled into the lot at Danny's for about the tenth time that day. Danny's was a tiny box of a restaurant on the corner of Gloster and Jackson, right where the Kentucky Fried Chicken is now. No more than six customers could sit on the bar stools inside, but the parking lot could hold thirty cars. Hoss Williams was there in his Ford, the Black Bomb he called it, a forty-eight coupe with a chopped top and moon hubcaps. Hoss was sitting in the driver's seat with the door open, a cast from when he had broken his leg in spring practice protruding from his cut-off jeans. Two girls were standing in front of him, leaning over to read the signatures on his cast. They were both wearing Golden Wave football jerseys. The tails of their jerseys barely covered their round hips, with only an inch of their shorts showing—short shorts they called them, little pieces of red and yellow cloth that exposed a strip of white flesh above the tan line—a tempting sight for Charlie, who flicked one of the girls on the rear end with a rolled-up towel.

"Ow! Cut it out," she said. "Oh, hi ya Charlie. Hi Travis." She didn't speak to me.

Travis said, "Hi ya Betty. Rosie baby, what'cha say!"

"Ya'll seen Wanda around?" Charlie asked.

"She went to Okolona with Bitsy."

Okolona was a half-hour drive away. The kids liked to go to the swimming pool there because it was ostensibly an Olympic sized pool, because it had a slide, because it was away from the hometown.

"Howzaboutit fellow travelers? Ya'll want to go to Okolona?" Charlie asked, burning rubber as he wheeled out of Danny's parking lot. "How 'bout you, Johnny boy? Want to go swimming? Or scared it'll mess up your hair?" He reached across the seat and mussed my hair, swerving into the oncoming traffic lane.

"What are you trying to do, kill us?" I said.

"Whassa matter, you want to live forever?"

"I just wish you would be more careful."

"Yeah? Well how 'ya like this?" He swerved again and sideswiped a garbage can.

"Oh Christ!" I yelled. "You're going to wreck us." I knew as I said it that I was exposing myself as a sissy, but I couldn't call the words back. Charlie, naturally, mimicked me (badly). He said, "Ooooh, he's going to kill us. Oh Christ, Charles, you're going to kill us. We're all going to be very, very dead."

Travis slapped Charlie on the side of his head. He was the only one who could get away with that. "Cut the crap," he said. Then he really put Charlie in his place. Doing a perfect imitation of my voice, which Charlie had done so poorly, he said, "And Charles, would you kindly take your hand off my dick."

So Charlie drove us to our houses to get our swimsuits, and we picked up Sam Littlejohn along the way, and drove to Okolona with the top down on the red Impala. Travis drumming furiously on the dash board and singing along with the radio, "It was an itsybitsy teeny-weeny yellowpolkadotbikini that she wore for the first time today..."

Charlie said, "Wanda's got one of those teeny weenie bikinis. She ordered it from Frederick's of Hollywood."

"Ooh, this I gotta see," said Travis. Sam just laughed.

When we got to the pool, sure enough, Wanda was there in what must have been the skimpiest bikini anyone in Mississippi had ever seen (it was, after all, nineteen sixty; such suits were just beginning to show up on beaches in places like California, but not at small town swimming pools in Mississippi). She was standing on the diving board, trying to work up the nerve to jump. Charlie hollered, "Hey, baby!" and suddenly everybody moved. Travis and Charlie grabbed each other and pushed-wrestled-jumped into the pool with a humongous splash, and Sam guffawed and took a mighty leap into the pool, looking like a hippopotamus trying to fly, and Wanda bounded off the board with a competition class swan dive. They all surrounded her when she surfaced, with a barrage of splashing water and a chorus of rebel yells. They horsed around for ten or fifteen minutes, then Charlie and

Wanda climbed out, spread a towel near the edge of the pool and stretched out to stare goo-goo-eyed at one another.

Travis and I sat at pool's edge with our feet dangling in the water. Travis said, "Why is it, why oh why? He gets Wanda Ramsey and I get you."

Sam was standing in line to climb up to the high board. Travis shouted at him, "Hey Sam, five bucks says you won't do a belly flop off the high board."

Charlie shouted, "Don't do it, Sam. It's too dangerous. You'll kill yourself."

"Naw I won't. You really gi'me five bucks if I do it, Travis?"

"Sure. You got the guts, I got the bucks."

"I mean it, Sam," Charlie shouted. "Don't do it."

Somebody said, "He won't do it. Who you kidding?" And pretty soon Travis was collecting bets. Sam pulled his large body slowly up the ladder and edged out on the board with shuffling steps, testing to see if it would hold his weight. Travis grabbed a megaphone from the lifeguard stand and, imitating the announcer on the Friday night fights, cried out, "And now ladies and gentlemen, in the white trunks, weighing in at seven thousand, two hundred and ninety-four pounds, the pride of Nawth Miss'sippi, the entire Golden Wave defensive line, the chug-a-lug champion of Lee County, the one and only Samuel Alison Littlejohn the Third (and last) will perform from a height of twenty meters or thereabouts, his world famous belly flop.

"We need quiet now, ladies and gentlemen. We need your rapt attention. We need an ambulance—and a crane."

Boys nudged one another; girls covered their eyes and peeked between fanned fingers. The lifeguard hedged on his perch, unsure of what to do. Travis announced, "He is making his approach now, ladies and gentlemen. Notice the intensity and poise, the sure grasp of prehensile toes..."

"What kind of toes?"

"Some big word. It means he wears toenail polish. Shut up and listen."

". . . the mass of blubber engulfing his trunks like a globular froth of lava, the protruding pink tongue, the slobber of concentration. Remember now, Littlejohn will be judged not only on height and position at entry, but on survival. You will notice that he is using the classic penguin approach. He springs! And he's off!"

Sam bounced a few inches off the board and his body lurched forward, flat-out, with arms and legs spread, back almost arched. From my viewpoint at the edge of the pool he looked, for an instant, like an airplane silhouetted against the cerulean blue sky, like a blimp with wings, hovering. Then the instant was over. He plummeted. He cracked the water in a solid sheet from knees to neck, and for a moment he was lost in a wall of water. Then we saw him, still horizontal, with arms and legs splayed out, the airplane now gliding in a reflected sky. He sank to the bottom and stayed there, immobile. Swimmers crowded the edge of the pool. The lifeguard dove in and swam to a position above him, waiting. Travis counted through the megaphone, "One Mississippi, two Mississippi, three Mississippi . . ."

At the count of ten Sam pushed himself off the bottom and propelled his body to the surface, breaking the water like an actor parting the curtain. The crowd whistled and cheered.

Charlie whispered to Wanda, "He almost had me fooled that time."

"You mean the whole thing is an act?" Wanda asked.

"Sure it is. Sam knows how to jackknife just at the instant he hits the water, so it looks like he's belly flopping, and me and Travis always pretend to bet. It's all in fun. We never accept our winnings."

Wanda rode back to town with us and snuggled up to Charlie all the way. Sam and Travis sat in the back with me.

When we pulled into town Travis said, "Drop me at Zeke's Rexall, Charlie."

"What for? What's at the drugstore that you want?"

"Books."

"I didn't know you could read." To Wanda, Charlie said, "I'll bet'cha he's gonna buy a *Playboy*. Travis spends all his time in the bathroom with *Playboy*, pulling his pud."

"He draws from the pictures," I said.

Changing the subject, Charlie asked Travis, "What'cha doing tomorrow?"

"We're going out to Tombigbee. Family outing, you know."

Charlie said, "Yeah, well maybe we'll just head out there our own selves. Maybe we'll see you at the lake." For Charlie, as for me, family outings were something that simply didn't happen. He lived alone with his mother, as did I, which was something Travis could never understand. I mean no matter how hard he might try to put himself in our shoes, and he was the kind of guy who would give it his best, he could never do that.

A couple of minutes later we dropped Travis off at the corner, and he went into the drugstore. He browsed the spinner rack of paperbacks until he spotted a cover that attracted him. It was trashy looking, a crude drawing of a moody man wearing a black striped T-shirt, with a scarf tied around his neck. The blurb on the jacket said, "This is the bible of the 'beat generation'—the explosive bestseller that tells all about today's wild youth and their frenetic search for Experience and Sensation."

Travis bought the paperback *On the Road* and a pack of Juicy Fruit and a *Playboy*.

Labor Day Weekend

The day dawned and—swoosh—all over the great old house doors opened and people darted to their various chores and preparations: Travis skipping down the stairs with a drum roll on the banister and a giddy song gushing from his throat, Cassie and Marybelle chattering loudly as they dressed to dash to the Esquire where they were going to buy new swim suits, Chuck gulping his coffee and grabbing the madras-print sports coat from the hall closet, Janet, up for a change.

Chuck drove the Buick to work that morning, leaving the sedate family wagon at home for Janet and the kids. The Buick was Chuck's plaything. It was a sky blue convertible with plush white interior trimmings and a terry cloth wheel cover. His favorite Lucky-13 fishing lure dangled from the rearview mirror.

At the Esquire, Cassie tried on six swimsuits before leaving with her new purchase in a box tucked under her arm, saying to Marybelle, "I should have bought the green one, don't you think? Do you think the color is right for me?"

"It's just fine, honey. I thought it looked precious."

While Chuck ate a light lunch at Mike's, the rest of the family gobbled peanut butter and jelly sandwiches on the run. Travis glopped mayonnaise on his sandwich.

"How can you eat that?" Cassie asked.

"Hey, it keeps the peanut butter from sticking to the roof of your mouth. You ought to try it."

They tossed their gear into the back of the wagon and headed out to Tombigbee State Park. By late afternoon all but Chuck were settled in at the cabin on the lake. Janet had

Store Credit issued for new and unread books and unopened music after 14 days or without a sales receipt. Credit issued at lowest sale price.

Full refund issued for new and unread books and unopened music within 14 days with a receipt from any Barnes & Noble store.
Store Credit issued for new and unread books and unopened music after 14 days or without a sales receipt. Credit issued at lowest sale price.

Full refund issued for new and unread books and unopened music within 14 days with a receipt from any Barnes & Noble store.
Store Credit issued for new and unread books and unopened music after 14 days or without a sales receipt. Credit issued at lowest sale price.

set up the barbecue grill and was playing solitaire on the picnic table while the charcoal flared in preparation of becoming chalk-white embers. Travis was alone on the pier, casting out into a clump of lily pads that floated around an old piling twenty feet from shore. Marybelle and Cassie were in the cabin slipping into their swimsuits.

Marybelle came out and said to Janet, "You'd better get in there and have a talk with your daughter. She's behaving like a perfect idiot."

"What's she doing?"

"She put on her new suit and took one look in the mirror and started crying. She's embarrassed to come out because of her lack of development."

"D'ya mean . . ." She cupped her breasts.

"Yeah, I mean . . ." mimicking the gesture, laughing. "The poor child. I guess I shouldn't laugh."

"No, you shouldn't." And they both chuckled. Janet said, "I'll have a talk with her."

She walked into the cabin. Cassie was posing in front of the mirror, eyes puffy, her face like young camellias in bloom. She blurted, "I know it's silly, Mama. There's nobody here but family anyway, but I can't help it. I look so juvenile. All the other girls have breasts! All I've got are these . . . these silly little fried eggs."

"Don't you worry, honey. It doesn't matter anyway, but I was just like you, and look at me now. I'll bet you anything that by Christmas you'll be as big as me."

"Great!" She sniffled, allowing herself a bit of a chuckle and wiping her nose with her forearm. "Then I'll just wait 'till Christmas to go swimming."

They talked a bit more, and then Janet said, "Your father will be here any minute now. Let's go out and start cooking the chicken."

Cassie changed into a pair of shorts and one of Travis's football jerseys. The chicken was already on the grill. Hickory smoke

117

evaporated into a lilac sky. Marybelle hovered over the grill with a sauce-smeared hand poised in front of pursed lips. A dab of barbecue sauce glistened on her chin. Drawn by the cooking aroma, Travis put his fishing rod down and walked up to the grill, where they were all gathered in hungry anticipation when Chuck drove up. There was someone with him.

Janet, stunned for a moment, stared at the unexpected apparition of an old friend they hadn't seen in almost two decades. Suddenly she rushed the newcomer, shouting, "Jay Pee! Jay Pee!"

She clutched him in a hearty embrace. Exuberant noises of welcome filled the twilight with merry music, with Chuck and Janet and J.P. twittering like birds. Marybelle and the kids were momentarily excluded from their circle, but were soon drawn in. Chuck said, "Hey everybody, I want you to meet my old college classmate and the best tap dancer ever seen on the Tulane campus, J.P. Hollingsworth."

Giggles seemed to bubble under the surface of his puffy cheeks and chin, and all around his puckish mouth. Wire rimmed sunglasses slipped down to the bulb of his nose. He wore a bright yellow shirt and held lightly by its collar a Navy blue blazer that draped across his shoulder. He looked like someone lounging on the lawn at a Great Gatsby soiree.

"Hello everybody," he said. "Hello, hello. I want to thank you for welcoming me to your family gathering." Clipped and rounded words popped from his lips like champagne bubbles. As Travis put it, you could even hear the "A" sound in his "want" (everybody else pronounced it the same as "won't").

Chuck did the introductions: "Marybelle."
"Hello, Marybelle."
"Hi. Nice to meet you."
"And her son, Travis."

"Hello, Travis."

"Hello."

"And this is our daughter, Cassie."

"Cassie. My goodness, you are such a beautiful young woman. You look just like your mother when I first met her. Same eyes. Same lovely lithe figure."

"Thank you."

Chuck said, "I think there's cold beer in the ice box on the porch. I could go for one about now. How about you?"

"I'd love one. Marybelle? Janet?"

"Sure."

"No thanks." Janet said she had a touch of a headache and was afraid a beer would make it worse. "But you know what," she said, "you could bring me some ice to rub on my neck. I'd love that."

Chuck said, "Wouldn't we all." With the temperature hovering in the nineties and the air wet with humidity, they could all use some ice.

They all went to the porch, leaving Travis and Cassie by the grill. Travis said, "Boy, I never seen Mama Janet perk up like that. That J.P. must be something special."

"I think he's a dreamboat."

"You would. Boy, he sure talks funny. Did you notice that?"

"If you mean he doesn't talk like a redneck, yes, I noticed."

That night Chuck and J.P. swapped tales of their college days, and J.P. entertained them all with some fancy tap dancing while Chuck played the hand jive, something the kids had never seen him do. After midnight, when the night finally became cool and after they had nearly all gone to bed, a gossamer mist settled over the lake. The moist air dampened the mournful night sounds. In the cabin, Janet lay sleepless, listening to the whistle of katydids, and to her thoughts. She slipped quietly out of bed and tossed on a robe and walked down to the pier. Dew-wet grass slapped at her cotton slippers and licked her bare ankles. J.P. was sitting on the pier. Even in the dark she could make out his silhouette, and she could see the pulsing glow of his cigarette, reddish-orange against the ashen veil of night. Other lights, pale yellow and pulsing according to another beat, encircled the lake like a battalion of fireflies. These were the lanterns that hung above piers, each aswarm with buzzing insects.

Janet padded out on the pier and sat herself down next to J.P.

"Can't sleep, huh?" she said.

"Nope. You either?"

A granddaddy bass broke the surface of Tombigbee Lake with a resounding splash and unseen insects made random plops of water all around. Pinpoints of light sparkled in J.P.'s glasses. He said, "What's going on, Janet?"

"What do you mean?"

"I think you know. You're not the same girl I knew. Even though you were in good spirits today, I can tell you're not the same."

"You didn't expect me to still be a cheerleader, did you?"

"That's not what I mean. You're getting too old too soon. The life's gone out of you. Chuck is worried. He says you're not interested in anything anymore."

"Oh Chuck! What does he know? What does anybody know? Oh, J.P., I surely don't know what's going on. I grew up and got married, or I got married and then grew up, and I had a baby, and now my baby is almost grown, and what have I done with my life? You spend half your life trying to grow up. You can't wait to grow up. You have all these dreams. You want security, a nice home, family. Then all of a sudden you realize that you're middle-aged and you've won the prize and it wasn't anything but a silver coated trophy to sit on the mantle and hold dust. The trophy: a successful man that you can point to and say 'He's mine,' a child that you can point to and say, 'We made her.' Oh, J.P., you can't know. You're a man. You've got your own demons. Remember what I was like in college? Head cheerleader, KA Sweetheart, engaged to the big man on campus, the center of attention. Yeah, great! But what did all that mean? It meant I was a good catch, a prize fish. My talents were good looks and charm."

J.P. interrupted to remind her she had had others talents. She had been a good artist and she was a wonderful dancer ("That's not a talent to scoff at") and that she had an amazing talent for understanding what makes people tick.

But Janet continued her train of thought as if his words of consolation had been merely more night sounds. "My God, J.P., you can't make a career out of being the life of the party. A girl grows up with only one goal in life, to catch herself a man. It's pounded into her head in a million ways. And if she's lucky enough to catch her man, then what? There's nothing left. From then on it's his life; her life is over."

"But it doesn't have to be that way, Janet. Hells bells woman, you're still young. There are all kinds of things you can do."

"Like what?"

"I don't know. Lots of things. And sure, maybe marital bliss isn't all it's cracked up to be, but take it from the voice of experience, the alternative is no great shakes either."

"That's what Marybelle says."

"Speaking of Marybelle, she is gorgeous. Who is she? I mean what's her . . . uh, is she . . ."

"Available? You bet." She smiled at that, paused a moment, then said. "I'd forgotten how shy you were. You still are, aren't you?"

"Yes, I guess I am."

* * *

The holiday weekend was over. The family was seated at the breakfast table, all but Travis. "What's keeping that boy?" Janet grumbled. "I declare he's going to be late for his own funeral."

"He's got to make himself beautiful," Cassie said.

Chuck said. "I thought that primping stuff was for girls,"

"Not this girl. I'm naturally beautiful. Don't have to primp. Daddy's friend said it yesterday. He said I was a beautiful young lady just like Mama."

Travis then bounded down the stairs, whistling. His hair was slicked back and he was wearing sunglasses, his team blazer slung casually across one shoulder. "Hello! Hello!" he sang out. "I want to thank you for welcoming me to your family gathering. Ah, Cassie. You're such a beautiful young lady, and to think, you accomplished such beauty without a moments primping!"

"Somebody's been eavesdropping," Cassie said.

"Well I'll be damned," Chuck said. "That was a great impersonation of my friend and yours, Jewel Pomeroy."

"Of who?"

"Whom."

"Jewel Pomeroy. J.P. That's his name."

Marybelle said, "No wonder he goes by J.P."

Travis started skipping around the table singing, "Jewel Pomeroy. Jewel Pomeroy. Allow me to introduce myself, my good people. I am Je-well Pomer-roy Hollingsworth."

Marybelle said, "Sit down and eat your breakfast."

Chuck said, "I didn't know you had such a talent for impersonations."

"One of his many hidden talents," Cassie said. She meant it. Cassie truly admired her brother.

Proud of himself, Travis made a performance of eating his bacon and eggs with primly expansive gestures.

Marybelle refilled everyone's coffee cups. She said, "Tell us more about J.P., Chuck. What's his story? What's he doing here?"

"He's a newspaper man," Chuck said. "A pretty big fish. Worked for a big paper in Atlanta and wrote a syndicated column that was published all over the country. He married a girl from Greenville—that's his home. She got sick and had to be put in Whitfield..."

"Whitfield! You mean the nut house?"

"Travis! Shame on you."

"She was mentally ill. She's dead now. Two, three years ago. So anyway, J.P. wanted to get away from the city. Wanted a simpler life, I guess. He applied for a position with the *Journal*, and of course they were overjoyed to get him. Hey! I just thought about it—we should throw a welcome party for him, a real Warner style party."

Janet shuddered. A Warner style party, to her, meant big preparations, big anxieties, and another migraine. But it was decided (with Chuck and Marybelle doing most of the deciding, as usual) that the party would be Saturday night.

"Enough talk," Marybelle said. "God Chuck, we're worse than the kids. You're going to mess around and be late for work, and you're going to make me late too. Ray's giving one of his infamous pep talks at the staff meeting this morning, and you know what he's like if anyone's late for one of his rah-rah talks. So let's get out of here. Come on everybody, scoot."

The dishes were left for Janet. Marybelle and the kids were already out the door. Chuck, who had gone into his study to pick up some papers and then cut back through the kitchen on his way out, stopped when he saw Janet still sitting at the table with her head propped in the palm of her hand. "Bad headache?" he asked.

"Just the usual. I'll be all right."

"Is something else bothering you?"

She said, "I don't know, Chuck. This idea for a party's got me upset I guess. The idea of having to cook and clean house. Sometimes I wish I could just take a vacation from housework."

"Well you can, honey. You don't have to do it all. I didn't know. I thought you liked it. Shucks, we can hire a maid if you'd like."

"You know that would never work. Nobody wants to eat anybody's cooking but mine."

"Well they'll just have to learn to like it. Or we can all pitch in and help with stuff. I mean, if you're overburdened . . . hell, you never said anything."

She stood up and started gathering the dishes. He grabbed a few plates. She said, "It's not the work, Chuck. I don't mind the work. I'd just like to be able to do some other stuff. Maybe take up painting again or try my hands at writing poetry. I always wanted to do that."

"Sure," he said. "I think that's a good idea. I think I recall telling you years ago you ought to start back painting. You never did, so I figured you just weren't interested anymore."

"No, it was 'cause Chuck and Cassie were little and always underfoot."

"So we'll talk about it some more. We'll make sure you have some free time or whatever you need. But I've got to go to work now. We'll talk later, okay? Bye."

He kissed her and rushed out the door.

* * *

When Marybelle got to work, the staff meeting was well underway. Prancing smugly in front of his seated employees, like a self-satisfied teacher lecturing a class, Ray Prichard said, "Well well, if it isn't the late Marybelle Coe. We're honored that you decided to join us."

"Tardy, not late. I'm still among the living. I'm sorry

I'm tardy. I . . ." she gave a half-hearted stab at manufacturing an excuse, but dropped it.

Ray said, "Now that we're all here, I have an important announcement to make. Billy White, as you all know, has been with us over a year now. He came in as a part-timer during the Christmas rush, and he pitched right in and made himself indispensable, and he has become a valuable team player and a real leader. Of course we have to credit Marybelle with doing a fine job of training him. Now I'm proud to announce that effective immediately, Billy White is the new Esquire marketing director."

Everyone applauded. A couple of the young salesmen gave Billy comradely punches, a sock to the shoulder and a slap on the butt. Alma Smith, the clerk in marketing who would now be directly under him and who had been working at the Esquire for six years without a promotion, shot Billy the universal gesture of contempt—the finger, the bird, the fuck-you-asshole. Naturally she concealed the gesture so that only Marybelle and the women behind her saw it. Marybelle shot Alma that other universal gesture—the thumbs up, the sock-it-to-him, the right-on-Sister!

Billy White stood up and gave a short speech with references to teamwork and carrying that championship spirit into every game. He thanked Marybelle for her guidance, pronouncing her name "Mara Belle."

Ten minutes later Marybelle burst into Ray Prichard's office on rubbery legs, fists clinched and trembling. "That was the most humiliating thing I've ever been forced to endure," she said—without even so much as a hello or a may I come in. "You patted me on the head like a good little puppy dog and you gave that pompous twerp head of marketing."

"Take it easy, Marybelle."

"I'll not take it easy! You . . . you Man! It's not fair. I wanted that job, and you knew it, and you should have given it to me, and you should have promoted Alma too. But no, you promote that green-gilled kid over both of us."

"Now you just calm down and be reasonable, honey. I understand how you feel. Really, I do. But you have to understand my position too. Billy was hired as a management trainee. He's been to college, for Christ sake. What do you think would happen to our management-training program if the young men we hired knew that a woman without college credentials could be promoted over them? We need to let our young men get on top."

His deep, resonant voice was soothing and conciliatory. He sat tall in his leather-upholstered chair, regally ensconced behind the mahogany desk. An attractive man, not what you'd call really handsome, but comforting in his appearance, his shoulders were slightly stooped and a soft shock of hair was brushed across a bald spot. He wore a tailored suit and sat at ease, with diamond rings flashing on fingers that lazily tapped the felt pad on his desk. A martial cadence.

Marybelle sat down, wearied by her tirade. She didn't like confrontations of any kind. She didn't know what to do with her hands. She looked past him, out the window. Her fingers picked up the rhythm he was drumming on his desk, and they played along in her lap. Her eyes wandered out to Main Street and took a walk past the fairgrounds and Clayton's Staff-O-Life Feeds, and on out to the red clay bluff on the eastern horizon. There was nothing special about that bluff, but it was solid, enduring, comforting, like Ray Prichard's voice, like the timbre of his voice, not the words he said. She could see the bluff from her front yard when she was a child, and seeing it now brought to mind her father's voice. Old Rudy Sullivan, proud of and fearful for his beautiful, precocious daughter. "You gonna be somebody some day, honey. You gonna make something of yourself. I kin feel it in my bones. But you gotta work hard and use that noggin of your'n.

And you gotta respect your elders and your betters and don't sass nobody."

Ray Prichard could not know her mind, but he could see that her thoughts had drifted far away. He allowed her the pensive moment, gave her time to trace the perspective of Main Street from its vanishing point in the shadow of the bluff in a hazy past to the bright glare of the present moment. He swiveled his chair and stood up. He stepped across the carpet to fiddle with the frame of a picture on the wall. It was a portrait of a man, presumably his father. The portrait hung on hidden hinges. At Ray's touch it swung away from the wall to reveal a hidden bar, complete with a tiny refrigerator, shot glasses, swizzle sticks and monogrammed napkins. He mixed drinks and carried them to the desk. Putting one in front of Marybelle, he said, "I think we can both use this. Now believe me, honey, I intend to make this up to you. As a matter of fact, I had something better in mind for you all along. I just didn't want to tell you yet."

Did he mean it? Or was he simply trying to make up for his insensitiveness and stupidity without 'fessing up to any of it? She knew that she would never know.

"I have plans to expand the business. I want this to be more than just another small town department store. I intend to start selling some real fashion wear, and to do that I need someone who can go to trade shows and talk to designers and help me develop a smart fashion line—something that'll put us in league with the big city shops. That's a job a woman can handle, a savvy woman."

Marybelle remembered when she was in the ninth grade and Ray was a senior. The high school band had won a regional contest and a chance to go to Chicago to perform in the nationals, but there was no money to pay for the trip. Ray wasn't even in the band, but he took it upon himself to organize a fundraising drive, and he raised something like three thousand dollars or some such huge amount—whatever was needed. If he said he was going to expand the business, then the business would expand. And Marybelle really liked the sound of that phrase: *savvy woman*.

"And you want me to be that woman?" There was a perkiness to her voice that hadn't been there moments before.

"Well, maybe. We'll see. There's a trade show in Memphis next month. I think that would be a good place to start. If you do a good job in Memphis, there's a designer in New Orleans I'd like for you to meet."

"It sounds exciting."

"It can be. But don't get too excited yet. There are no guarantees. Let's not get ahead of ourselves. First we go to Memphis—I've already reserved a suite in the Peabody; Josh Culpepper is going to fly us up in his Cessna—and if everything goes all right there, then we'll see about New Orleans."

He gave her some catalogues to study and suggested that she buy new clothes for the trip. "Nothing too formal. Everyone will be pretty casual, except—yes, you will need an evening gown for the banquet. Otherwise, dress sporty. Bring a tennis outfit, some shorts. Dare to be a little sexy. Check with Ellen in Sportswear. She's got some exciting new things I think you'll love. And don't worry about money. The company will pay for it."

So that afternoon Marybelle did some shopping. There was a daring jump suit on a mannequin in the window. She had noticed it before. It was a soft lavender, all-in-one-piece pant-and-jacket outfit made of stretch denim, one of those marvelous new synthetic fabrics, sleeveless, with a roll collar and a front zipper from crotch to cleavage. Oh, and what cleavage!

Marybelle asked Ellen if they had it in her size. Ellen pulled a box from under the counter and said, "Here 'ya go. Try this one on for size. I been dying to see somebody in one of these. Started to get one myself, but I'm afraid Wade would have a hissy fit."

Behind the curtain of the dressing booth, Marybelle stepped into and pulled up the clingy denim. It was like putting on full-body panty hose. She zipped it up and parted the curtain. "What do you think, Ellen?" she asked. "It's a bit too much, isn't it?"

"Oh no, honey. Not at all. That's you. 'Course I could never wear anything like that; I ain't got the figure for it. But if I was built like you—Hoo-whee!"

"But don't you think it's a little snug? And the collar—pretty low cut, huh?"

"Oh, I don't know. Maybe a little, but hey!—you sure look good to me. Why not turn a few heads while you've still got what it takes!"

How long had it been since her former husband had demanded that she wear clothes that hid her figure from view? How long since she had felt the thrill of knowing that all eyes turned when she entered a room?

Marybelle said, "I'll think about it. Let's see what you've got in a nice tennis outfit."

While Marybelle was trying on new clothes, Cassie soaked in the old upstairs bathtub in the big house on Magazine Street. The only things protruding from the sudsy water were her lobster red knees and her pert little face. She had just come home from dance class, the first class after a two-week break. Every muscle in her body ached, but the scalding water eased those aches deliciously, as she drifted into private reveries. The old tub with eagle claw feet became a barge adrift on a river, and she an ancient princess, a dancing girl in ancient Egypt, a queen of some dimly imagined exotic land bathing in a hot spring with ebony skinned servant girls dribbling precious bath oils over her body and massaging the muscles of back and thigh and calf. Soon the sounds of neighborhood boys playing football rushed in through the open window and brought her back to the moment. Her bathwater was becoming tepid. She lifted herself from the tub, wrapped herself in a large towel and rushed across the cold floor to her room, where she flung herself slantwise across her bed and lay still for the longest time, allowing her eyes to roam about as if it were some other girl's bedroom and she were an uninvited guest. The furnishings and various doodads in the room spoke of a much younger girl. There were fluffy stuffed animals piled on an easy chair and movie star magazines on the dresser. Over the dresser, a faded pom-pom was taped to one corner of the mirror. A dance poster dominated a wall of clipped and pasted pictures. In an unconscious reflex, as her eyes studied the poster, her body began to assume the dancer's pose.

    She kicked away the towel and stretched. The cool sheets caressed her. Fingers massaged muscles still slick with bath oil, a warm and languorous exploration of thigh and hip and stomach. She turned onto her belly and stretched to reach the record player that sat on the floor near her bed. There was a stack of 45s scattered on the floor, mostly older records she had bought three years earlier when the portable pink stereo, a twin of Travis's, was new. She put on an Elvis Presley record as she heard Travis's footsteps bound heavily past her door.

    Standing up, Cassie approached the mirror over her dresser and studied her naked reflection. "Fried eggs," she had bemoaned, but the image that greeted her was not so terribly immature. She shrugged and smiled and winked at her mirrored image and said to the image, "Not bad. Hmmm." Then she pulled pink silk panties from a drawer and stepped into them, and pulled a thin cotton tee-shirt over her head, and padded on bare feet across the hall to Travis's room, leaving Elvis all alone to sing "Love Me Tender."

    She rapped on his door: Shave and a haircut six bits!

"Come on in, Sis. Taint locked."

    He was working on a drawing in his sketchbook, struggling to correct an unresolved figure he had labored on the night before. Glancing up as she entered, he said, "Hi 'ya Sis. Looks like you forgot your pants."

She glanced down at her pink panties and shrugged. "What'cha doing?"

"Drawing. Trying to anyway."

"Let's see."

The sketch pad was opened to a drawing of a naked woman, face and hair beautifully rendered with delicate cross hatch strokes; shoulders, collar bone, breasts and delicate swell of belly solid and convincingly drawn. But there was something awkward in the pelvic region, where the drawing was smudged from repeated erasures.

"Not bad," Cassie said.

Next to the sketchpad was a book called *Nudes For Artists*. The cover illustration was a grainy, black and white photograph of a standard studio nude viewed from behind, with a towel draped coyly across her hips.

"Where'd you get this?"

"I ordered it from an ad in one of my art magazines."

"Is the one you're drawing from in here?"

"Yeah." He handed her the book. "It's on page, uh... close to the back."

"I'll find it."

She flipped the book open and started thumbing through it. Each page pictured an eight-by-ten full figured nude. They all looked alike. Expressionless. Bland. In the photographs, as in Travis's drawing, there was something wrong with the pelvic region. It took her a moment to realize what it was. Pubic hair had been airbrushed away. Cassie started giggling.

"What's so damn funny?"

"These women. They don't have hair."

"Well, they touch 'em up. They can't show ... you know."

"That's the silliest thing I've ever heard of. It's grotesque."

As if her comment had been directed at him—as if she were saying that he was the unnatural, grotesque prude who had airbrushed the photographs or as if he in his infantile stupidity didn't know the difference (after all, he could not positively say that women didn't look like that; he had never seen a naked woman; God forbid she should make fun of his innocence)—he rebuked her, snidely saying, "So what? You don't have any hair down there either."

"I do too."

"Yeah? Prove it."

"No way!"

"Ah Sis. You ain't a woman yet. You're nothing but a scrawny, no-hair nowhere girl child."

She turned red in the face and stretched herself up to her full five-foot four and thrust out her chest and cupped both hands under her breasts to tighten the cloth and make her nipples poke out against the thin, cotton T-shirt, and she said, "Since when do little girls have tits like these?"

They were both laughing and grimacing at the same time, because they could see that the argument was silly (they were, after all, the same age and both almost grown, and who cared anyway?) and Travis's facial muscles spelled out fleeting expressions of shock and lust and confusion, because it was a time long before it became fashionable for girls to go braless or to wear natural form bras, it was in fact a time when girls wore hard, pointy bras like Medieval breast plates, and the clearly defined shape of small breasts and firm nipples under the thin cotton was the nearest thing to nudity he had ever seen other than in photographs and in nightly dreams that drove him crazy, but it was, after all, only Cassie, only Sis, and her strutting was downright comical to boot, so the hieroglyphics of expression on his face relaxed into an accustomed sneer and he taunted, "Ah, that's not real. You probably stuffed toilet paper in your training bra."

"Oh yeah!" She grabbed her shirttail and inside-outed the shirt over her head in one frantic jerk and shouted, "There! See!"

For an instant like the click of a camera shutter in painful slow motion, they confronted one another with naked trembling and delicate pride and confused sex emerging in an explosion of hormones. The myriad emotions that tortured them in their fantasies and unspoken wishes played themselves out like the jerking images of old-time movies in their eyes and on their lips and in the electric space between them, and Cassie ended the moment by clutching her shirt to her chest and rushing out of the room.

In her bedroom the record went "shee-taw, shee-taw, shee-taw," but she did not notice it for a long time. Finally she turned off the record, and she laughed at herself and got decently dressed in blue jeans, with a brassiere under the flimsy T-shirt.

Marybelle's old Plymouth pulled into the drive, and a few moments later the front door slammed shut with its usual double bounce. Later, Chuck came home. Janet shouted upstairs to Travis and Cassie, and they all gathered for supper. Marybelle told them about her new job. She said, "I went on a real shopping spree. I bought an evening gown and a tennis outfit and shoes and a new purse, and some naughty French underwear (you should see it—no, you shouldn't either) and a beautiful, sexy, lavender jump suit that I'll probably never have the nerve to wear."

Chuck said, "With this new job, which doesn't seem to have any real definition, was there any mention of a pay raise?"

"Well no, not exactly. But I'm sure there will be."

* * *

Saturday night was the night of the big party at the Warner house. The house was festooned with crepe paper streamers and a banner that said, "Welcome J.P." The huge dining table was overflowing with snacks. Simply everybody came to the party—that is everybody in Tupelo who anybody there would call anybody, and a few that some of them wouldn't. Even Wallace Jones, who had been blind since World War II, showed up. Even Mabel Cook, with her hair let down. Travis and Cassie's aunt Becky, who lived in New Orleans, brought her beatnik friends. The beatniks huddled together and never took their cigarettes out of their mouths. Ray Prichard arrived about three sheets to the wind already, escorting his mousy wife, whom he instructed to go into the kitchen to see if there was anything she could do to help. Marybelle's parents were there, too. Rudy found himself a seat near the front window where he could watch everybody and swap jokes with the men who huddled nearby. Nora Lee, like Mrs. Prichard, but of her own volition, went to the kitchen to help Mama Janet and the maid. Even my mother came to the party. That may be the only time I can remember her ever going anywhere. Mama was pretty much a homebody.

The guest of honor, J.P. Hollingsworth, talked to everyone and smiled and laughed easily, but he seemed a bit nervous. He kept glancing at the door up the stairs as if expecting someone special to make an appearance. Of course that someone was Marybelle. Marybelle was late, but when she did finally make her appearance—Hoo—whee!

I don't think I ever saw such a gorgeous woman. She appeared at the top of the stairs and everybody—I mean everybody—stood stock-still and gaped at her. We could have been in Hollywood at some Beverly Hills extravaganza. But there we were in plain old, provincial Tupelo, Mississippi, and the goddess who descended the stairs was plain old Travis

Earl Warner's mother, Mama Marybelle. Her hair was a burnt gold waterfall that cascaded freely over her shoulders. She was wearing the new lavender jump suit. Like the cascade of hair, it flowed down her body, soft over her breasts and snug across the angular jut of her hip. The only jewelry she wore was a deep burgundy choker with a single faux diamond.

As if Marybelle's entrance were an awaited signal, the party became suddenly lively. Somebody put an old fogy song on the stereo, a funny thing called "Do The Huckle Buck," and a bunch of people formed a line and started dancing: left foot out, left foot in; right foot out, right foot in; left foot up, left foot back; now everybody forward, hop, hop, hop. I think what they were doing was the bunny hop, but the music was the huckle buck. It was all stuff from before my time, anyway.

The dancing line went out the door and up Magazine to Church Street. There were six dancers when they left the house and about fifteen when they hopped back in. Meantime someone had put "Stardust" on the turntable, and couples were dreamily swaying to the lush music. Marybelle was standing by the dining room table. Ray Prichard, slightly wobbly and slurred of speech, put his hand on her shoulder and said, "Would you care to dance?"

"Sure. Why not? It's not everybody that gets to dance with the boss."

He danced gracefully, even if he did have some slight problems with balance.

"Boy, I'll bet you're a devil on the dance floor when you're sober," she teased.

Chuck, dancing with Janet, overheard Marybelle and winked at her.

Ray said, "Fred Astaire should have such moves."

Marybelle's hand rested lightly on Ray Prichard's shoulder; he tightly encircled her waist. His fingers pressed firmly into the small of her back. Former bunny hoppers or huckle buckers encircled the dancers, holding hands and humming as they swayed to the beat of the band. Louis Hutchinson kissed his wife while swirling her in a dizzying circle. When the song ended, Ray dipped Marybelle, and grasping her firmly, he bent forward and lightly kissed her lips.

"Ooh, what was that for?" She asked,

"For you being so gracious and lovely," he slurred.

"Oh."

"I didn't mean anything by it, honey. I just feel good."

"Well don't get to feeling too good, Bub. You'll get yourself in trouble."

Like a polo player beating his opponent to a shot, J.P. swooped down and grabbed Marybelle away from Ray. "May I have the next dance?" he asked.

Marybelle said, "And Janet told me you were shy!"

I was having the time of my life. One of my greatest pleasures has always been to sit back and observe others, especially groups of people. I've always loved the syncopated patterns of movement at parties and the unconnected snatches of conversation, word bubbles bursting. J.P. and Marybelle were dancing right in front of me. I heard her whisper to him, "Thank you for rescuing me."

Behind them I could see Chuck and Janet and the Hutchinsons. They were laughing. Louis Hutchinson had his arm draped across Chuck's shoulder. By the window, Travis was talking to Becky's beatnik friends, and through the window I could see Cassie leaning against the rail, looking into the night sky. I saw my mother chatting with Mother Warner on the couch with such animation you'd think they had a lifetime of memories to catch up on.

Old Rudy Sullivan, peg leg and all, slipped up behind Mabel Cook and clamped his hands over her eyes and said, "Guess who."

"Get your hands off me, you dirty old man!" She jerked away and took a playful swipe at him. "What do you think you're doing?"

"Why I'm just trying to be friendly, sweet thing—for old time's sake."

Everybody laughed, and Rudy started slowly and menacingly advancing on her. To everybody's surprise, she let him catch her. Travis put some rock and roll on the turntable and Rudy and Mabel performed a stiff and clunky jitterbug.

They all partied late into the night, giddily dancing and hugging one another, stuffing themselves with food and liquor, telling jokes and repeating often-told tales. And as they danced and as they walked around and as they gathered in parting groups and arriving groups on the front porch, and as they sat here and stood there, Marybelle kept bumping into Chuck and Marybelle kept bumping into J.P. and Marybelle kept bumping into memories and hopes and reminders of the joy of the moment, and dancing bodies met in tender touches and glancing eyes met in melded vision of accidental recognition of love and beauty and joy, and there seemed there could be no sadness anywhere.

Then it grew late and some of the people had gone home and I was sitting on the porch steps with Travis. Marybelle was perched on the rail watching a group of people by the curb who were noisily and drunkenly wishing Louis and Jenny Hutchinson good night. Ray Prichard staggered onto the porch and sat down next to Marybelle. Once again, and this time not so playfully, he kissed her. She pushed him away and said, "I think maybe you had better go inside and see if your wife needs you."

"Yeah, I guess I'd best do that. Don't be mad, honey. I was just having fun. Wee bit drunk, 'ya know. Didn't mean anything by it." But saying this, he draped his arm around her and she had to push him away, trying to keep it light, saying, "Go on, you lecherous old so-and-so."

Before the party ended I somehow wound up on the porch alone with Marybelle, and she spoke to me as though I were an equal, an adult. She said things to me that she probably couldn't say to any adult. We sat on the steps and smoked cigarettes, our smoke floating desultorily into the morning dark. Veiled light from the corner lamppost filtered through our smoke, washing her hair with the glow of smoldering embers. She said, "Have you ever been in love, Johnny?"

"No," I said, "I haven't." And I hadn't either, not then and not for a long, long time afterwards when I finally met Jimmy and fell head over heels. That moment sits in my memory like an intrusion of a reality so surreal that I can't fit it into any of the other patterns of my life. Here I am now, an aging queen who never in his life slept with a woman, and never even wanted to. Yet the most precious memory I have of anything remotely like falling in love was when I was eighteen years old, and the object of my love was my best friend's mother.

She said, "I've been in love. Long time ago. But I've never really made love to a man."

"But you must have," I said. "You had a baby. You had Travis."

"No, Travis's father and I had sex, but we never made love. I don't know what it was, but it had nothing to do with love. I wish I could fall in love. Still. If only once in my life, I'd like to know what it is like to make love to a man, to feel a man inside of me, and to know that he loves me and I love him, to know passion and tenderness. I'm forty years old, Johnny. That must seem ancient to you, but it's not. Still, it's probably too damn old for dreaming silly dreams of romance."

She said, "I sat right here once and talked about these same things. It was such a long time ago, fifteen years ago. Travis was still pretty much a baby, and in some ways I was too. It was a night like this night, after a party like this one. It was right after the war. Chuck and I sat right here, and we talked about love. You know we grew up together. My mother was his mother's maid. We were practically brother and sister. We were kind of sweethearts too, growing up. But we couldn't—you know—follow through on that. We were so much like brother and sister that it would have been like incest. It would have been like if Travis and Cassie married each other. They could, you know. They are not really related at all. It wouldn't be incest, but it would be *like* incest. Isn't it funny how patterns repeat? Now Travis and Cassie are growing up as brother and sister just like Chuck and I did."

Her words circled and danced in the night air like the smoke rings we blew. Her thinking seemed so convoluted that the concepts she was trying to articulate kept tripping on one another, but I didn't mind. I was entranced with the sound of her voice.

"Chuck was a couple of years ahead of me in school. He went off to college and I stayed behind, and he fell in love with Janet and they got married, and on their wedding night I met John Coe. Pretty soon we got married, John and I, even though I never did love that man. Then the men went off to war and John got himself killed. It was after the war that Chuck and I sat right here on these steps and talked about these things. He said tell me what I am to you. And I said you're everything to me. He said do we love each other? And I said haven't we always? He said I don't mean like brother and sister. I mean like a man and a woman. Did you ever want to make love with me? I said, of course I wanted to. If I let myself think about it, I guess I still would, but you know we can't do that. Not now. Not ever. He said it's so goddamn hard sometimes, because you're always here, a constant reminder. I ache for you so much. I'll never forget him saying that, I ache for you so much. Then I asked him if it would be better if I moved out on my own. He said no, I don't want that. Afterwards we just sat right here, sat until daylight came, not saying a word. That was a long time ago. We never talked about it again, but from time to time we would catch one another's eye, and it was all said in a glance."

She put her hand on my hand and she smiled at me. "You'll have to forgive this silly old fool," she said. "The party tonight made me feel like a young girl again. It brought all that stuff back."

It would have been so nice if we could have sat right there until daylight came. Nobody would have had to say a word. The few last party stragglers could have gone on home and we could have sat right there. Quiet. Listening to the intermittent night sounds. The soft, high chirp of crickets, the dull whistle-hum of unknown insects that fill the void of night, the occasional whoosh of a car driving down Gloster Street, five blocks away. But Marybelle said, "You better run along home, Johnny. It's getting awfully late."

With that, the spell was broken. It was not so much what she said, but the very typically adult tone of voice that reminded me she was not my personal, private and secret confidant; she was the mother of my best friend.

* * *

Marybelle called the newspaper office and asked for J.P. He picked up the phone. "J.P. Hollingsworth speaking. May I help you?"

"Oh God, I hope so," she blurted. "This is Marybelle."

Either he didn't catch the desperation in her voice or he decided it best to make light of it. He said, "Ah yes, Marybelle. Marybelle of the beautiful flashing eyes, Marybelle whose son, I'm told, does impersonations of yours truly."

"Yes, that's me. Flashing eyes, huh! Do my eyes really flash?"

"Oh yes, they do. They do." His voice sang over the line. Perky. Exuberant. Like a jazz piccolo twittering over Ma Bell's taut cables.

"Oh God, J.P. You can't imagine how good it is to hear a friendly voice."

There was no denying the desperation. "Is something wrong?"

"There was. Maybe I'll tell you all about it sometime. But meantime, would it... would it shock you terribly if a woman you hardly knew called you up and asked for a date?"

"Yes it would. Indeed it would, but if you're asking, I'm accepting. I'm flattered."

"Thank you. I'm flattered too. I feel kind of silly, but... well... I just bought a brand new evening gown and the occasion for wearing it was ruined. I simply want someone nice to take me out. You are nice, aren't you?"

"Oh yes, I'm nice. I may be a little flabbergasted by this conversation, and I may feel a little stupid because I didn't ask you out first, but yes I think I am nice, and I'm honored, and I think I blabber too much. But tell me, where does one go in formal attire in Tupelo?" There was a short pause, then he said, "Oh never mind. You put on your new evening gown and I'll be by to pick you up at seven. I think I know just the place."

That evening he arrived at the Warner house dressed in a tuxedo, with a white carnation pinned to his lapel, bearing a bouquet of paper flowers which he had fashioned himself out of toilet tissue. She said they were the most beautiful flowers anyone had ever given her.

J.P. escorted her to his black Ford sedan and held the door open for her. As they were pulling away from the curb, she asked, "Where are we going?"

"We are going to dine at Chez Michael, my dear."

"Chez Michael! There's no... where is Chez Michael?"

"Very near, my dear. Very near indeed." He curbed the Ford. They had not gone more than three blocks. "So near, in fact," he continued, laughter in his voice, "that we're here.

To plebeian folk it is merely Mike's Cafe, but tonight it is Chez Michael. I made special arrangements with Mike."

Mike's was a long, narrow cafe nestled between a barbershop and a music store on Broadway, half a block from Main Street. A chubby woman with a tangle of coarse black hair stood behind the Formica counter. Connie. Mike's wife. The restaurant was crowded. A couple of teenagers spun on swivel bar stools. A hefty policeman with his shirttail hanging out behind was hunkered over an ice cream sundae. His gun belt and his cap occupied the empty stool to his left. Ray Prichard and his wife sat in a booth near the front. Ray nodded and mumbled his perfunctory greetings as J.P. escorted Marybelle past them, and past Mabel Cook, who was eating soup and reading a book, and past the Longs, with their twin boys who were kicking each other under the table. Mike himself, wrapped in a white apron, stood expectantly at the rear of the restaurant, waiting for J.P. and Marybelle. He was sparking with pride. Mike had created for them a private dining section, partitioned from the rest of the cafe by a folding Japanese screen brought from home. A sky blue, silk cloth spread across their table, upon which sat a floral centerpiece and a tapering candle. Mike held chairs for them to be seated.

"I love it," Marybelle said. "It's wonderful."

"Thank you, Mademoiselle," Mike said. "May I suggest an appetizer?"

"We'll leave it up to you," J.P. said. "And coffee, please."

Wine was out of the question, since Lee County still hadn't repealed prohibition. Mike went to fetch the coffee and appetizer. J.P. glowed with self-satisfied pleasure. Marybelle clasped her hands over his and exclaimed, "This is the most wonderful date I've ever had."

"But it's only just begun, my dear. Wait 'till you taste Mike's steak special."

Travis and I had dates of our own that night, with a couple of girls he had met at the pool in Okolona. One of them lived in Verona, a tiny town nearby. The other one was her cousin from Jackson. We were taking them to the dance at the Teen Center. After the dance we were going to park with them at a special place Travis knew about in the woods by Tombigbee. Travis said, "These girls like to do it. Mine told me so, and she said her cousin will do it too. So, the plan is, we're going to get laid tonight. I mean, if that's what you want."

I wasn't too sure that I liked that plan. I didn't know if I wanted to or if I could, but I went along anyway. It seems that most of the things we did were done with no sense of personal volition, but simply by going along. Besides, I figured it wouldn't happen anyway.

Not only was I scared, not only was I very doubtful about whether or not sex with a girl was something I wanted to try—although God knows I was curious, the thing that really bothered me was that Travis talked about those girls the way Charlie Speed would. It wasn't like Travis at all, talking about girls doing it, putting out. As if girls either did or didn't. As if personal choice, determined by taste or any other consideration, had nothing to do with the matter. To hear the guys talk, you'd think that a vagina was something like a beautifully decorated birthday cake ("Don't you dare pick at it before the party!"). Let somebody pluck the cherry off the top and you might as well pass it around for everybody. I remember Charlie saying that the best pick up line in the world is simple and straightforward: "Would you like to screw?" And I kept thinking it would be great if they answered him: "Yes I would, but not with you."

Before picking up the girls we went to Zeke's Rexall and bought two packs of Trojans. Travis put his in his wallet. I noticed the circular imprint it made and was determined that I didn't want to pull my wallet out in public and have people see that, so I dropped mine in my shirt pocket.

On the way to the dance I tried to engage in small talk with my date, but I couldn't think of much to say. Fortunately,

Travis was entertaining enough for all of us. He told jokes and did impersonations of a Negro revivalist preacher and in general saved me and the girls from the burden of being sociable.

A local band played for the dance. Almost every song they played was some version of the twist. Kids were twisting all over the place. Travis was great. His legs and arms gyrated so fast and loose it looked like parts of him would surely fly off at any moment. I went through the motions. Anybody could do the twist. After a while I really got into it, twisting away with abandon, just like Travis. God it felt great! For the first time in my life I felt like one of the gang. I actually had a date, a girl—not bad looking either. Me, the skinny, big-nosed kid who the other kids were beginning to suspect as queer—me with a good looking chick, twisting the night away! My girl was smiling at me and Travis shouted out, "Go Johnny, go!"

Then suddenly that goddamn rubber went flying out of my shirt pocket. It sailed across the dance floor and ricocheted off Wanda Ramsey's shoulder and skidded over Charlie Speed's foot. Hoss Williams picked it up and held it aloft and shouted, "Somebody dropped their rubber!"

Twenty voices joined together in the immediate response: "It's Johnny's. I saw it."

"Johnny Lewis? No way! Can't be!"

"Hey Johnny boy, planning on oiling your gun tonight?"

Hoss threw the rubber over Bitsy's head. Charlie Speed caught it and tossed it to Sam, who dropped it and stepped on it and kicked it under a table. Wanda Ramsey, of all people, got down on her hands and knees and crawled under the table to retrieve my pack of Trojans and ceremoniously returned it to me. Everybody was laughing and shouting and I heard from somewhere in the crowd the thing that had never before been said in public. It was as if a lightning bolt ripped through the Teen Center. The tumultuous den of locker room humor suddenly died. That last sentence hung over us like a glob of party streamers left out in the rain. "Johnny don't need that rubber. Don't ya'll know? He's queer as a three dollar bill."

Once again, as he had done so often, Travis came to my rescue. He tried to turn it back on the boy who said it. Tried to make a joke of it, but none of his usual tricks worked. He couldn't diffuse that bomb. When all else failed, he grabbed my arm and said, "Come on, Johnny. Let's get the hell out of here. Escorting me out like I was his date or something, right smack dab in front of everybody, he turned to our real dates and said, "I'll be back for you both real soon."

"Forget it!" one of them said. "There's plenty of real boys here who'd just love to take us home."

"Well fuck you!" Travis shouted, and he hustled me out the door.

It was all so embarrassing and disgusting. But then that whole period of my life was nothing but one big, disgusting embarrassment. I was a young white boy living amongst other young white boys who thought the world was created especially for them—and by God that seemed pretty much the case. Every white boy in Mississippi was a prince awaiting his chance to be king. Black people didn't count. They hardly existed in our world. Even though the population of Tupelo was pretty near fifty-fifty black and white, Negroes were functionally invisible. Women didn't count either. A girl wasn't a person; a girl was a pussy. Period. And if a guy acted in any way like a girl, then he was a pussy too. Here's what our world consisted of: football, fast cars, beer guzzling, rock and roll, and pussy. I fit into that world like a turd in the swimming pool. Yet I was accepted as one of the guys. I never knew why, but it must have been mostly because I was Travis's friend. Sometimes the guys teased me and there had always been veiled hints that they suspected I might be gay, but I had always been invited to go along with the gang and nobody, until that night, had ever come right out and called me a queer.

Travis never had such problems. Not only did he fit in, he could get away with things any other guy would be ostracized for. He could dare to show affection to another male, for instance, as he did with me, and nobody would dare call him a sissy. He could dare to pursue his dream of being an artist when art was considered a sissy thing. He could even dare to take me by the arm and escort me away from the frenzied crowd of queer-baiters at the teen dance. Travis could do all that because he was a football hero. His masculinity, in other words, was unimpeachable. At least it seemed that way to me. But maybe it was much tougher for him than I realized. In some ways, though, he caved in to the pressures of the crowd. He didn't like getting drunk, for instance. He had a very low tolerance for alcohol. So when all the guys gathered in the parking lot at Danny's to guzzle beer, Travis would surreptitiously pour half of his beer on the ground, or he'd tongue the hole in the can, turn it up and gulp air. And he wouldn't admit to any of the other guys that he was a virgin.

Charlie Speed was sleeping with Wanda. Everybody knew it. Plus he could go to Oxford any time he wanted and pick up girls on the Ole Miss campus who would put out for him. Hoss was doing it with Bitsy, and there was this girl in East Tupelo they called "Number Eighty-sith" who they all gangbanged. She had a speech impediment. The first time they took her out, Hoss (whose nickname referred to the size of his cock) was wearing his football jersey, number eighty-six. After they all had her in the back seat of Charlie's Impala, Charlie asked her, "If you get pregnant, who you going to name as the father?"

She said, "Number Eighty-sith," which is how she got her nickname.

When Travis told me about it, he said, "The poor girl is probably retarded and unloved, and she probably hates letting the guys do it to her. And then they make fun of her. Jesus! It's sick."

Yet he admitted there were times he'd almost be willing to go along. There are very few things in this world powerful enough to stand up against the combined persuasive power of raging hormones and peer pressure. Morals and conscience seem puny by comparison.

At the Teen Center dances Travis danced almost every dance with a voluptuous sexpot whose name was—I'd swear it on a stack of bibles—Rosie Peach. What Rosie and Travis did on the floor gave a new definition to the idea of dancing. Fucking through their clothes was what they did. They rubbed their groins together so hard and so long that sometimes Travis would go home at night bleeding from the friction. All the guys assumed he was sleeping with her, but he wasn't.

One day after the usual Friday night dances Charlie called Travis and said, "We're going to gang-bang Number Eighty-sith, and you're going with us this time."

I guess Charlie caught him in a vulnerable moment. For whatever reason, Travis agreed to go along. Charlie picked him up shortly after lunch. Bobby and Hoss were already in the car, and they were going to pick up one more boy, a new kid who had just moved to town. They were all wearing purple and gold team sweatshirts and new, short haircuts. Suddenly ducktails were out and the really cool guys sported the new style haircuts that they called Ivy League. The new style was no style at all.

The new guy was waiting on the curb when they got to his house on Church Street. He was draped around the stop sign on the corner, a cigarette dangling from his mouth. He wore a bright red T-shirt with the printed legend: "I Got Mine At The Chicken Shack!"

Travis shouted, "Wow man, a Chicken Shack shirt!"

"No shit, Sherlock." The new guy hopped into the convertible.

"Where'd ja get it, man?"

"At the Chicken Shack, natch. Four bucks."

"Aw-RIGHT man," Travis bellowed, "I gotta get me one of those."

"Let's all get 'em," Charlie said. "We'll be the Chicken Shack snatch squad."

"Aw-RIGHT!!"

The Chicken Shack was a popular bootleg joint out past the fairgrounds on East Main. It has once been a fried chicken restaurant, which is where the name came from. It was a one-room, rundown wooden house with a sagging roof over the front porch. Attached to the peak of the roof was a giant plaster chicken painted white with Chicken Shack lettered in blue. The people who ran it paid off the cops and ran their illegal operation with such impunity that they had the audacity to sell T-shirts.

The boys drove out to the Chicken Shack to buy shirts, and then they drove farther out East Main to where they saw the girl standing at a bus stop, a forlorn hump of a figure standing in the dirt, hands hanging listlessly from the ragged sleeves of a tan sweater. A pink dress with a brown and yellow flower print fell over her form like laundry on a line. She was short and heavy. Her eyes were green, and they darted about nervously. The only bright thing about her was the too-red lipstick that was streaked across her mouth.

Charlie pulled the Impala to the side of the road, and Travis hopped out to hold the door open for her. She got in and sat between Travis and Charlie. Her dress was crumpled in her lap like a used hanky. Over the dress the faded cardigan sweater was unbuttoned and drooping like forgotten laundry. Charlie reached under her dress and gave her thigh a squeeze.

"You stoff that now," she admonished. "Cain't you wait?"

They drove to an old Negro cemetery. Nobody spoke. Charlie parked next to a mimosa tree, his right front tire wedged against a decaying tombstone. Silently they climbed out of the car. The boys walked away and huddled. The girl crawled into the back and laid herself down like a slab of pork on a butcher's block. Leaving her sweater on, she unbuttoned her dress and let it fall open; the floral print was like spilled flowers strewn about the unkempt graveyard. And she waited.

The boys argued in excited whispers over who was going to be first. They decided on the new boy. He walked to the car. He stepped in. The other boys scanned the cemetery. Travis picked up a dry iris and placed it back in its cracked vase. Charlie and Hoss told jokes. Travis slid one foot back and forth, watching the grass turn alternately yellow and green as his foot switched the blades. The new guy got out of the car, hitching his pants up, a silly grin on his face. Hoss said, "My turn," and walked to the car, giving the new guy a sock on the shoulder as they passed.

Travis wiped his sweaty hands on his pants. He had to piss. He urinated on the trunk of the mimosa.

Hoss hopped out of the Impala, laughing and making obscene gestures with his meaty arms. He looked like a gorilla. Charlie was next. He stayed in the car a long time, at least half an hour. Then it was Bobby's turn.

Travis had to piss again. Again he walked over to the Mimosa and cut loose. Bobby pulled himself out of the car, over the door. The door opened behind him and the girl got out. She stood by the car and started buttoning up her dress. She said, "Ah cain't do no mo'. I'm all wore out."

"Aw come on, gal," Charlie said. There ain't but one more. Ain't nobody but Travis left. You ain't gonna leave the old redhead out, are you?"

She said, "I thowwy. No mo'."

Hoss said, "Shit fire, Travis. You don't have to take that crap. Just grab her and screw her brains out. What's she gonna do? Holler rape? Her?"

Travis stepped toward her. I think what he was going to do was get in the car, to get them all in and take the poor girl back where they had picked her up. But the guys thought he was going for her. They thought for sure he was going to grab her and sling her onto the back seat and force her, just like Hoss had said he ought to. She must have thought the same thing. She thrust her hands out to ward him off and she screamed, "Oh no! Noth yew!"

The guys broke into hysterics. They all started shouting, "Noth yew! Noth yew!"

"Travis is some stud, huh?" Hoss said. "He ain't good enough to fuck Number Eighty-sith!"

"Jesus, man," Travis said, "How can you talk like that right in front of her?"

"Oh shit, listen at'm now boys. Takin' up for the cunt that turned him down. You're a real pussy, Travis. You really suck. Shit, I bet you're a virgin. Bet'cha cain't even get it up."

A year earlier Travis would have creamed Hoss for that, and Hoss and everyone else knew it, but Travis was beginning to change. Hoss obviously sensed it. Knew he could get away with taunting Travis. Travis did nothing but set himself defiantly in the shotgun seat of the Impala and wait in silence for them to take him home.

In the hall at school the next day Hoss shouted, "Hey Travis! I got a call from you-know-who. She said to tell you that you still ain't good enough."

After P.E. a bunch of boys rushed into the shower and skidded to mock halts when they saw Travis taking a shower. They backed up as if horrified, pushing at one another, laughing, shouting, "Noth yew! Noth yew!" Travis didn't even know those kids.

* * *

The phone rang at the Warner house. Marybelle answered it. "Hello."

"Hi there. It's me, J.P."

"G'morning."

"It's Sunday. I didn't know if I should call or not. I thought you might be a churchgoer."

"Nope. Nobody in this house is big on going to church. I tried it for a while, but I had a falling out with the preacher and haven't been back since."

"Really? That sounds juicy. You'll have to give me all the gory details. Meantime, I thought maybe if you were not doing anything I'd drop by. Maybe we can take a ride out to the lake."

"Yeah, sure. Sounds like fun."

It was a brisk morning, but the sun would soon burn the chill away. Chuck and Travis were passing a football on the front lawn when J.P. pulled up. Marybelle was waiting on the porch. She was wearing a plaid skirt and a white blouse with a lightweight cardigan sweater tied loosely around her neck. As soon as J.P. parked she ran to the curb and dashed around the car to hop in.

"What's with the sweater?" he asked. "It's not cold. Heck, I thought maybe we could take a dip in the lake."

Chuck said, "I told you he was crazy." And they were off.

Heading into the sun, J.P. lowered his visor. Marybelle draped her sweater over the back of the seat. There was little traffic. The only sound was the swish of tires against pavement. At the lake a soft breeze set the hanging branches of a willow to dancing. Sunlight reflected off the rippled water. Dancing diamonds. J.P. parked in the shade of a large oak. They stepped out onto grass that was still wet with dew—wet in the shade, but toasted dry where the sun lay down patches of gold.

They walked to the water's edge and sat on sun-toasted sand. It was warm to the touch at first, but cooled quickly as they settled in. J.P. poked his fingers into the sand. It was wet below the surface. He pulled off his shoes and socks and wiggled his toes, edging them crablike into the lake. "Ooh, that feels great. You ought to try it."

"All right, but if I get frostbite, you've got to pay Doc Littlejohn.... Ahh, not bad."

"You know," he said, "there was something you said that day you called me. Before we went to Chez Michael. You said the occasion for wearing your new evening gown was ruined, and you said you'd tell me about it sometime."

"Yes, I will. But not now, please."

"Okay. So tell me about your sparring match with the preacher."

"There's not much to tell. Like I said, I'm not much on going to church, but I tried it for a while, mostly for Travis's sake. They roped me into teaching a Sunday School class. One Sunday the lesson was supposed to be on temperance. I couldn't teach temperance, not with Travis in the class. He knows we drink. I couldn't get up in front of that class and teach that drinking is a sin when I don't believe it. So I asked Brother Barnes to let someone else teach the class that Sunday. Well, he started preaching at me about the evils of alcohol. He said, 'I'll pray for you, Sister.' Boy, that got my dander up. I know I shouldn't have done it, but I let him have it right then and there. I said 'I'll pray for you too, you pompous, hypocritical so-and-so.'"

J.P. burst out laughing. Grabbed her hands and lifted them high over her head like a referee at a boxing match. "And the winner is . . ."

With that they went absolutely insane with laughter. She threw a fistful of sand on him, and he scooped up a glob of mud from the bottom of the lake and rubbed it in her hair. Tears of laughter streaked both of their faces. She pushed him backward; he stumbled and fell on his butt in the shallow water. She hiked her skirt above her knees, and holding it out like a little parachute, jumped on top of him. A fisherman about thirty yards out into the lake cranked his motor and high-tailed it to a quieter spot, while J.P. and Marybelle wrestled with one another in the lake. The fisherman's boat was well out of sight (as if they cared) when he kissed her. It was a long kiss with wet lips pressing firmly and dripping hands wrapped around soaked clothing, and neither of them had to lean over or stretch upwards, because they were the same height.

* * *

Autumn announced itself with early morning chills and the pennant-waving hoopla of football games. The Golden Wave was in contention for the Big-Eight Conference championship. They trounced their first three opponents. Travis played his defensive tackle position like some kind of possessed animal. Once he broke through the line and tackled the enemy quarterback and the halfback simultaneously as they were handing off. The sports writer at the *Daily Journal* said that Travis, almost single-handedly, was responsible for the fact that no opponent had scored a touchdown against the Golden Wave.

As the days grew colder Travis became more and more ferocious on the field and more aloof at school. He disdained hanging out with the boys on weekends, staying home to draw instead. Cassie and I were usually nearby. Our presence never seemed to distract him. We would talk while Travis drew. There was an openness between the three of us that was unique. We could and did talk about everything—or almost everything. I felt at home in Travis's room. I would imagine that we all lived together in some major city far away from Tupelo, that Travis was a famous artist and I was his agent. Cassie, of course, would be a dancer. Those idyllic days did not last for long.

In the Deep South autumn is repeatedly interrupted by a false summer—right up until Christmas. It was one of those false summer days in November. Chuck was grilling hamburgers in the backyard. He and J.P. and Mama Marybelle and Mama Janet were on the patio. From where I sat with Cassie on the upstairs window sill, they looked like paper cut-out figures, an inky, purple-black on one side and gold on the other, depending on where they stood in relation to the amber colored light bulb that dangled from an overhead wire. Their voices were carried upward by the evening breeze. Marybelle said, "Warm night and good company. Makes me bubble like champagne. I don't know when I've felt like this."

"Me either," Janet said. "Must be something in the air."

"It's the changing season," Chuck said. "Does it every time. Makes you feel young."

Marybelle stood up and twirled around, her skirt billowing. "I feel like a teenager again! Travis and Cassie are old fuddy-duddies by comparison."

I looked at Cassie to note her reaction. She was enthralled with the scene below. Didn't notice me at all.

J.P. said, "If you really were sixteen again, what would you do right now?"

"I'd do this!" skipping to where he sat and plopping onto his lap, flinging her arms around his neck and nuzzling him.

Helium balloons of laughter floated up to Travis's bedroom window where we sat. Cassie turned to Travis, who was doing sit-ups on the floor. "They're really having a great time out there."

Travis grunted. He pulled his body up, with fingers locked behind his neck, and jerked to touch elbows to knees. A fine spray of sweat flew toward us. I could smell it, sweet and mildly pungent.

"Can you smell the hamburgers cooking?" Cassie asked.

"Nah."

"Boy, I can. They smell great."

"They sure do," I put in.

We kept watching the scene below. Chuck said, "Marybelle, if you weren't so busy trying to seduce J.P., I'd ask you to go inside and get us all some more beer."

"Well I might as well do just that." She hopped off J.P.'s lap. "This seduction thing's not working too well anyway."

To Mama Janet, but with no attempt to keep anyone else from hearing, she said, "Either he's a perfect gentleman, or he's terribly shy, or my charms are simply insufficient. He actually kissed me once—right on the lips, a real man-woman kind of kiss—but that was ages ago, a month or two anyway. Since then . . . well, there have been hotter romances."

Spinning to face J.P., she admonished, "Why J.P., you're actually blushing!"

Cassie swung her legs off the windowsill. "You're missing a great show, Travis."

"Hunnh! What?" He sat up with a great huff of breath and rolled his arms and neck to work out the kinks.

"I said you're missing a great show. The folks are acting like teenagers. Mama Marybelle was sitting in J.P.'s lap and teasing the Dickens out of him. I've never seen her like this."

"She's in love, Sis. Whadda'ya think. Head over heels. Hell, grown-ups aren't any different than us."

He got up from the floor and squeezed in between us on the windowsill. His naked upper body pressed against us, his sweat soaking into me, suddenly cool in the night air. I felt myself shudder and sensed my involuntary shudder run through Travis and into Cassie like an electrical charge. He put his arm around her and she cuddled her head onto his shoulder. His other arm—naked, hard, smooth, hot—pressed against me, shoulder to elbow, like some great snake, coiled muscles at rest but ready to strike. His sweat dried and his body was a furnace. We were enveloped in his heat, drowsy with it.

Cassie said, "It's funny, you know. They're all right down there, only a few feet away, yet it seems they're a million miles away."

"Who?"

"Everybody. Whadda'ya mean who? Mama Janet. Chuck. All of them. It's like they are actors on a stage, with heavy makeup and lavender-tinted footlights reflecting off their faces, and we're sitting in box seats, far, far away, spying them through opera glasses."

Travis stretched his arms and pressed against the window frame. His odor mingled with the aroma of beef cooking on the grill. I felt a little dizzy.

Cassie sighed, "I feel like I belong right here, precisely here in this window sill, like everything that's ever happened in the whole world from the beginning of time was geared toward the end goal of placing each of us in the precise spot we're in at this moment; yet, at the same time, I think I don't belong here at all. I'm here for the moment, on loan, on a mission from somewhere else. I'm content for the moment to stay here and observe these people, these strange and wonderful people down there who belong to me but don't. But I guess sooner or later I'll have to leave, to search for the place where I really belong. Do you ever feel like that?"

I said, "Uh huh."

Travis said, "Yeah, sure. I guess. Maybe I'm not as dreamy as you, but if you mean do I feel like I don't belong in Tupelo, you're darn right."

If Cassie was watching the people below as if from afar, I was even farther away, watching us watching them. She said, "I look down there and I see our parents and they seem so contented, but they are like laughing marionettes. I get the feeling that there is a great circus out there beyond horizons we've never crossed. It's the most marvelous circus in the world, and I've just got to find it. They are contented because they not only don't know about the circus, they couldn't see it if . . . if . . ."

"If they had front row seats center ring," Travis completed her thoughts for her.

"Yes! Yass!"

"I like the way you said that. Yass! There's such great satisfaction in that. There's this guy in a book I read. His name is Dean Moriarty. He's always saying Yass! like that, like he was so damned wonderfully in touch with everything in the world, like he'd see things: colors, movement, patterns, common things that everybody else takes for granted, and it would all come together for him in some wild, fantastic improvisation, and it would be like ... like it was just too stupendous for words. And then he'd shout out this great big Yass!"

"Cass! Travis! Hey you guys!" It was Papa Chuck hollering from below. "It's ready. Come and get it!"

We went downstairs. Travis said, "Race ya!" and we raced to the backyard as we often did, Travis heading out the front door and tearing around the garage, me darting straight through the kitchen. Of course I won. I always did. His route was twice the distance or more, but he always swore that one of these days he was going to beat me. We all helped our plates off the grill and sat around the picnic table. Just as we started to eat, a sudden and unexpected squall ran us inside. It came down fast and hard. Grabbing plates, we rushed into the house. We ate on the big dining room table, each of us in our own little puddle, dripping, laughing, chattering away, the music of our chattering and chomping and slurping almost drowned out by the violence of the rain storm. Strobe of lightning. Crack of thunder. There's nothing like a thunderstorm in the South—nothing so sudden or so ferocious. We used to call them electrical storms, because they nearly always put out the lights.

Chuck brought candles in and lit them in anticipation. And sure enough, in a moment there was the snap of blackness. Black, flash, after image—the eerie, funny, romantic flicker and flash of light from pulsing candle flame and crackling slash of lightning. Everyone animated, joyful. Only Marybelle was quiet. She who had been so playful earlier had lapsed into a private reverie. I think I'm the only one who noticed. Then she spoke:

"Will I ever be anything but daddy's little girl? The daddies keep changing, but I stay the same. I've got to do something." I don't think anyone said a word in response. I can't remember, but it seems we were all too stunned. Her words made no sense, seemed to come from nowhere.

The thunder and lightning slackened, but the rain continued to beat down relentlessly. Marybelle's monologue was voiced to no one in particular. It was as if she didn't know we were there. I could see that Travis was embarrassed. Nobody knew what to say, so nobody said anything. Nobody save Marybelle.

"I've always been somebody's plaything or somebody's little girl or somebody's mother. I have no identity aside from what I am to others, no self that's just me. I've got a mind, but I've never been able to use it. I'd give anything if I could quit my job, but what else can I do? I've got a high school education and I've never been anything but a sales clerk. I've never even lived alone. God! Could I even take care of myself if I had to? I don't know who I am or what I'm supposed to do. Supposed to do! It's always what I'm supposed to do, what's expected of me, never what I want. That big shot Ray Prichard tempting me with talk about going to fashion shows and working with designers. Hell, all he wants is to be my sugar daddy. You know what he tried to do in Memphis? Yeah, you can figure it out. He figured I owed it to him. He ordered me to buy new clothes to wear, and then he acted like I was in his debt, and we all know how I was supposed to pay off. He said he'd divorce his wife. The liar. I'm going to quit. I swear I am. I don't know what else I can do, but I'll find something."

She scanned the table as if waking up and noticing there

were people there. She perked up. "Hey, J.P.," she said, "Do you think I could get a job at the newspaper?"

"I don't know. Maybe. What can you do?"

"I can type. I could probably write. I made straight A's in English. I can answer the phone and file and . . . hell, I can sweep the floor and carry out the trash."

He said, "I have a feeling you could do anything you set your mind to."

Chuck said, "Give it a shot."

Proud of herself, she crossed her arms in front of her chest and nodded her head in a gesture of determination and said, "I'll do it by golly."

Chuck said, "Good for you."

"Yeah. Good for me. It's time I took charge of my life, huh? Time I quit worrying about what's expected of me and do what I want to do." Then staring at J.P. with a I'm-gonna-get-you-sucker gleam in her eye, she said, "And as for you, Mister Jewel Pomeroy Hollingsworth, it's high time you did something about this romance stuff. I'm tired of waiting for you to make a move."

We started laughing. Travis choked on one of his monumental bites of hamburger. J.P. blushed so bright you could have seen his glow from Willis Heights. He was tongue-tied and he stammered, but he said the right thing. He said, "How 'bout we do something about it this summer, with a ring and a license and a lovely ceremony on the shores of Tombigbee?"

Marybelle shouted, "Yes! Yes!"

And Travis and Cassie and I all together shouted, "Yass!"

During all this, Travis managed to wolf down three hamburgers and two whole baked potatoes.

Spring of 1961
Tupelo

Anticipation, alive and palpable like a covey of quail flushed by a hunting dog, fluttered over the town of Tupelo. Elvis Presley was coming to town, coming back home to perform at the Mississippi-Alabama State Fair and Dairy Show—at the fairgrounds anyway; the actual fair had come and gone back around Halloween. A week before the concert J.P. finagled an interview with Elvis. He drove up to Memphis with Marybelle in the morning. After school that day a sizable chunk of the senior class besieged the Warner house and set up camp in the front room, waiting for them to come back home. We wanted to know what Elvis had said.

"I'll tell you one thing, and one thing only," J.P. said. "If you want to hear more you'll have to wait for Sunday's paper. The one thing I'll tell you is this: Elvis said that when he lived here the only way he could get into the fairgrounds was to climb over the fence behind Clayton's Staff-O-Life. He never had the price of admission. Now they're paying him ten thousand dollars to come sing a few songs."

Travis cut me a look. I immediately knew what he had in mind, what he simply had to do, what he would surely talk me into doing with him. Sure enough, a week later I found myself on the loading platform behind the feed store, with Travis and Charlie Speed, climbing up the metal ladder on the side of a box car and jumping over the fence into a hay stack in the fairgrounds. Would you believe it? I landed right smack in a cow turd.

That idiot Charlie started howling, "Johnny stepped in cow shit! Yah! Yah! Yah!"

"Shut up, Charlie!" Travis hissed. "You want us to get caught?"

We hurried around the big top searching for a loose flap where we could crawl under. Acrid dust rushed up my nostrils, making me sneeze. Pulling myself out of the sawdust and brushing my clothes, I hurried to catch up with Travis and Charlie, who were running around among the girders under the grand stand. Charlie suddenly stopped. I almost ran into him. He grabbed Travis's arm and pointed upward, signaling us to shush, hardly managing to keep from laughing out loud himself. We looked up to see what he was pointing at. The underside of people, a worms-eye view of big legs and foreshortened figures. There was a woman standing above us. We could see right up her dress. We could see heavy legs with puckered and splotched skin and stockings and garter belts, and what I guess was a corset, and stained panties. To me the sight was disgusting, but I guess Charlie thought it was sexy, and funny as all get-out. He was clutching himself around the middle to keep from laughing, and he was making disgusting gestures like he was jerking off. I suppose his obscene gesture was supposed to indicate that the illicit view turned him on. Travis whispered, "You're sick, man, really, really sick. Come on, let's get in with the crowd before somebody spots us down here."

We scuttled out from under the stands and merged with the crowd. We found empty seats on the top row. All around was a static of excited murmuring like bird wings beating the air. Wind whipped the tent top, intensifying the bird-wing illusion. A flock of raucous people, all talking about Elvis. A lady to the left of Travis said, "Elvis come into Danny's this one time and had his self a big ol' ice cream cone. After he left, my Jennifer, she went right up and kissed the stool where he was sittin'. I swear she done it."

"That's terrible," her companion said.

A man in front of her said, "I knowed him back in grammar school. He weren't nothing but po' white trash back then. We used to make fun of him. I'd come home from school and my mama, she'd say, 'What happened at school today?' and I'd say, 'Aw nothin'. Elvis brung his gee-tar agin'. Like him playing that gee-tar was the dumbest thing in the world. Look at him now. Look at what playing that gee-tar got him."

Everybody had an Elvis story. After all, this was Elvis's hometown. A lot of these people had actually known him when he was a kid living out by where Mama Marybelle grew up in East Tupelo. But most of the stories they so proudly told were probably second-hand and only half true.

Charlie said, "Me and Hoss saw him once. We pulled up right alongside him at the red light at Gloster and Jackson. It was summertime and we were both driving convertibles with our tops down. I was driving my Impala and old Elvis was driving a big, white Caddie. Hoss, he hollered at him, 'Hey, I know you! You're . . . ' and he paused like he was trying to recall the name, and old Elvis he just smiled real big, reared back behind the wheel of his Cadillac convertible like he owned the whole damned world. Then Hoss said, 'You're Carl Perkins!'"

Charlie laughed a regular knee-slapping laugh, and a woman on the next row shot him a quizzical look and said, "Who's Carl Perkins?"

Travis spotted his mother in the crowd and waved at her. She was sitting with J.P. Suddenly the lights were dimmed and a single spotlight focused on a point mid-stage. The curtain rose. I could feel the electric shock of anticipation shoot through the crowd. The band started playing an introductory riff, playing the same refrain over and over, each chorus a tiny bit louder, each chorus a tiny bit faster. It went on and on and on and the huge tent was otherwise silent and everyone pitched forward on their seats and only the single spot light broke the blackness. It lit a bare spot on the stage, a chalky, luminous spot of worn wood that shone like an old coin under water. Then Elvis walked out and stood in the spot light. He reached for the microphone, pulled it to his mouth, sneered that famous lip-curled sneer of his, winked at the audience, opened his mouth, and the tent exploded with a blitzkrieg of screams and clapping and foot stomping. Elvis sang and thousands of voices screamed at him. I don't think anybody in that tent actually heard his voice. You couldn't even tell when the song ended, because the screams were so loud. Then he sang another song, and another. People were jumping up and down and the seats were shaking and the noise was a constant roar.

After about two hours of bedlam, Elvis simply stepped out of the spot light and vanished. The band went into the same number they had started with. Nobody seemed to notice. They didn't know what was happening on stage. They had come to scream and clap, and that's what they were doing. An electrified voice began repeating a single phrase over and over: "Elvis has left the fairgrounds. Elvis has left the fairgrounds." It was like someone trying to break into a dream. Eventually the message was heard. Gradually, as if in a trance, everyone wandered out of the tent and across the sawdust trail to the main gate by Long's Laundry. There they fanned out to get into cars that couldn't move because of the congestion. We had come in Charlie's car. We climbed in and sat, unable to pull out into traffic. Finally Charlie said, "To hell with it. Let's hoof it. I'll pick up the car tomorrow. It's party time, boys!"

Charlie's mother was out of town for the weekend. He had the house to himself. The word had flown around school all week: it was going to be one hell of a party, one of those where no one is actually invited, but damn near everyone shows up.

From the outside, Charlie's house wasn't much to look at. Not a tiny house like ours, but nowhere near as big as the Warner house either. Old, in need of a paint job. A profusion of flowerpots on the little front porch. Inside, it was something else. Simple. Elegant. You could tell that Charlie's mother had impeccable taste, but very little money. We stepped through an arched doorway into a small foyer, a welcome mat on the floor. An umbrella stand and coat rack. An Impressionist style landscape on the wall. Another arched doorway led into a living room that was much more spacious than I expected. The floors were a worn but highly buffed hardwood. The area rug was probably homemade. No overhead lights; the room was softly lit by a pole lamp next to the couch and spotlights on prints that hung on the walls. These were frame-shop variety reproductions of landscapes by Degas and Monet.

For a little while I felt at peace in Charlie's house. Then the party arrived. Hoss Williams and the Casey boys and Wanda and Bitsy and Sam Littlejohn, who immediately spilled a beer on Mrs. Speed's rug, and some girls from the women's college in Columbus and Josh Culpepper, who always turned up where he wasn't wanted. And others: some I vaguely knew, some I'd never seen before. In the unseasonably hot night, it was a witch's brew of boys and girls all dolled up in men's and women's bodies, all thrown together in the cauldron of a small house on Green Street, all terribly, painfully, self-consciously aware of the hormones that raged in their young bodies. Guys trying to out bravado each other, spewing beer and cussing and slapping each other on the back, every word-sneer-look laced with sexual innuendo, and rock and roll throbbed in the melee.

Charlie draped his arm around Wanda, his hand casually (innocently?) brushing her breast, a beer clutched in his other paw. He shouted, "Ya'll know Wanda has different color panties for every day of the week!"

"Do not!"

"How do you know?" someone challenged.

"How ya think he knows?" someone else asked—a rhetorical question if ever there was one.

Everybody had something to say on the subject of Wanda Ramsey's panties.

"You're asking for it, Charlie."

"What color is today?"

"Five bucks says it's red!"

"Yellow. Gotta be yellow!"

"Let's find out!"

Charlie clutched the waistband of Wanda's pants. Grabbing his hand and glancing quickly at the gathered crowd with an expression that spoke of some kind of strange combination of panic and pleasure, Wanda said, "Don't you dare!"

Charlie and Hoss grabbed her. She squealed, wrestled with them, slapped at Hoss. Hoss held her and Charlie yanked her pants down to her knees. She was wearing pink panties.

"Assholes!" she shouted at everybody, slapping and laughing and pushing them away. It was all in fun, but I sensed that Wanda felt hurt and used, especially by Charlie, but didn't want anybody to know how she felt.

Then Josh Culpepper was bragging about some pseudo Klan type organization he had recently joined. "You gotta be free, white and twenty-one," he said. "Ain't none of ya'll old enough yet, but I figger you got your hearts in the right place."

I was sitting next to Travis on the couch. We both heard Josh. "Who invited that guy anyway?" I asked.

Travis said, "Nobody invited him, man. When you go to a party like this it's like going skinny-dipping at Blue Hole. You gotta figure you're gonna bump into at least one asshole."

Charlie had wandered over by us. He put in his two cents worth: "What I don't understand is why everybody seems to think he's such hot stuff."

"He's slick as snot, that's for sure," Travis said. "Got a lot of folks fooled. Hell, look at Sam. Josh used to beat him up all the time, and he still makes fun of him, but Sam thinks he's cool." Much older than any of us, Josh was in law school at Ole Miss, a school whose main purpose at the time was the training of attorneys who could defend the Southern Way of Life. We all figured Josh would have flunked out already if his old man hadn't been slipping somebody some big money.

We heard Josh say, "We ain't got anything against niggers. 'Member what Brother Dave Gardner said on the Jack Parr show? He said, 'I like Negroes; I think everybody ought to own one.' Haw! Haw! Oooh! Naw, seriously. We probably care more about our colored people than most Yankees do. Treat 'em better, too. What these civil rights people don't understand is that they're being used by the Commies. If them outside agitators would leave us be, we'd work out our race problems."

It was getting late. Everybody was drunk. Somebody came running in and shouted, "The cops just raided the Chicken Shack!"

One of the Casey boys came stumbling up the hall from the bathroom with his pants tangled around his ankles. His skinny butt was covered with droopy boxer shorts. He reached the rug, flopped down to his knees and put his head on the edge of the couch and started snoring.

Somebody I didn't know hollered at Travis, "Hey Travis!"

"What?"

"Noth yew! Noth Yew!"

Travis said, "What's that you say? I can't hear you. Didn't your mama teach you not to talk with shit in your mouth?"

Everybody started laughing. All but Charlie and Wanda, who were cuddled together in an easy chair. Wanda was sleeping. Charlie's eyes were closed, but his hand was moving, slowly caressing her shoulder.

If the party had begun as a great, boiling cauldron, it had slowed to a simmer. I grew drowsy, but didn't want to leave. Other people did leave, or they passed out, or wandered off to Charlie's bedroom or the den in search of a place to sleep.

I watched Travis pull himself up from the couch and stagger down the hall. He propped himself against the bathroom door for a long time, then finally lurched into the bathroom. The whole house was now silent. Travis must have stayed in the bathroom for half an hour. I heard the toilet seat clap down; after a while the rush of running water. Eventually he came out. He stumbled across the hall and into Mrs. Speed's bedroom. I sat on the couch, wanting very badly to go in there too. I had a hard time breathing. There was a sharp pain in my shoulder and it felt like something was pushing on my chest. I rubbed my chest and was surprised at how bony it felt. I don't guess I'd ever noticed before.

I slipped off my shoes and tiptoed down the hall, holding my shoes in my hands. In my mind I could see myself sneaking through the house like a parody of some inept thief. Thinking about it now, I see the animated cartoon character the Pink Panther. Pausing in the doorway I could see Travis in the spilled light from the corner street lamp. The light oozed through Mrs. Speed's chintz curtains and spread its subtle pattern across the floor and onto the bed and over Travis's recumbent body. His clothes were in a pile on the floor. His stomach rose and fell in deep breaths. I realized after a while that I was trying to slow my rapid, shallow breath to match his more satisfying rhythm. As quietly as I could, so as not to attract the attention of anyone who might still be awake in the house, I pulled the bedroom door shut behind me and stood just inside the door watching Travis sleep. I watched him for the longest time, then quietly removed my clothes. Everything. Even my Jockey briefs. I carefully folded my clothes and placed them on a chair, and I eased down onto the bed.

Carefully avoiding any sudden moves, so as not to wake him, I squirmed into as comfortable a position as I could, and tried to fall asleep. But there was no denying my closeness to his naked body. There was no denying my lust. I wanted him. I wanted to squeeze those muscular legs as hard as I could. I wanted to press my face into his rippling belly, to feel his body hair against my lips. I was dying to grab him between the legs and feel him grow hard in my hand and nuzzle my cheek against the shaft and take it into my mouth. Yes, I had finally admitted to myself that I was gay, that there was something in me I couldn't deny that compelled me, despite my attempts to fight it, to seek out other men. But it scared me to death. In my mind, I could hear Hoss and Charlie, could hear their sniggering bravado. So often I'd heard them say it: If any man ever tries to touch my dick I'll kill the son of a bitch! Any guy that tries to do it with another guy ought to be locked up in a nut house. Any guy that blah blah blah . . . sicko scumbag queer. I could hear that word splattering in my mind like spume spat from the mouths of the righteous: Queer, queer, queer . . . the *Bible* calling it an abomination, Brother Barnes preaching against it, polite people so repulsed by it that they can't even mouth the words for it . . . and me knowing in that moment that queer was what I was and would always be. I could not resist. I didn't even want to try and resist.

My hand was on his leg. I was afraid to move it. What if he woke up? What would I say? I could pretend I was asleep. Didn't know what I was doing. Guy can't be held responsible for what he does in his sleep—or for what he does when he's drunk, for that matter. Bullshit. I was goddamn every bit responsible. Please God, why do I have to be this way? Please let him want it too.

I moved the hand an inch. Two inches. He never stirred. Maybe he wasn't asleep. Maybe he did want it too. I moved my hand another inch. The back of my hand was resting against his scrotum. It felt hot. He moaned and stretched (in his sleep?) and resettled in the bed. Now my hand was on his penis and still he seemed to be asleep. He didn't touch me. He didn't make a sound. But he was hard. Guys get hard in their sleep all the time. It didn't mean a thing. He could wake up and catch me at it and beat the shit out of me. Worse yet, he could wake up and catch me at it and never speak to me again. Forever after he would look at me with disgust and I would slither away like a worm.

The house was silent. An ever so tenuous breeze ruffled the curtains. It was probably two o'clock in the morning. Maybe even later. For at least twenty minutes (it seemed like an hour) neither of us moved. With agonizing care, still terrified that he'd wake up, I began rubbing my hand up and down the shaft. The throb of his heart pulsed in my palm. I lay my cheek against his thigh and inched upward. Finally I closed my mouth on him. He let me, still feigning sleep.

I didn't see anyone. I didn't hear anything, but it started to feel as if someone was watching us. As if suddenly awakening from a dream (and right in the middle of my first ever love-making of all times, goddamn it) I realized that it was growing light outside the window and that someone was behind me in the doorway. Travis must have seen what I only felt. Violently he wrenched away from me and flung himself out of bed and threw on his clothes and rushed out of the room. I don't think he was after whoever it was that had been spying on us. I think that person had run away before Travis even got a clear look at him. Travis was just running for his life.

By the time I got myself dressed, Travis was gone. Charlie and Wanda were still asleep in the living room when I hurried through. Hoss was on the floor with his head against the couch. Bitsy slept with one hand flopped over Hoss's head. Sam Littlejohn was sitting up on the floor, his back against the wall. He, too, seemed to be sound asleep. I saw all of that in a glimpse. Nobody stirred when I ran through the living room. On the front porch, I almost tripped over Josh Culpepper, who had found a sleeping bag and curled up in it.

Keeping my distance, I followed Travis. He was already five or six blocks ahead of me. He walked to Magazine Street, but instead of turning up the walk to his house, he cut behind the Casey's and across the tracks. In a clearing about twenty yards into the woods there was a concrete slab, the foundation of what had once been a little house. Years ago we had called it the Pirate Shack. Back then there had been walls and part of a roof. Long since abandoned and rotting away, it had been the inspiration for many a fantasy adventure.

Travis sat on the old foundation and smoked. He never touched cigarettes during football season, but now that he was a senior and next year's team was beginning spring practice, he smoked like a chimney—Chesterfields snitched from Papa Chuck.

He smoked a couple, grounding them into the earth when done, and made patterns in the dirt with his heel. He looked up at the sound of approaching footsteps. Someone parted the leaves of an oak tree and stepped into the clearing. It was a young black man from the Alley, apparently on his way to work. He stopped when he saw Travis, paused for a moment, and then called him by name—a rising inflection on the name, asking, "Travis, is that you?"

Travis stared at him and paused, then finally he said, "Man?"

"Uh huh, it's me. 'Cept I don't go by that name no mo'. I'z Raymond. Raymond Carver."

"Well I'll be damned," Travis said, "I never knew your real name."

"Me neither. Still don't. But I goes by Raymond Carver now."

"Well okay, Raymond. So howzabout you pulling up a tree or something and sit down and join me for a smoke."

"Okay."

He plopped down beside Travis and said, "Man, it's been a long time."

Travis laughed. He said, "I'm supposed to say that. I'm supposed to say man it's been a long time."

"Naw, you 'posed to say Raymond it's been a long time."

"That's right man—Ray-man."

I felt stupid and perverse spying on them. I crept away and walked to Mike's for a cup of coffee. J.P. and Marybelle were there. She had started working at the *Journal* and breakfast at Mike's had become a daily routine. On the stool next to J.P. sat that fat cop, Lieutenant Norman. J.P. was talking to him. He said, "What's new in the world of crime, Fats?"

Norman said, "We shut down the Chicken Shack last night."

"What did you do that for?" Turning away from the cop, he said good morning to me. Marybelle said, "Hi Johnny."

"G'morning."

"Have you seen Travis? He didn't come home last night."

"He's okay. He stayed over at Charlie's."

The cop said, "What'd we do that for? Hell man, they were selling booze. That's illegal in this county in case you didn't know."

"So why now? And why not some other bootlegger? They quit making their pay-offs? Or could it have something to do with the color of their skin?"

Norman blushed. "Hey man, it wadn't nothing like that. Shit, they were selling T-shirts advertising the damn place. You can't let a bootlegger advertise. That's rubbing our noses in it." As an afterthought he said, "Hey, don't you go putting none of that in your goddamned newspaper."

The sixties

We all graduated from Tupelo High in the spring of 1961, all but Sam Littlejohn, who had to repeat a year and eventually dropped out. Cassie graduated with top honors. After graduation she went to New York to study dance. J.P. and Marybelle were married in June. Travis enrolled in the Memphis Art Academy in September. The year after that he transferred to the University of Alabama, where he stayed for six years—the last two as a teaching assistant in the Master of Fine Arts program. We saw each other every now and then: when he came home for holidays, once in New Orleans at Mardi Gras. And during all that time there was never a repeat or any mention of what had happened at Charlie Speed's house the night of the Elvis concert.

J.P. and Marybelle became active in the Civil Rights movement, which did not endear them to the community at large. Surprisingly, Mabel Cook, who usually loved any opportunity to berate just about anybody, defended them. "At least you've got to admire their courage," she said. "They stand up for what they believe in. The rest of us run around like chickens with their heads cut off, trying to fight off what we know damned good and well is right and inevitable."

By the end of the sixties, the only people from our old gang who still lived in Tupelo were Josh Culpepper and Sam Littlejohn and Wanda Ramsey. Hoss Williams was sometimes around. Hoss married Bitsy, moved to Jackson, got divorced within a year, married another woman, moved to Oxford—which is practically a suburb of Tupelo, but don't dare say that to anyone who goes to Ole Miss—became a hot-shot salesman and coached his boys' Little League teams.

Josh Culpepper got his law degree and came back home to become the youngest assistant District Attorney in the state. Sam dropped out of school and spent a few months, on two separate occasions, in the state mental hospital at Whitfield. Back in Tupelo he got a job cleaning stables for a local man who raised show horses. Wanda spent a few years in Atlanta where she tried to make it as an actress. She did a few TV commercials and some bit parts in local theater, and after while she moved back home and never told anyone why she had given up her acting career. Man trouble probably.

Charlie Speed went to Ole Miss on a football scholarship and then went to Vietnam and was killed in the war. They might as well have killed his mother too. First she lost her husband in World War II, and then she lost her only son to Vietnam.

As for me, I got out of Tupelo as soon as I could, vowing never to return. I moved to New Orleans, got a business degree from Tulane, admitted to the draft board that I was gay (which kept me out of Vietnam, thank God), and I went to work for an investment firm. I told myself that since I could never be an artist like Travis or a dancer like Cassie—I had no talents of any kind—I might as well spend my efforts on building a fortune, which I did. Along the way I also built an enviable art collection, which included a number of Red Warners.

The last time I saw Travis was during Mardi Gras in New Orleans. It must have been 1965 or 1966. He was on the patio at Pat O'Brien's, drinking a Hurricane. I joined him and he introduced me to his companions. They were all grad students from Alabama. I had one drink with them, and then Travis and I took a walk through Jackson Square and Pirate's Alley, a Mecca for hack artists who do pastel portraits and French Quarter street scenes. Travis was ecstatic. He shouted, "Hoo-whee! Looka there! Arteests!"

Tourists—the ones who were sober enough to notice—gaped at him and laughed out loud. I tried to shush him, but he was on a roll. "Shee-it, these guys are the real McCoy! They got them berets. They got them goatees! Oh Mister Artist Man . . ." He approached one who was doing pastel portraits for ten dollars. The guy sat on a fold-up stool in front of his easel. A wooden tray attached to the easel with c-clamps held piles of pastel sticks. On the easel was a drawing of a woman who appeared to have been lifted from the cover of a *Cosmopolitan*. His little area of the street was fenced off by a display of portraits propped up with folding metal stands. Most of them were portraits of celebrities such as Elvis and Bob Hope and John F. Kennedy. Beside the easel was a chair you could sit in to have your portrait done. I thought about him lugging all that stuff down the street.

Travis sat for his portrait. Sat? He plopped his butt on the stool and grinned his monkey grin and started scat singing and stomping his feet and drumming his hands on his thighs, singing out, "Doo-wop a dwap dop ah do me right Mister Artist Man!"

The artist gave up, because Travis would not sit still. Travis said, "You got to catch my movement, my man. I'z the moving man, movin' right along. Thass my essence and my being. Ee-rupting, kee-rupting, effervescent energy captured in glorious pastel! You can do it, man! Move that marvelous drawing hand!"

The artist said, "Forget it man. You're crazy as a bed bug."

"Why thankee anyway, Mister Artist Man. I'm obliged for the attempt." He bowed and tipped a make-believe hat and was off at a trot, dancing along the street to the music in his head. I tagged along behind.

I had witnessed moments of his high-energy clowning back in high school. I remembered that he had fallen in love with Kerouac's character—the one based on Neal Cassidy—

and had tried to emulate his way of speed rapping. I also remembered that he had studied and tried to impersonate the speech patterns of black preachers at revival meetings, but this was the first time I ever witnessed the full-blown persona that he was later to become famous for. Frankly, I was embarrassed. I didn't know what to do. Luckily, he dropped it. He suddenly grew calm and pensive. We were in the park. He stood still and looked me in the eye with a sad expression and said, "I worry about Sam Littlejohn. What's going to become of Sam?"

I didn't know what to say, so I said nothing.

Travis said, "Remember when he used to do the belly flop off the high board? He was scared shitless. He never let anybody know it, but he was scared. He did it because it was the one thing he could do that the rest of us could admire. I always felt guilty for goading him into it. I was always scared he'd hurt himself."

Hearing Travis say that made me think of him in ways I never had before. I'd always thought of him as independent, a guy who never game a damn what other people thought about him. It was strange to discover he had been just like the rest of us back then, a bundle of insecurity, scared to death somebody might think he wasn't so cool after all.

* * *

Wanda Ramsey was killed in the summer of 1967. I read about it in the *Times Picayune*. According to the article in the paper, her body was found in an alley beside Page's Market next to a parked truck. Her skirt was bunched around her waist, and she was wearing nothing underneath. When I read about that, I couldn't help but remember the night of the big party at Charlie Speed's house and the big ruckus over what color her panties were. The police surmised that she had been raped. As near as I could tell, this assumption was based on the flimsiest of circumstantial evidence. If there was any medical evidence of rape, the paper failed to mention it. A black man identified as Raymond Carver was arrested and charged with rape and murder. I knew who Raymond Carver was, of course. He was the man I had seen Travis talking to at the old Pirate Shack, the black man who had been his childhood friend, the kid whose friendship with Travis had been destroyed because of racism before we were even old enough to know what racism was, although we had lived with it and in it every day. Travis was also mentioned in the newspaper. He was a witness, not to the actual crime, but apparently to the whereabouts of the accused at the time.

I wanted to call the Warners and find out what was going on. I even thought about driving up to Tupelo. But there was a part of me that wanted nothing to do with Tupelo or anything that related to my past.

I followed the reports on Channel Four and in the *Times Picayune*. There wasn't much information. It looked as if the police had arrested the first suspicious character they could lay hands on. They had no reason to suspect him except that he was black and he was there. Neighborhoods were still segregated, and it was highly unusual to find a black man in a white neighborhood late at night. Not only that, the police had a vested interest in being able to pin any rape of a white woman on a black man. It perpetuated a myth that needed to be fueled in order to maintain the status quo.

The alleged crime was first reported by Mabel Cook, who called the police around ten o'clock that night to report a disturbance at the diner across the street from her house. She saw a male and a female arguing in the parking lot. She said there was some pushing and shoving, then the female took off running toward Crosstown. She couldn't identify the female, but when later asked if she fit the description of Wanda Ramsey, Mabel said that she did. The male was Travis; Mabel did recognize him. What happened next was confusing to her. Her phone rang and turning to answer it, she missed some of what was going on across the street. But she said there was another man talking to Travis and a third man joined them. And she said she could have been mistaken about that; the third man could have been at a distance; maybe it only looked from her vantage point that they were all together. At least one of the men followed after Wanda, this much Mabel was sure of, but she couldn't tell which of the men it had been who followed after Wanda. One of the men, she said, was black. That was the extent of the eyewitness account. Apparently Travis could identify the black man as Raymond Carver and could say whether or not it was Carver who followed in the direction Wanda (assuming it really was Wanda) had gone.

To me it seemed awfully slim evidence for charges of rape and murder, but I had heard of cases being won on less—especially when race was an issue.

The trial opened less than a month after the crime was committed. J.P. reported the trial for the Tupelo *Daily Journal*, and the New Orleans papers picked up the story. His article was more literary than factual, full of metaphors for race relations. A beautiful read, but confusing. He said that all during the trial Sam Littlejohn sat in a seat directly behind the defense counsel and cried. Sam, who never really grew up, always had a schoolboy crush on Wanda, as did most of the boys in school. Also like many of us, he had looked up to Josh Culpepper, begrudgingly. In his article, J.P. used Sam and Josh as literary devices, casting them as symbols for the town as a whole. Such a device was needed; the actual proceedings were pretty boring.

Man was convicted of the lesser charge of attempted rape and involuntary manslaughter. He was sentenced to thirty years in the state penitentiary at Parchman.

The day after the trial ended Travis threw a few clothes

and his paint and canvas into the trunk of his car and drove to New York. The next time elections rolled around in Lee County Josh Culpepper won the D.A. post. Sometime later, Man won his appeal and was set free. I don't think Travis ever knew that. Sam Littlejohn became more and more dysfunctional and eventually became a permanent resident at Whitfield. I heard about that later, from Marybelle.

Four years later, maybe five, I was reading *Art News*, and I spotted an ad for an exhibit at the Broome Street Gallery: "Four To Watch: James Streeter, Marlo Davis, Kim Kyo, Red Warner." I didn't know it was him, but the name registered. I watched for it when the reviews came out. (I had not started my collection at the time, but I had ideas about investing in art and dreamed of discovering the next Jasper Johns, so I had to keep up with the reviews; I subscribed to all the major art magazines, as well as the Sunday *Times* and the *Village Voice*.)

The next week's *Voice* reviewed the Broome Street show. Randall Jarrett wrote the review. He called it an exhibition of emerging artists, a common euphemism for artists who have been busting ass for years, trying to get a tiny bit of recognition. He described Red Warner's paintings as "the abstract equivalent of portraiture"—whatever that is. (I remember reading somewhere that all painting, abstraction included, is either landscape or portraiture, depending on whether the format is horizontal or vertical. But I had the feeling that Jarrett mean more than that.) He also mentioned that Red Warner was a Southerner, and called him "the wild man of SoHo".

I was becoming a detective, putting together bits and pieces of art reviews to prove my suspicion (hope?) that Red Warner and Travis Earl Warner were one and the same. Same last name. Red hair. Southern-born wild man. I couldn't find anything in writing to prove it, but in my heart I knew. (In Your Heart You Know He's Right: the Goldwater poster that hung on the wall at Danny's Diner. I bet it was still there, faded and grease splattered, the night Wanda Ramsey was killed.)

I clipped Jarrett's review and put it in my scrapbook, along with sports write-ups on Travis and the stories on Wanda, and the report of Charlie Speed's death in Vietnam.

Three years went by before I saw anything else on Red Warner. Then he was suddenly all over the place. *Art News*, *Art Forum*, *Arts*, *Art In America*, they all ran feature articles on him. He was in the *New York Times* and the *Village Voice*. His name even appeared in gossip columns in *Cosmo* and *Rolling Stone*. The papers told us if he was seen at Max's Kansas City or Club 57 or Warhol's Factory. Suddenly he was a star. We read about his clothes and his sexual exploits and his comic shenanigans. We read that he partied all night and painted all day and that he loved to shock the hoity-toity by bringing prostitutes and drug addicts and other low-life characters to their parties.

I wondered what Marybelle thought of all this. I wondered if he was ever in contact with her. And what of Cassie? She was, I assumed, still in New York. Did she see Travis? I could picture her fretting over him, patiently waiting to pick up the pieces of him when he finally crashed. And crash he surely would. Nobody could sustain such a frantic life.

It seemed like he wanted to crash, like maybe he was pushing himself beyond all limits in an attempt to punish himself for what he might have done to Man, and maybe because he despised himself because he was afraid that he was homosexual. I imagined that simply because he had had one homosexual experience, forced upon him by yours truly, that he would seek out others in an attempt to discover for himself whether he was really gay or not, or maybe to punish himself in moments of despair. Or . . . or . . . oh, I don't know. Perhaps I was projecting my own feelings onto him.

All I knew for sure was what I read, and I had sense enough

to figure half of that was hype. But I knew Travis. He painted with burning concentration, and when he quit painting he had to escape. With Travis escape would be drugs, sex, wildness. This I knew about Travis Earl Warner: he was the kind of man who would go to orgies at night and confession the next morning, only he wasn't Catholic, and probably wouldn't go to confession anyway. Instead, he'd wallow in guilt, and go out and fuck some more to put it out of his mind, and then dive back into his painting. He could not allow himself a moment of quiet introspection. Every time a quiet moment managed to sneak up on him, Man would be there, accusing; the whole damned senior class from Tupelo High would be there, reminding him of the time he escorted me out of the dance; Brother Barnes would be there, preaching hell-fire and brimstone; and Papa Chuck would be there as a perfect example of what a young boy from Mississippi could grow up to be. I'm sure that all of Tupelo followed him to New York. They were even in the paintings, abstracted and hidden under layers of scratched and scumbled paint.

I saw the paintings only in reproduction, and frankly I was perplexed. I wanted to like them, but I couldn't see what all the fuss was about. A typical Red Warner painting consisted of one or two simple shapes on a flat background, minimalist blobs painted with a sloppy, Abstract Expressionist application of Roplex, an acrylic medium. All I could see was a generally wedge-shaped form of some unnamable, murky color in a ground of some other unnamable, murky color. Of course I was willing to withhold judgment until I saw the real thing, not only because I was aware of the tremendous difference between small photographic reproductions and paintings, but because it was Travis.

When I finally went to a Red Warner exhibit and was confronted by his paintings, it was as if I were locked in a room with another man, a stranger, a man whose presence threatened me, scared me, made me want to run, a man who looked into my eyes and saw my soul. He was big and he was ugly, dirty, slovenly, as heavy as guilt. From the canvas, his eyes locked onto my eyes and I could not turn away. Slowly, doggedly, like a rising flood, his gaze revealed to my gaze the startling truth that his ugliness was a mask, a stereotypical ugly mask worn for protection. The man under the mask was beautiful, so beautiful that I could not help falling in love with him. What I saw in paint on canvas was Travis Earl Warner's heart. What I also saw was myself. And I had the feeling that I was not the only person who experienced such a personal, emotional response to his work. Randall Jarrett had not been able to express it aptly—who could?—but now I knew what he meant when he called Travis's work the abstract equivalent of portraiture.

I went back to the gallery three more times. After my third visit I went back to my hotel room and called Leo Garner, the owner of the Broome Street Gallery. I didn't want to talk to him in person, an unnecessary precaution probably, but I didn't want to give him a chance to try and influence me. "This is Johnny Lewis," I said into the phone. "I want to purchase Red Warner's "Hungry Frederick." I'll send a cashier's check tomorrow, along with instructions to shipping it to my warehouse in New Orleans."

"Thank you," he said. "That's an excellent choice. We'll have to hold the painting until this show is over, and until your check clears the bank. Is that agreeable with you?"

"Yes it is. You'll have the check within the week, and I'll expect shipment by the tenth of next month."

Over the next decade I bought four more Red Warners.

1982

I first heard about it on the morning news. I was in bed at home in my Garden District Apartment. Jimmy was beginning to wake up and nuzzling against me, purring the way he does in the morning. I had my cigarettes and a cup of coffee. With chicory (practically a requirement for living in New Orleans). I was propped on heavy bolsters, watching the morning news on Channel Four. My normal morning routine. The talking head of the Channel Four anchorman was displaying his usual sincere look, while bad drawings and uninspired headlines behind him let us know what he was talking about. A computer-generated likeness of Red Warner flashed on the screen behind him, along with the headline "Artist Vanishes."

I grounded my cigarette in the ashtray and scooted closer to the set. The anchorman said, "Notorious abstract artist Red Warner apparently vanished last night, following a bizarre accident in his studio loft. Reports are sketchy and unconfirmed. The famous artist was said to have been despondent on the heels of bad reviews of his latest exhibition at the Broome Street Gallery. Friends said he had been drinking heavily. Last night the artist threw a party for over two hundred people. During the party he reportedly wielded a butcher knife and started swinging it wildly while quoting scripture in one of his famous evangelist parodies. Witnesses report that he began hacking at himself, blood splattered and people ran out of the loft screaming. An unidentified woman stayed to nurse the injured artist. As of six o'clock this morning, New York City police report that Red Warner's condition and whereabouts remain unknown. He did not check into a hospital. It is suspected that the so-called mystery woman took him to a private doctor and is keeping him hidden from the public. In other news, Creole frog legs are the latest hot item in French Quarter restaurants. Here's Jane Curtis to tell us all about it..."

    I was stunned. I don't remember thinking anything for a long time. It was as if my mind simply switched itself off. It said, Oh no. We're not going to deal with this shit. Not yet. I remember that I pushed my glasses against my nose until the pain of it shook me out of my stupor.

    The next day Jimmy and I flew to New York. I spent a couple of days in the city reading about Red Warner and hanging out in SoHo bars where he was the main topic of conversation. I don't know what I thought I was doing. Playing detective, maybe. But I didn't get anywhere. Nothing but rumors. There was one thing happening around the New York art scene that would have tickled Travis if he had been around to know about it. All the critics suddenly retracted their original reviews (with convoluted justifications). Some of them were magnanimous enough to admit they had been wrong. They said that Red Warner's new paintings were such a radical departure from what they had come to expect of him that they had been too quick to condemn. All of a sudden the latest trend in art criticism was admitting, "I was wrong."

    Finally, I went to the Broome Street Gallery to see Red's latest show. Being there! Standing in that gallery, my feet planted, my eyes locked on the paintings, a cigarette in my hand, conscious of my gestures as I smoked with a studied air! It was like being in some surrealistic scene out of a Fellini movie. That moment haunts me. I looked back on it and see it as a metaphor, or as multiple metaphors (mixed). It was crowded. People wandered in and out, talking, posing, gesturing. Peripheral vision of street action glimpsed through a window. Horns honking, people shouting, shoppers, gawkers, walkers, all like some kind of circus act. I remembered something Cassie had said years ago about there being a marvelous circus somewhere and people sitting front row center and not even knowing it was there. And there I was, trying to watch the high wire act in the center ring and being distracted by animals ring-left and jugglers ring-right. The action swam around me. Fish in a tank. I was seaweed, my feet rooted to the floor of the tank, my head awash in the current. Outside, a Volvo pulled to the curb. My peripheral vision caught sight of a woman getting out of the car. She went into the New Cedars Bar. Consciously I paid no attention, but unconsciously something about her registered. Whatever it may have been about her that was trying to dig into my awareness was wiped out by the immediacy of the Red Warner paintings. Nothing else could take root in my brain.

The paintings were unlike anything I had ever before seen. I didn't know what to make of them. At first glance they were like color field paintings, only rough and highly energetic, with frantic, all-over line work as in a Pollock. The surface was a dense field of scumbled, scratched and layered paint, which was in some ways very much like typical Red Warner paintings from the past. The color and the paint application were the same, but there were recognizable figures, something he had never done. The figures weren't exactly there on the surface. They emerged through the surface. Hints of figures, a line here, a shadow there: clues to hidden figures; and oh yes, fully-realized figures too, painted with loving care and then painted over with glazes that obliterated them, imprisoned figures that struggled to get out.

My initial reaction was, I think, disorientation, perhaps even revulsion. But as I stood there and took them in, the elements that had put me off at first glance became enticing. It was the same reaction I had experienced when first coming upon his earlier paintings.

As I stood there, my mind was worked on two or three

levels simultaneously. On one level it was just me and those goddamned awe-full paintings locked in a stare-down; on another level I was aware of all the movement around me: other people milling about, in and out of the gallery, a trucker across the street loading paintings into his van; and on yet another level I was aware that the owner of the gallery, unseen, was watching me, trying to guess whether or not I was going to buy one of the paintings.

I bought them all. The whole damn show. It cost me a hundred and eighty thousand dollars. It was either the wisest or the most foolhardy investment I'd ever made. At the time I had no idea which (still don't). I only knew that I had to have them. Now, of course, each of those paintings is worth twice that.

The next day we rented a car and headed south. I let Jimmy do the driving. I didn't want to go back to New Orleans, and I didn't want to fly. I wanted to go to Tupelo. And I wanted to take it slow, give myself time to let it all bounce around in my head.

"There was something going on," I told Jimmy. We had stopped for lunch at a truck stop in New Jersey. "I'm not sure what it was, but there was something going on outside the gallery when I was there. You know. Sometimes you catch something out of the corner of your eye, and you don't pay any attention to it, but later you realize it was important and you should have paid attention. It was like that. There was a woman. She got out of a car and went into a shop, or maybe the bar. Yeah, it was the bar. She did go into the bar. I remember, because she was still there when I went in later, or she had just left and people in the bar were talking about her. Oh, I don't know. Probably nothing. It's just . . . for some reason it keeps gnawing at me."

It was the next day, driving through the mountains near Knoxville, before I began to put the pieces together. I had seen the woman get out of her car and walk into the New

Cedars. I can't remember if it was before or after I went into the bar that the trucker pulled up and she let him into a building. Of course I had no way of knowing at the time, but it was Travis's loft they were clearing out. She was the woman who had been at the party, the so-called mystery woman who had whisked him away. When I went into the bar after leaving the gallery, people in the bar were talking about her. They said things like "I'll bet she's the one." But they were speaking in pronouns: she and him; they never used names, and I didn't make the connection.

What an idiot I was! But then, how was I to know?

* * *

We pulled into Tupelo around noon on a Sunday afternoon. The streets looked more narrow and congested than I remembered. The people looked like people in New Orleans or anywhere else. Where were the familiar faces? I should have recognized somebody, even after twenty years. Tupelo wasn't supposed to change, but it had. Magazine Street was nothing like I remembered. When we'd lived there hardly anybody parked on the street. They all had garages, and most families had only one car. Now many of the old homes had been converted into apartments and the curbs were congested with cars. The little house where I'd grown up had been made into a duplex—it hadn't been big enough for a single family to start with—and I couldn't even find the Warner House, which had been the biggest house on the street. It must have been torn down.

We headed downtown with the intention of stopping at Mike's for lunch. But when we drove down Broadway, there was no Mike's Restaurant.

We parked on Broadway and walked around town. And I did see a familiar face in a coffee shop on Main Street. It was Mabel Cook. She must have been well over eighty—maybe pushing a hundred, yet she didn't look much older than I remembered. I introduced myself.

"I remember you, Johnny. You used to be a skinny little runt. How are you?"

"I guess I've put on a few pounds over the years." I thought the extra weight looked good on me. "I'm doing well, thank you. How are you doing?"

"Not bad for an old biddy that should have been dead long since."

We chatted for a few minutes. "Whatever happened to Mike's?" I asked.

"Oh, Mike passed away about eight years ago. Just about everybody's passed on. Mike's son is still here, though. Remember him? Constance? He's got his own restaurant. One of those fast food, fried chicken places. Calls it the Chicken Shack. Now isn't that a silly name? But I hear the chicken's pretty decent."

"What about Chuck Warner? I assume he's still around."

"Of course, Chuck and Janet are still here. Only that wonderful old house of theirs on Magazine Street was torn down to make room for a parking lot. Shameful thing. The Warners live out by the airport now."

"What about Marybelle and J.P.?"

"Oh, they're in Oxford. J.P.'s a hotshot professor at Ole Miss. Marybelle still works for the *Journal*. She commutes. Seems to me like they could have stayed put and let him do the commuting."

It was good talking to Mabel. It felt as if she were the first person I'd spoken to in ages who had feet planted on the ground.

I called Marybelle and she invited us to spend the night at their home in Oxford. I tried to decline, but she insisted. We ate, we talked about old times, and of course we talked about Travis. "He's all right," she said. "Yes, they came here after leaving New York. Nobody knows where he is, and he asked me not to tell, but he's fine. Don't worry. Oh, you don't know how I worried about that boy. Worried myself sick. When he first left here, he was in bad shape. He blamed himself for Man being convicted. I was afraid he was going to do something terrible to punish himself. In a way, I guess he did. Maybe his whole time in New York was a kind of self-inflicted purgatory. All that wild living! I'd read about him in the papers. It worried me to death. But he told me most of what the papers wrote was exaggerated. Anyway, he's okay now. Cassie's with him. She'll see to it that he's okay."

Cassie! How obvious! Cassie was the woman who whisked him away, the woman who cleared out his studio. I sat right across the street and watched her and it never dawned on me. I still pictured Cassie as the girl in high school we called Sis. And of course I never would have expected the premature gray hair. It dawned on me then that if I failed to recognize Cassie, she and Travis would be even less likely to recognize me. Twenty years older, beard and glasses, thirty (or so) extra pounds: I looked nothing at all like the Johnny Lewis they would remember.

"So where are they now?" I asked.

"I don't know. Well, yes I do, but I promised I wouldn't tell anyone."

"Not even me?"

"I'm sorry. I can write him, though. I bet'cha if I wrote him he'd say it's okay to tell you. I mean, after all, it's not like you're some snoopy reporter from the *National Enquirer*."

"That's okay," I said. "I understand." I knew then that if I persisted I could get her to tell me where he was. She was dying to tell me, but by then I was in no hurry. I knew, somehow, that I would find him soon. Besides, even though I was still anxious, in some ways, I had started enjoying playing detective. I wanted to figure it out on my own.

While we were talking I kept eyeing an old copy of the *Times Picayune* poking out of a basket. I knew it would contain a needed clue. "Do you subscribe to the *Picayune?*" I asked.

"No. Travis left that here. I just never got around to tossing it out."

"Good. I'd like to read it."

I took that paper to bed with me, convinced that something in it would tell me where to find Travis. It told me, all right. It was laughably blatant. He had circled an ad in the classified section: Fishing camp for sale, Mary Walker Bayou . . .

Mary Walker Bayou

Mary Walker Bayou crawls through the mosquito beds of the Mississippi coast bending around little towns with exotic names like Escatawpa and Gautier and Pascagoula. It flows into the Pascagoula River, which is vomited out into the Mississippi Sound with the outgoing tide and is sucked back into its own gullet when the tide rushes in. Hidden among canopies of hovering pine trees are fishing camps, typically run by retired couples. It was to one of these camps that I went looking for Travis. I went alone, having first taken Jimmy back to New Orleans. He had work to do—impatient clients, and city boy that he was, he wasn't about to go hang out with me at a fishing camp.

I drove along a narrow road paved with broken seashells and shaded by tall, scraggly, long leaf pines. The road turned out to be a cul-de-sac. A ramshackle whitewashed house sat at the end. Spaced around it, partially hidden by the trees, were seven or eight small cabins. The big house begged for a paint job. The screen porch was rusted. Behind the screen a small woman sat. She was quilting, a cascade of patchwork colors falling across her lap. I stepped out of my car onto pine straw and seashells and chalky earth. Pine cones littered the ground like spent grenades on a battlefield. I kicked one as I walked to the porch, halfway expecting it to explode, remembering games played as a child.

"Hi there," the woman said. "You looking to do some fishing."

"Well yes. I was thinking about it." I didn't know what to say, but somehow that seemed right. She didn't recognize me, which was what I expected. Beautiful, earthy, dimly viewed behind the screen, dressed all in black with a fall of hair the color of storm clouds, there was an aura of mystery and sadness about her. No wonder her appearance in SoHo had caused such a stir among the rumor mongers. She had changed, but she was definitely Cassie. My heart was racing. I couldn't untie my tongue to speak.

She said, "You need to see Travis if you want to fish. He's down't the docks. Right down that path."

I swallowed air and nodded stupidly and walked in the direction she had pointed. A few shaky steps down a dirt path and I saw him. He was standing on the pier, shouting at an elderly couple who were paddling out into the bayou. "Ya'll watch out for snakes now, ya' hear. I killed a moccasin last week that was twenty foot long. Sis skinned him and made a belt out of his hide. That bugger had a head as big as my hand."

Hearing me, he turned to wave with a meaty, red-splotched hand. That monstrous hand held into the glare of sunlight shocked me. It was like a gnarled cypress stump. At some point since I had seen him last he had lost two of his fingers. He shoved that hand at me, waiting for me to shake it, looking right in my face with a gleeful twinkle in his eyes. I shook his hand and said, "You don't know me, do you?"

"Nope. Can't say as I do. Why? Should I?"

"Probably not" Maybe I felt insulted that he didn't recognize me. Maybe I wanted to see how long it would take. Travis was still playing games, pretending to be a country bumpkin. I decided to play along.

"My name is Lewis. I'm from New Orleans. City boy. Never been fishing in my life, but I'd like to learn." I was proud of myself for thinking so quickly that Lewis could be either a first or last name. If Travis was going to play games I would too.

"Well hell, son, we kin take care of that. We'll go out and catch ourselves a mess of shellcrackers."

"What are shellcrackers?"

He laughed. Looked at me like he pitied my ignorance. He said, "Evidently, son, you don't know shit from shinola 'bout fishing. Shellcrackers are the granddaddy of pan fish."

"Do you mean bream?"

"They's something like bream, but they ain't. They's the utmost hellacious fightingest fish you'll ever get on the end of a line."

We climbed into his boat. Travis sat on a swivel seat that was clamped to the bow. His weight forced my end of the boat out of the water. With a short paddle clutched in that gnarled hand, he silently eased us out into the bayou. The paddle slipped into the water without a splash, leaving a trail of circular ripples behind us. He didn't talk, but chain-smoked Chesterfield cigarettes, flicking the glowing butts in wide arcs into the still water when done. I remembered that he had smoked the same brand back in high school. He snitched them from Poppa Chuck. After silently rounding a few bends in the bayou, he eased us alongside a tree stump and dropped anchor. He rigged up a fly rod with a long, thin hook and a lead sinker that he crimped on with his teeth.

"Put-jew a worm on that hook and toss 'er over them lily pads," he said.

Nervously I tried to hook a squiggly worm.

"Naw, not like that. Shellcracker'll slip your worm offen that hook without nary a budge. Looka here. You gotta skewer that sucker on like this," putting the worm on the hook the way some men bunch up their socks to pull them on.

We cast out and settled back to wait. "Watch your cork real close," he whispered. "Shellcrackers don't bob 'em up and down like bluegills. They ease 'em under and run. You gotta watch for that, and when you see it, set your hook good and hard."

"Set my hook?"

"Give 'er a yank. There! Now!"

My float slipped under water and started moving laterally along the border of lily pads. I jerked on the rod and my line flew up and slammed the side of the boat. Empty.

"I said give 'er a yank, man." Travis guffawed. "I didn't say jerk 'er guts out."

The next time I hung onto one. My rod bent double.

"Hot damn! Reel 'er in, son."

Frantically I pulled on the line. It played from the reel like live spaghetti, like twine on a kite when it's taking a nosedive. I was grabbing and pulling at that tangle of fly line and the fish was tugging against me and Travis was laughing and shouting, and before I knew it I was hefting a big, fat fish over the gunwale. It was ten inches long and as fat at Travis's hand. He grinned and reached into his ice chest for a can of beer. Handing the beer to me, he said, "Beer don't taste right 'til you get the smell of fish on your hands."

Snapping the beer open, I lifted it for a well-deserved, hefty slug. That was when Travis said something that no one else could have said. I loved it. I sat on the aluminum seat in that little boat with my jaw dropped open in hilarious, stupefied joy and heard Red Warner say, "Don't drink yet, son. You gotta savor the moment. It's the virgin fish of the misty American morning. It's the sacrificial moment. Did you know, son? Can you comprehend it and dig it in your All-American redneck soul, that you did not catch that fish without his knowing it and shouting a great big yes? Think about that, man. The ecological balance is a jazz rhapsody, and we're disturbing it with discordant notes. It's only by the grace of the gods that we're allowed. Now drink that beer like Eucharist wine."

The drawl was gone. His voice thundered ecstatically, tumbling like salmon over a waterfall. His shoulders jerked and his massive, but firm, belly heaved, and an almost malicious, boyish gleam radiated from his face. He was speed rapping like Neal Cassidy in all his beat splendor.

"That country drawl is a total fake," I said, on the verge of saying, Don't you know that I know who you are?

He shrugged and reached for another beer, gripping the can like an arthritic, with two fingers and a thumb, stubs of the missing fingers pointing skyward.

"What happened to your fingers?"

"Gator got 'em. Used to wrestle 'em when I was younger. That's what they call sport around these parts."

About then he hung onto a shellcracker and quit talking; then I got one, and for half an hour we pulled them in as fast as we could re-bait. Travis was jerking and cursing and spewing poetry and talking doubledeclutch, non-stop, beat jargon, and bounding and swiveling on that little seat that threatened to rip loose, shouting like a circus barker, "Whoo-wee! We done run into a veritable tribe of them mothers! It's a shellcracker review. Count 'em, boys, one hundred beautiful fishes. See 'em wiggle, see 'em turn; see 'em flash they bellies in the sun. Whoo-hee!"

The boat was rocking. Waves rippled to either shore. Tears literally poured down my cheeks, and I was sloshing my beer all over the place. Fish, jerked hastily off hooks and tossed in the bottom of the boat, were jumping in a jumble of rods and boxes and cans that littered the boat, and Travis Earl Warner was jerking about so wildly that the boat nearly capsized.

Then, as soon as the feeding frenzy had started, it stopped. I looked at Travis. He looked at me. I think I saw love in his eyes. I know I saw deep satisfaction. We were quiet for a while. Finally I said, "Goddamn it Travis, don't you know that I know who you are? Don't you know who I am?"

"Yes, Johnny. I know. It took me a while. You've changed. But I know."

He stood up in that unsteady little boat and lurched toward me—and I thought for sure we'd be thrown into the bayou—and he gave me a big bear hug.

I stayed with Travis and Cassie for a week. We talked about old times, about Tupelo and about New York, but the things I was dying to find out he avoided. One day when we were standing on the bank talking I said, "You know, Travis, I envied your popularity back in high school. I never had any real friends, other than you. The other guys, they just tolerated me. Barely. But you were different. Maybe we never talked about it, it wasn't exactly the kind of manly thing teenagers brag about, but you were extremely sensitive, and you had an exceptional talent. I always knew that you were going to make it big some day. I wanted you to. I envied your talent, knowing I didn't have any. I loved art more than anything, but I couldn't draw at all. Somehow I was able to experience it through you. Maybe that's why I followed your career so closely."

Travis said, "Wow!" And I realized that even after a decade of almost legendary fame, he was still flabbergasted that anyone could look to him as a hero.

"Did you know that I own the largest collection of Red Warners in America?"

He didn't even answer that. He just smiled at me quizzically, as if I were some kind of strange animal. I said, "I do. I bought three early paintings, and I bought out your last show."

"Hell, the critics killed me on that one."

"Yeah, but after you left New York they recanted. They put you in a class with de Kooning and Pollock now, and you don't even know it. Do you miss it? The fame? The excitement?"

"No, I don't miss any of that. That wasn't me in New York. I don't know who it was, but it sure as hell wasn't me. Maybe this cockamamie fisherman ain't really me either, but it's a hell of a lot closer than anything I've found so far."

I smiled at that. No other comment was called for. Travis said, "A fish don't have to be nothing but a fish. He don't even have to know what a fish is. But a man's got to spend his whole blessed life trying to figure out what it means to be a man."

He scooped up a flat rock and skimmed it across the bayou. It skipped six times, ricocheted off a piece of sheet metal on the other shore and stuck like an arrow in the trunk of a pine tree. Travis jumped up, spun around, let out an Indian war cry and said, "Fish ain't nothing but a fish, but a goddamn man can sometimes do things you'd never believe."

Later, back at the house, he handed me a notebook and said, "I think you ought to read this. There are things you're dying to find out that are best answered here. It's rough. Sketchy. But all the essentials are there. I wrote it when I was recuperating, when Cassie and I first came down here."

RED WARNER'S JOURNAL

I'm a has-been hero, and I've got the clippings to prove it. What I wish more than anything else is that I could just BE a simple fisherman down here on the bayous, and purge myself of memory. Memory's a son of a bitch.

My earliest memories are all about war, a house-of-mirrors collage of war stories that span years and are confused with movies and comic books. GI Joe and John Wayne. We fought the Japs and fought the Krauts and fought the Koreans, and we rose Old Glory on Iwo Jima and stormed the beaches at Omaha (Nebraska?) and remembered the Alamo and the Maine; and Babe Ruth and the Manassas Mauler could beat the daylights out of any old slanty-eyed Jap any day of the week, and God was on our side.

From the earliest time I knew, as well as I know that fish swim, that the duty of a man is to fight the enemy, to carry the ball across the goal, to love and protect women and children, and to never ever cry. I also knew that thou shalt not kill any but the avowed enemy and that no matter what, a man's gotta worship Sweet Baby Jesus and never for a moment be weak like a woman.

A few lines scratched out, then:

God. God lived at the Calvary Baptist Church. CAL-VAR-EEE! Marching to Cal-var-eee! The shrine of the holy of holies. It was a fort, a monument, a place of silence and reverence and fear and awe, where they sang, "Jesus loves the little children, all the children of the world. Red and yellow, black and white, they are precious in his sight." But there were no black children at Calvary Baptist. To find black children you had to cross Magazine Street and dart down the little path that led between Casey's and Doc Littlejohn's, and cross the railroad tracks where you could walk the rails, pretending to be a tightrope walker in the circus (and if you fell off with bare feet, the cinders hurt like the Dickens). Across the tracks was the Alley. Man lived there. Man was my best friend for a little while.

I can remember old Brother Barnes scaring the shit out of me, preaching about the wrath of God. I didn't even know what a wrath was, but whatever it was, I damned sure didn't want any truck with it. I thought I saw it for sure when I was five years old. There was a terrible electric storm. Lightning flashed the sky an icy blue that was immediately crushed by blackness. Thunder rolled and crashed and cracked, and windows and doors rattled in their frames like castanets. I stood inside the screen door and taunted the storm, pretending to be a big, brave man. "Go on, you dumb old lightning," I shouted. "Hit something. See if I care. You can't hurt me. Why don't you hit the church? Burn the church to the ground." I dreaded Sunday school and got sick headaches every Sunday morning. Me and Mama Janet.

A few more lines scratched out, then:

Who cares what church or when? I'm not about to let anything as paltry as the facts fuck with my memories.

And he continued:

When the church did burn down, it wasn't our church. It was First Baptist, about four blocks further up Church Street. It wasn't right after that either. It couldn't have been, because it was summer then, and it was snowing the night First Baptist burned to the ground.

We heard the fire trucks and Papa Chuck shouted, "It's a big one! Grab the kids! Let's go!" When there was a fire in town everybody went.

Black silhouettes scurried frantically against a backdrop of flame. There were cars and trucks, and two big fire engines with flashing lights. Heavily corded hoses stretched across the street in a jumble of black-booted feet in sheets of icy water. Flames stretched to a sky laden with heavy clouds of smoke that tumbled glowing embers of black wood and ash. On the fortress-like face of the church a jagged wall dropped as if someone had pulled the bottom from under it, and a shower of sparks shot right at us.

I couldn't stop shaking. My hands and feet were freezing. I started bawling, and Cassie squeezed my hand.

Mama Janet put her arm around me and said, "It can't hurt us here. We're safe."

And Cassie said, "It's okay, Travis. Jesus won't let it hurt us."

But it wasn't the fire that scared me. It was the wrath of God. They didn't know that I had caused that fire. They didn't know it, but He knew.

* * *

When you're a kid you assign magical powers to certain moments that loom off in the future: moments like the first time you get to go to the swimming pool without your parents, or when you get to order real coffee in a restaurant instead of hot chocolate. Fifth grade was one of those magical times, because in fifth grade you got to take art. There was a teacher, Mrs. Fields, who taught art one day a week. She was a large woman who wore a dark blue smock over her dress and pinned her hair on top of her head with a big rooster-tail comb that was all covered with rhinestones. She wore gold-rimmed glasses that hung like a necklace on a gold chain. She never peered through those glasses, but sometimes she perched them on the end of her nose and looked over them. Mostly they just dangled over bulbous breasts encased in yards of cotton and lace.

I waited forever for that first art class. When it finally arrived, I was so excited I ate my shirtsleeve. Mrs. Fields came in without saying a word. She marched from table to table and placed in front of each child a large sheet of paper, a mimeographed illustration of a wasp out of Colliers Encyclopedia, a sharpened H-B Eberhardt-Faber drawing pencil, and an art gum eraser. Even those names were magical. No plain old writing pencil, but an ART pencil and ART gum eraser!

"You shall each draw the wasp," she declared. "Take your time and be very careful. If you make a mistake, that is what the eraser is for. Now let's all get to work and we'll see what good little artists we can be."

It wasn't exactly how I had pictured it. Well, what the heck. I went to it. Grabbed my pencil and sketched in the outline of the wasp's body in one bold stroke. For the stripes I made an energetic, zigzag mark. Wispy lines formed the feelers, and staccato shading with the side of my own Eberhardt-Faber drawing pencil gave to the wings an illusion of flight. I finished in a few minutes, and to kill time until she gave us something else to do, I started flying my wasp, buzzing it and swooping it over my head and dive-bombing the kid in the next seat.

Mrs. Fields jerked my wasp away from me, glanced at it, and crumpled it in her hands and slammed another sheet of paper onto my desk. "Now start over," she demanded, "And this time do it right."

I couldn't do it the way she wanted. My hands were shaking and I was trying to hold back the tears. Suddenly I bolted. It was as if some powerful force were pushing me out of there. I dashed out the door, across the playground, under the bushes by the fence, over the fence to the football field, under the bleachers, out to the street. Surely someone was after me. They wouldn't just let me go. I ran like crazy, darting between houses, jumping hedges, cutting through backyards, imagining I was a soldier on a secret mission far behind enemy lines. There was the church! The perfect place to hide. Those strange basement windows that opened into a bricked-in recess below ground level. We always thought of them as dungeon windows. I dropped down to where the windows were and found one that was open enough to push it up and crawl into the basement room that was used as a childcare center during Sunday services.

Hiding in the church I imagined I was hiding from a German patrol in an underground labyrinth, my freedom dependent upon my skill and daring. I'd never done anything so brave. Even Josh Culpepper wouldn't break out of school and hide in the dungeon at Calvary Baptist Church.

I explored the church, all the secret places behind the pulpit, the choir room and the stairway that led up—to heaven, I imagined. Up there was where Brother Barnes baptized sinners. It was like a little swimming pool on a balcony perched majestically over the alter, glass fronted to waist height like saloon doors and draped with heavy velvet curtains.

I couldn't resist. I stripped buck-naked and went for a swim all alone in that heavenly pool. I was happily splashing in the pool when Brother Barnes stormed up the stairs and screamed at me that I would go straight to hell because I had profaned the house of God.

* * *

All of my life I've been running away. I ran away from Man when he needed me. I ran away when Johnny Lewis tried to love me, because that was not the kind of love I wanted and I couldn't tell him that. I ran from Tupelo over and over, but no matter where I went, Tupelo was there, watching me, judging me. Mabel Cook and Brother Barnes and that goddamn pesky cop named Norman, who looked like Lou Costello, the people who said I'd never amount to anything and the people who expected me to amount to something, and the people I never wanted to let down.

I got out of Mississippi as soon as I could. Went to Memphis, to the Art Academy. As far as running away goes, that ain't much. That's a chicken-shit escape, like packing your bags and moving next door. Still and all, it was different. Memphis is a city, and the kids at the academy were sophisticated kids who had been around. At first I had a hard time fitting in, but I soon found the way.

What I did was this here: I developed my Redneck Dean Moriarty persona. I started speed rapping, mixing in a large dose of Negro preacher talk and hillbilly slang, slurring and drawling and getting that rolling rhythm going like the preacher man calling them sinners to repentance, and I stirred that stew together with doubledeclutch jive talk straight out of Kerouac's *On The Road*. Shee-it! I was on stage all the time.

At the Art Academy we had heroes who were not athletes. Can you dig it? In Tupelo that would have been unheard of, but at the Art Academy we shared those heroes: Matisse and Picasso, Allen Ginsberg, Walt Whitman, John Coltrane and Dizzy Gillespie, Willem de Kooning—de Kooning was de King!

My God, what de Kooning did to my brain! At first I couldn't get it. There was something in his painting that grabbed me and, at the same time, put me off. I kept coming back to his works, to let them enfold me in their awful grasp. And their grasp was like a torrid romance. The raw power! The daring! The rage and humor and even the lyricism! Those vicious, raw, vibrant paintings of women distorted almost beyond recognition, with grimacing mouths and bulbous, detached breasts, claw-like toes and fingers lost in a cacophony of great slashes of heavy paint and jagged shapes like shards of broken glass!

And Pollock! Oh Lord, to see a Jackson Pollock and let yourself fall into the vortex of his spaceless space until you taste the very viscosity of his marvelous skeins of paint! If only sex were half as good!

UNTIL THE DAWN

* * *

There was a time after I got my degree, a dead, lost summer spent back in Tupelo, trying to figure out what to do next. Heat like a wetted funeral shroud drained the lifeblood from the people until they shuffled around town in slow motion, looking like a dream sequence in a Fellini movie. I decided to go down to Danny's Diner. Driving up Gloster toward Jackson in my VW bus, I could see cars in Danny's parking lot. Under the wavering blue lights they looked like beached whales. You could see the heat in the air. Groups of teenagers were lolling in the lot like wavering ferns in a fish tank, like those strange and monstrous goldfish that still swam lazily in that out-of-place pool in the lobby of Poppa Chuck's bank.

Inside the diner the only customers were Sam Littlejohn and Wanda Ramsey. Ol' crazy Sam and sad and sexy little Wanda. The diner was brightly lit, with mirrors on the walls and lots of chrome. Behind the counter, looking like forgotten photos from somebody's scrap book, were: a purple and gold Tupelo Golden Wave pennant, an autographed photograph of Elvis Presley, a copy of a newspaper photo of John F. Kennedy's assassination (the one with Jackie leaning out of the car), the cover of an Ole Miss football program with an action shot of Charlie Speed throwing a pass (also autographed), and a Barry Goldwater campaign poster with the printed legend: In your heart you know he's right.

Fluorescent light reflecting off white, plastic tablecloths cast Sam and Wanda in cool, blue tones. He wore a dingy white shirt with a frayed collar. Gaps between buttons stood open like stretched tent canvas. His right leg jerked like a jackhammer, an unconscious, violent, nervous tick. Wanda had bleached her hair. It looked thin and dry. She wore a short skirt that pulled like elastic across her midriff and a man's yellow shirt, with the shirttails tied in a bow under her breasts.

She had put on a little weight, but not enough to detract from that tantalizingly body that had driven us all nuts back in high school. As a matter of fact, sitting down with her belly exposed, I could see a little roll of fat creasing her belly right across her navel, and the word that popped into my mind was ripeness. Ripe for the plucking, juicy and full. I felt this crazy urge to slither my tongue along that crease. I pushed that thought out of mind and said hello to them and grabbed a bar stool, attempting to be polite, but distant.

I wanted them to see me as someone who had outgrown them, no longer the fun-loving kid from high school, but an artist, an intellectual, someone with more important things on his mind. I ordered a Coke and sipped on it while staring at the wall as if in deep thought. Stupid, I know, but I did things like that.

Wanda wasn't buying my act. She started flirting with me, and we talked about old times, and we joked around. She kept moving, swiveling on her stool, crossing and uncrossing her legs, bending near to me to deliver punch lines in a stage whisper. With all of that moving around, she allowed me to see a lot of cleavage and a lot of thigh, and even glimpses of yellow panties. Must be Saturday, I thought. Yellow for Saturday. Boy that goes back.

Wanda was trying to get me hot, and it was working. She was flashing thigh and exposing that yellow flag very purposefully. The only thing was, I couldn't tell if she meant it or not, if she was trying to see if she could still get me aroused out of some kind of vanity, just to see if she could still do it. I couldn't tell if she wanted me or just wanted me to want her, or if her whole, crazy sexy game was nothing more than a reflex action, going through the motions of what we had always done. All through high school we had flirted outrageously, but I never thought she ever meant more and I was too loyal to Charlie to pursue more.

But now Charlie was dead and gone, senselessly killed in a stupid war that I so far had managed to avoid.

Wanda and I kept on flirting there in Danny's, and after awhile we went out to my VW bus and messed around a bit—nothing serious, a little playful petting. I didn't know it at the time, but to Mabel Cook, who was watching from her porch across the street, it looked like we were fighting.

Playful petting escalated into something pretty heavy. The night air was wet and hot, and so were we. Take a wet towel and slap it over your head and sit in a sauna for an hour. That's what it's like in the summertime down South, and it doesn't let up when the sun goes down. Before the invention of air conditioning it's a wonder anybody ever had sex down there, yet there we were getting all rabid and raunchy in a VW bus. Bodies sticky and glistening slick as molasses. Panting and sweating, we had to come up for air. I stuck my head out a window and glanced around, and I was struck again with the thought that the cars cruising the lot and the teenagers sitting on and leaning against them were like fish floundering in stagnant waters. The floundering fish were all kids younger than us. Most of them were acting out the same kind of mating rituals Wanda and I were engaged in. Suddenly what we were doing seemed meaningless. I was playing a ritualized mating game with a girl from high school days and I wasn't even particularly attracted to her. Well, yeah I was. I was far from immune to her obvious sexual attraction, but there was no personal connection. She was nothing to me but a memory and an object of my lust. What were we doing? Trying to bring back something that had never been there in the first place? Like a fish, I was hooked, and I wanted to get away.

Wanda didn't notice. She kept teasing and flirting, and I kept vacillating between wanting her and wanting to get the hell away.

"Let's get out for a while," I said. "I'm melting in here."

It was barely any cooler standing in the parking lot, but at least I could breathe. She asked me if I remembered how she and Charlie and Bitsy and I, and some of the other kids, used to chase each other from Danny's to Page's Market, about ten blocks north on Gloster. Sure, I remembered. The payoff had been that if the guy caught the girl before she got to Page's, he got to make out with her. How far it really went, of course, depended on the individual couple. I know I had done a lot of chasing, but I never got any payoff.

"Come on, Travis," she challenged. "Let's see if you can still run. Just for fun. For old time's sake. Catch me or not, we'll go to my apartment."

Before I could answer she started running toward Crosstown. She got half a block away and turned to shout, "Two blocks head start. Remember?"

Yeah, I remembered. That had been Charlie Speed's standard challenge. He swore he could give anybody a two-block head start from Danny's and catch them before they reached Page's Market. He could do it, too. But God damn it all, Charlie was dead. Suddenly I realized what Wanda was doing. She was trying to bring him back through me. I had been his best friend and she had loved him. This wasn't right.

I thought about chasing her all right, to catch her and shake some sense into her and hold onto her and let her cry it out if that's what she needed. But I got distracted. The unexpected appearance of Man (or Raymond Carver as he now called himself) hoofing past Danny's all by himself put Wanda out of my mind. The lily-white neighborhood of Danny's Diner was not a safe place for a black man to be.

Man stopped to talk to me for a few minutes. I said, "Man, you'd better high-tail it away from here before some rednecks decide to use your head for a basketball."

"Don't I know it!" he said.

Only a few weeks before that a black man had been beaten by a gang of whites a few blocks from where we were.

We talked for only a minute, two at the most, then he took off toward Shakerag, in a hurry to get away from whitey's territory. I should have offered him a ride, but I just didn't think about it. And I shouldn't have let Wanda run off thinking I was going to chase after her. At the very least I should have gotten into my bus and gone looking for her and given her a ride home. There are so many ifs.

* * *

Wanda's picture was on the front page of the *Daily Journal* the next morning. It was a murky picture. She was lying on the ground. Dead. How could she be dead? This had to be some kind of horrible dream. The article said that she had been killed in an attempted rape. It had happened shortly after I had last seen her at Danny's. Police found her body while cruising the Crosstown area following a reported disturbance at Danny's Diner. A disturbance at Danny's? Couldn't be; I was there. The paper said a black man by the name of Raymond Carver was being held as a prime suspect.

Why had they arrested Man? Because his skin was dark. Because there was an invisible line that meandered through Tupelo, circumscribing areas as black and white. Man was picked up inside a white area minutes after Wanda was killed. If it had been twenty years earlier they could have simply taken him out behind a barn somewhere and hung him from an oak limb and been shut of it. But in the 1960s the authorities were expected to at least go through the motions of an investigation and a trial.

Josh Culpepper handled the investigation and the prosecution. He questioned me the day after, and again on many occasions leading up to the trial.

I had never liked Josh Culpepper. Never. He was slimy, conceited, a bully and a cheat and an avowed racist. I never thought he was very smart, either, but I discovered during the course of the investigation that he was damned good at his job, despicable though that job was.

The first time he questioned me he was very polite and apologetic. Every time he asked me about a particular detail he said things like, "I know this probably doesn't seem important, but you never know." Or, "I know it probably seems like I'm grilling you, but I just don't want to take any chances on missing something."

He wanted to know everything about what I had seen, heard or done that night. "Who was with you when you were inside talking to Wanda?"

"Sam Littlejohn."

"Anybody else?"

"Nope. Just Danny. He served me a Coke and then went back into the kitchen."

"Did he leave the diner?"

"Who? Danny? No. I never saw him again after he went back to the kitchen."

"What about Sam? Did he follow you when you left?"

"No, I don't think so. Look, Wanda and I were . . . you know, kind of messing around. I wasn't paying any attention to anyone else."

He said, "What I'm going to ask you now may seem like something that's none of my business, but please bare with me. So you and Wanda were kind of flirting. Messing around, as you put it. Well I know Wanda. I know that she's—she was—a big time prick tease. I know this doesn't seem nice, but I've got to ask it. The way I figure it, she was probably giving you a few well-planned squirrel shots. I've seen her do it with other guys right there in Danny's. That's the way she operates. She likes to sit on one of those spinning stools and spread her legs and look at the lust on a guy's face. Gives her a feeling of power, like she can reduce us all to slobbering maniacs. Thing is, she was naked under that little skirt. Right? And she let you see it all. Am I right or not?"

I knew that Josh Culpepper couldn't keep up the nice act for long. I knew that the slime had to come out, and there it was. It did me good to say, "You're wrong, Josh. She wasn't naked under her skirt. She was wearing panties."

"You saw 'em, huh?"

"Yes, I saw them. What of it?" He even asked what color they were. He was starting to really bug me. What I didn't realize was how neatly he had tricked me. He wanted to pin a rape charge on Man, but he had no proof that Wanda had been raped. The bit about the panties at least made rape plausible. If it could be proved that she was wearing panties before she was killed, and she wasn't wearing them when her body was found, then it would be logical to assume the person who killed her would have been the one who removed her underwear. And now he had proof courtesy of my own damned stupid mouth that she was wearing panties of a particular color right before she was killed. It would be laughably simple for Josh Culpepper to plant a pair of yellow panties, preferably torn, in a bush somewhere between the crime scene and where Man was picked up. Or simply claim they found them in Man's possession. Nobody could prove otherwise, and I sure as hell wouldn't put it past Josh to pull a stunt like that.

I was surprised that when he asked about Man he didn't push harder than he did. He seemed to take my word that Man had walked away in the direction of Shakerag, which would have taken him away from the crime scene.

The next time Josh questioned me he took an entirely different tact, one that really shocked me. He told the truth about what he knew and asked me to lie. He offered reasons that were sincere, and he almost had me convinced. For the first time I knew exactly what had happened and what I could expect to happen at the trial, depending on my testimony. At least I knew part of what could happen. Josh still had a few tricks in reserve.

What he explained to me was that when Wanda and I went outside, Sam followed us. Naturally, I didn't notice. Sam was sometimes so taken for granted that he was invisible. For nearly two decades he had been the member of the gang who was never really there, the athlete who never got off the bench. He simply wanted to belong. And he also probably longed for love and sex as much as any other man, even though we had always assumed he was somehow sexless. Wanda and I were playing sex games, and Sam wanted to play too.

When she ran away, it was Sam, not Man, who chased after her. When he caught up with her, she turned to greet him, thinking he was me. He grabbed her clumsily and she fell to the sidewalk. Her head cracked against the curb. Death was instantaneous. Sam, confused and afraid, and maybe somehow thinking in that muddled mind of his that they were still playing, saw that her dress was bunched around her waist and that her panties were showing. He pulled them off. He told Josh all about it. He said, "I didn't mean to hurt her. I didn't know she was dead. I thought she was playing. I never saw a girl's underpants before and I never saw what was under them neither. I just wanted to touch. Then I got scared and ran away."

Josh said, "No one knows this, Travis. You and me and Sam. That's it. Now I know that the nigger we arrested didn't do it, but Jesus Travis, he's just a nigger. The damage is already done. I can't let it get out that I arrested the wrong man. 'Specially not a nigger. Them Civil Rights folks will have it all over Mississippi that I arrested him out of racist motives.

"To tell you the God-awful truth, I've already fucked this thing up so much that even if we convict him he'll beat it on an appeal. But that's okay. You see? That's really perfect. If we convict him I'll get the credit and Sam will not have to worry about the truth coming out, and then the nigger will get out anyway. We won't have to worry about an innocent man going to jail, and my reputation won't be hurt 'cause most people will think he was really guilty and got set free by his liberal lawyers on a technicality. So you see, you've gotta help me. It's the only way we can save Sam. All you got to do is say that what's his name, Raymond Carver, took off after Wanda when he left you."

It would have been tragic if Sam were charged with Wanda's death. Surely they wouldn't charge him with anything as severe as murder, but I imagined that he could be charged with something like involuntary manslaughter. At the very least he would probably wind up being committed to the state insane asylum and probably never would get out. But I didn't think that would happen anyway. Even if he couldn't convict Man, Josh would never divulge Sam's secret. There was no way I was going to tell a falsehood in court for Josh Culpepper.

"You've got to," Josh said. "Don't you see, it's much bigger than just a matter of your honor, telling the truth at all costs. We've got to save Sam. If he's convicted they'll put him away for life. So what if he can call lawyer and claim insanity? So maybe they put him in Whitfield for life instead of in the state pen? Do you know what they do to people in that fuckin' hospital? Shit man, it's worse than prison. Much worse. You gotta save Sam from that, Travis. You just gotta."

I didn't know what to do. I needed time to get my thoughts together, but Josh wouldn't give me time to think. I should have talked to Papa Chuck and Mama Marybelle. God knows I had always gone to them before in a crisis and I knew I could always count on them to help me figure out what to do, but for some reason I had this stubborn determination to handle this one on my own. Stupid, just stupid. That's what it was.

When everything else failed, Josh threatened to tell the whole goddamn town that I was queer. "You think I don't know. I saw you and Johnny going at it in Mrs. Speed's bed that night Charlie had the big party after Elvis was at the fair. You saw me looking in the door. You just didn't know it was me. Man, if I tell people around here about that you'll never be able to show your face in this town again. Is that what you want? Is saving that nigger's hide worth all that?"

He said, "I don't even have to prove it, you know. All I've got to do is plant the seed. Matter of fact, even if I didn't know you were a damn fag, even if I hadn't seen you and Johnny Lewis getting it on that time, even if you were straight as an arrow, I could start rumors and get certain people to say they know it for a fact. Once that happened, you'd be dead around here. Yo' mama would be so ashamed she couldn't even show her face in public. You think about that."

I tried to bluff him, saying that the people who really mattered to me would never believe it and I didn't give a shit about the people who would believe it, but he had frightened me deeply. I knew that there was no way I could be sure about what I would say when they put me on the witness stand until that moment arrived.

Josh couldn't have known how effective his threat was, but he came up with one more trick, just in case.

I fell apart after that. I was depressed, I was scared, I was confused. I started smoking heavily and drinking, and I couldn't sleep. For days and days, I don't know how many days. I was afraid to leave the house during the day and couldn't stand to stay in my room after everyone went to sleep. I would sneak out late at night, and wander the streets of Tupelo. I drove up to Memphis a few times and hung out in bars on Beale Street, where lonely insomniacs nursed their sorrows in isolation long after the bands had gone home for the night. Wherever I went, I felt like someone was following me.

One night in Memphis I let a guy pick me up, a skinny young black man who wore mascara and lipstick. He said his name was Jasmine. I thought he was disgusting, and at the same time there was a strong attraction. If it was lurid or illicit, I was drawn to it. And nothing could be more lurid to the fine folk of Tupelo than a black drag queen. Maybe I figured that if I was going to be destroyed for my depravity, I might as well be really depraved. Or maybe I just wanted him. When it was over and I got back into my VW, I decided to drive off the bridge into the Mississippi River. But I couldn't do it. I chickened out.

The next day Josh Culpepper came to see me again. He said, "I need you to come with me. There's someone you have to see."

He drove me down to Shakerag and parked next to a restaurant called Lulu's, and he walked me to a door and knocked. The man who answer Josh's knock was Jasmine, the queen from the night before. Jasmine was all prettied up with green eye shadow and red lipstick. There was a purple glow to his high, ebony cheeks, and a crazed look in his eyes, eyes that darted like bugs on the surface of a pool. He wore a yellow, silk blouse with an open front that showed off his oily, hairless chest. It was like the blouse Wanda had worn that night.

Jasmine flung open his door at our knock and screeched, "Travis! Honey Buns! It's so good to see you!"

I spun around and rushed out to the street, with Josh hot behind me. He grabbed me by the shirt collar. I started cursing him. I was shaking all over. My voice was trembling and shooting up to a screechy high register. "God damn you, Josh! You sneaky son of a bitch. How could you?"

We were standing in front of Lulu's. Somewhere off in the distance I heard the military rumble of a marching band. In front of me was Josh Culpepper. He was gripping my shirt collar and talking to me with his face inches from my face, but I couldn't hear a word he was saying. It was as if another person who was not me took possession of my mind. Josh's mouth was flapping and his teeth were gnashing and slobber sprayed from his lips, but all I could hear was marching music. A parade was heading our way. Black folks were positioning themselves along the edge of the street and there we were, two crazy white men in the middle of Shakerag, screaming at each other.

The drumbeat grew louder. All of a sudden the whole thing seemed ridiculous to me. All of a sudden the only thing I cared about was the Carver High Marching Band, one hundred high-stepping Negroes. Here they come!

The drum major reared back so far that the tassels on top of his high hat brushed the pavement behind him. He blew two short blasts of his whistle and thrust his baton high in the air, and the band broke into "Tiger Rag." Hold that tiger! Hoooold that tiger!

The band strutted by, with the drum major high-stepping and the saucy little majorettes switching their short skirts like happy puppydog tails, row after row of horns, then snare drums and bass drums, and finally the big tubas. Deliriously dancing kids trailed in their wake. I wrenched out of Josh's grasp and ran out into the street and started jiving and strutting behind the band, a white caboose to a black train, twitching my butt to the pounding rhythm and waving my hands. I left Josh Culpepper standing in front of Lulu's, wondering what the hell had come over me. At that point he probably figured I was too crazy to be put on a witness stand.

When I danced behind the Carver High School Marching Band I felt really free for the first time in my life. It was also the first time I heard that tiny warning voice in my head say, You're going crazy, Travis Earl Warner, and I said to myself, Fine! That's just fine and dandy. See if I care.

* * *

The same dumb little voice spoke the same impotent warning many other times: when I started hallucinating during the trial, during that frantic flight to New York, the first time I dropped acid . . . many times. And every time I said Fine! That's just fine and dandy.

Impending insanity is a great orgasmic release when you let yourself flow with it. That ought to be a quote from some famous psychiatrist.

What I would like to say about Man's trial is that it was an excruciating ordeal. That's what I'd like to say, 'cause it sounds so good, but it wasn't like that at all. It was more like a dull toothache that refuses to go away. I endured it with a wandering mind and with flashes of that craziness that, as I said, was already beginning to seep in; then I ran away—and Tupelo followed me.

Oh, it was a freaking circus, all right. There should have been barkers in red and black plaid sports coats standing between the columns at the court house, ugly barkers with greasy hair and yellow, gapped teeth, with "Mother" tattooed under a heart on their left shoulders and hula dancers on their right shoulders (although only Superman with his X-ray vision could have seen them under the coats).

Yessiree, they should have been there, and there should have been hot dog vendors and cotton candy stands, and out on Highway 78 there should have been signs painted on barn roofs, like the See Rock City signs, only they should have said: See the Nigger Squirm! Rape and Murder—Hear All the Gory Details!

That's what the people came for.

They came from all around: from Pontotoc and Oxford and Water Valley, from Guntown and Aberdeen, from as far south as Starkville, farmers in pickup trucks with grain sacks tied to their bumpers, good old boys with kitschy do-dahs like plastic Jesuses and foam rubber dice and baby shoes dangling from rear-view mirrors; ladies with starched, white dresses that crinkled like paper when they sat down, pale ladies with paper fans in hand, daintily decorated fans adorned with farm scenes and pictures of Jesus walking on water and advertisements for Moore's Funeral Home and Brother Bobo's Hardware, fans that (thank the good Lord) would not be needed because the city had finally installed air conditioning in the court house (but, of course, Mabel Cook and a couple of other women would use theirs for appearance sake); teenage boys in outmoded outfits, jeans with rolled cuffs and T-shirts with rolled sleeves, crumpled Marlboro packs enveloped in that twist of sleeve at the shoulder; businessmen in cotton and polyester and seersucker suits, coatless, or with coats slung over their shoulders, ties loosened and collars open, sweat circled armpits; round, Negro women with umbrellas to protect them from the sun.

They came and they clustered and shuffled for seats, a legion of characters and types mixed like Campbell's soup, with the blacks segregated into a shadowy, ashen-gray section in the back.

Into this human menagerie came I. Yes, I went in just like everybody else, but unlike everybody else—except, I guess, Man (and maybe Samuel Allison Littlejohn)—I didn't want to be there. I walked through the smoky outer court and jostled bodies to make my way to the heavy double doors, and I sidled down the aisle muttering, "Excuse me" and "Pardon," and I took my seat on discomfort itself.

And I waited. Waited while feet shuffled and throats rasped themselves clear. Waited while sounds sounded and movements moved morbidly in a breathless burlesque of any awaiting crowd at any old dance or revival or funeral or any other such major event. Waited while feet stomped and scuffed and squeaked, while knuckles cracked and papers shuffled and slid, dresses crinkled, doors slammed, hinges squawked. Waited while whining, laughing, whispering, mumbling voices murmured an antiphon that could not even be called noise, but just a lot of audible stuff.

Every person, every sound, every smell was as deadeningly familiar as the infernal hangnail I'd been gnawing on all day. I knew 'em all, had known 'em all my born days. I knew the kids and I knew their daddies, and their daddies knew my daddy and his daddy and on and on for generations—only, of course, they didn't know my real daddy, but only Papa Chuck. Well, yes, most of 'em knew about my real daddy too. It's that small-town knowing, everybody knowing everything about everybody. Even if there happened to be somebody there I didn't know, they were all types that I knew only too damned well, and we were all in that soup together, boiling in an endless repetition of our present gyrations and pronouncements.

So I waited. My mind darted in desperate search for escape. I waited for the dreaded moment when I would be called to testify. I waited while jurors were sworn in, while officers Norman and McDonald (I finally remembered his name, the one who looked like Bud Abbott) told about finding Wanda's violated body, while they described in detail how her skirt was rumpled and her genitals exposed—oh how deliciously they lingered over every detail—how I, me, that guy over there, Travis Earl Warner, had snuck a peek at her little, yellow, bikini panty briefs only hours before her body was found, and how those now famous little, yellow, bikini panty briefs were no longer on her body because they had been viciously ripped off by the perverted perpetrator of this horrendous crime. I waited while they told of finding the Negro, Raymond Carver, who goes by the name Man near the scene of the crime. I waited while Mabel Cook told what she had seen; waited while the trial droned on and on, while court recessed and reconvened, while the crowd thinned out and then built up again when time for the defense case drew near; waited while fingers combed unruly strands of hair and tugged at itchy collars, while fingers drummed on table tops and chair backs, while impatient, stubby fingers clawed sweaty bellies, while slim, elegant fingers tipped with ruby red nails flattened folds in dresses and tugged at bra straps and wrestled with bunched-up pantyhose elastic. And I thought of fingers on my leg, heavy, hairy fingers forcing their way up to cup the cheeks of my buttocks, while the machine-like rush of slavish breath assaulted my ears. I remembered being excited and hating myself for being excited and the voice screaming in my brain, "He's a man, you fool! A man!" And I remembered Wanda on the stool at Danny's with her legs crossed and my fingers itching to insinuate themselves where hot-flesh thighs met, and that same voice sneered, "You're heartless and cruel, Travis Earl Warner, and not worth killing."

That was when I started to drift. Memory and imagination merged, and I still don't know if what happened next was hallucination or vision or dream. I was staring at Sam Littlejohn. Flaccid as a water-filled balloon, his head was swaying like a buoy anchored in rolling waves. I saw his body swell up and float over the courtroom, with drops of his unsightly fat, like globules of paint, dripping on people in the room. He dripped on Mr. Preston's waxed head, and old man Preston, retired from his job as principal at Tupelo High, wiped that glob of lard off his head and said, "You go straight back to your class, young man," and I heard him say, "You spell principal with an A because your principal is your pal," but he was no pal of mine.

Deflating, Sam descended into the wrinkles of Mabel Cook's lap, and I saw all of us back in high school: Charlie and Hoss and I grabbed her and carried her into the boy's shower in the gymnasium and we ripped off her dress while she squirmed and screamed with a wail like the screech of brakes on a subway train, and there—under her dress—was nothing, no breasts, no nipples, no vagina, no hair, no navel, just orificeless skin like latex stretched head to toe and seamlessly sealed. Then I saw her not in this fantastic transmogrification, but in her disgustingly dull normal state, sitting in a beauty parlor with her hair in curlers and her pudgy fingers dipped in a bowl of green liquid, and she's saying, "Dish washing liquid!" and the lady from the TV is saying "You're soaking in it," and a chorus of rosy-cheeked fat boys is shouting, "Gossip! We want gossip!" And Mabel says, "I'll tell you the story of a boy who never had a chance. His father was a drunk and a womanizer and his mother was a loose woman and a nigger lover to boot, and his mother's mother was a maid and her husband was a bum, and even though the boy was taken into the king's castle and raised as a prince, he never had a chance, 'cause blood will out."

Then the cops were there, an army of cops aiming their guns at me, Norman and McDonald heading the phalanx, only they had turned into Bud Abbott and Lou Costello, and the fat one was pointing at me where I scrunched in the corner like a spider trapped in the back of Page's Market. Fat like lava flow oozed from his body, rolled on the floor like balls of mercury from a broken thermometer, mated with Sam Littlejohn's fat globules already dancing on the floor, and began to creep toward my ankles. Like a search party marching through a mucky swamp, the cops and the judge and Man and Mabel Cook closed in on me, pointing fingers and chanting, "He ain't none of Chuck Warner's nohow."

* * *

"Will Travis Earl Warner please approach the witness stand? Travis Earl Warner. Young man, will you please step forward?"

I shook myself out of my dream. I took the stand. I answered questions as best I could. Legions of faces faced me expectantly. Mama Janet was there, and Mama Marybelle, Papa Chuck and J.P. Brother Barnes was there, and Ray Prichard, and just about every teacher I'd ever had, even Mrs. Fields, whose art class I never went back to. Against the back wall slouched that skinny black man with the bright, yellow shirt, Jasmine.

Josh asked, "Is it true that you and the deceased had a fight, or an argument, in the parking lot at Danny's?"

"No, we didn't fight. We were playing."

I could not focus my attention on his questions. Sam Littlejohn, sitting in front of me with his bloated body slumped like something melting, mesmerized me.

For a moment there was no one else in the courtroom, just Sam. Josh asked more and more questions. I guess I answered them somehow. I can't recall.

Finally he asked the question everyone was waiting for: "After you finished talking to Raymond Carver and he walked away, which direction did he take?"

I said, "He took off that way. You know . . ." motioning vaguely with my hand.

"Could you please be more specific? Which way is that way?"

"Toward Crosstown."

Hell-fire, Crosstown ain't even a place. It ain't like Shakerag or the Alley or even Highland Circle. Those places have personality. They deserve a name. Crosstown ain't nothing but an intersection with a stupid arrow atop a pole that says Tupelo, First T.V.A. City.

I don't know why I said Crosstown. Yes I do. I said it to save my lily-white, All-American-boy reputation.

There was nothing left but the summations. Man's lawyer gave it his best, but it was useless. All he had on his side were the facts. Josh gave an impassioned speech loaded with black and white imagery: the black of night, Man's black skin hidden in shadow from the white glare of the street light, Wanda's pure, white skin on black pavement (even though it was actually light gray concrete). It's a wonder the rednecks in the courthouse didn't rush Man and lynch him on the spot.

He was sentenced to thirty years in the state pen.

*　*　*

I got the hell out of Tupelo. I drove day and night, stopping only for pee breaks and lunches on the run, all the way from Tupelo, Mississippi, to New York, New York. I carried with me a dream of freedom and fame and fortune, and voices from the past chased after me, nipping at my heels like pesky puppy dogs. To get away from them, I had to drive faster, work faster, live faster. I had to be somebody new: Red Warner, the manic genius, the wild and woolly beatnik from the South. I vowed to grab the Baghdad on the Hudson by the balls and make it take notice.

Bah! For the first year or so I existed in dull anonymity, a comatose fisherman adrift in a concrete sea, casting a wide net and hauling in nothing but the shattered shells of dreams. My home was a four-by-eight cubicle on the third floor of the Bleecker Hotel. The Bleecker was a prison where you paid for your cell. Mercifully, it has since been put out of its misery. There was no lobby, but only a tiny foyer with an elevator on the right and a locked door on the left coated with peeling forest green paint (who knows what goes on behind the green door?) and a counter, behind which the man took your money and handed you your mail (what mail?). The elevator was a cage. It went to the third floor, no higher; the upper floors were condemned. The cage opened to a bare hall. At the end of the hall was a bathroom with dirty urinals and a metal shower stall and once white, now stained and graffitoed walls. The whole floor shared this bathroom.

In my room there was a cast iron bed and a nightstand. No chair. No dresser. A pole for hanging clothes. The transom over the door was open and paint-stuck forever in that position. The window was barred, with missing glass. The view out that window was a courtyard. Once, perhaps, it had been landscaped. Perhaps there had been tables or benches.

Now it was a garbage heap. The tenants all slung their trash out their windows.

In the winter I stuffed a Salvation Army field jacket into the broken window to keep snow from blowing in. I slept in my clothes under a scratchy, green Army blanket. I ate on the soup line on 13th Street. Occasionally I picked up jobs from the day labor pool in a basement shop on MacDougal.

Sometimes I didn't make it back to my room at night, but would ride the subways until dawn. The trains were warm, and I liked their drumbeat sound. I was alone and scared, and I detested myself. Sometimes I'd head down to Christopher Street and hang out in the bars.

Days and days and dazed days I walked the streets of Manhattan with Tupelo still in my mind, down around Wall Street, up through China Town and SoHo, the East Village, across to the Bowery and up to Washington Square, peeping in shop windows, yakking with the drunks and junkies and whores on the streets, sleeping in the grass at Washington Square Park. Once I saw some wacko walking around talking to himself, one of the hundreds that you hardly ever notice, and I started hollering at him and he started hollering at me and our voices bounced back and forth over the heads of the old Ukrainian gentlemen who played their endless games in the park at Houston and First Avenue. A whacked out, off-key jazz improvisation of strident shouts. The whacko shouted at his gods and demons and I shouted at mine, talking back to Josh Culpepper's oily elocution and Hoss Williams' taunting "Noth Yew! Noth Yew!" and the mumbling voices of all those good old boys and mild mannered matrons who had crowded the court room and salivated for just-ice to quench their thirst, and the holier-than-thou boom of Brother Barnes warning 'bout hellfire and damnation.

Oh, mister preacher man and all ya'll self-righteous mothers, don't you know that our God is a loving god? Don't you know He loves them po' niggahs and dirty white trash and perverts and sickos mo' than anybody! Vengeance is mine, saith the Lord. Oh Lord, I wish you'd strike 'em all dead!

The Southern Baptists didn't believe in purgatory, but somewhere along the line I picked up on the concept, and it made sense to me. I sought my own purgatory. I wanted to bottom out, to indulge in my most depraved fantasies. I dressed myself in metaphorical hair suits and flagellated myself mercilessly, believing that miraculously, through all that, I could cleanse my soul and come face to face with God and transcend this grimy world.

And I thought about Cassie. What would she think if she saw me? Would she even recognize me, or had I transformed myself like a werewolf prowling the night and slinking into hiding in the glare of day. She was in New York. She didn't know where I was, but I knew where she was. She worked at a restaurant near Washington Square and sometimes danced in off-off Broadway shows. Her apartment was a small studio above Ye Waverly Inn at 16 Bank Street. I saw the nameplate over the buzzer: C. Warner, printed in that delicate hand of hers. I stood at the door many a time, staring at her name, imagining her upstairs, practicing her dance steps on the hardwood floor. But I couldn't bring myself to push the buzzer.

And the famous artist who had come from the South to take New York by storm could not paint. How could I? I had no money for paint or canvas, and even if I had, there was no space for painting in my little cubicle. I bought Crayola crayons and did thousands of little studies for paintings that I told myself I'd some day do in oil. I worked at them obsessively, with little joy.

Eventually I pulled myself together, got a job, found a bigger place to live, and started painting for real.

I wanted to paint New York as only I could see it, to capture the color of oxidized metal and the suffocating mass of aged brick and stone buildings with scarred and layered, graffitoed walls, to recreate the indefinable hue of the lights under the West Side Highway and the purple shadows they cast, to build skeins of paint like the layered grit of shopping bag ladies with their many coats, to find an abstract form that spoke of the faded, Army green aura of alcoholics sleeping on the sidewalks, ashen faces and dull, boozy-pink rims around whitened eyes.

I wanted to distill it to its essence, to symbolize it with a few simple shapes. I tried, I tried. If the devil had come along and offered to buy my soul for the price of making me the artist I wanted to be, I would have signed on the line in a New Yawk second, but there weren't no devil except for the devil in my head, so I did the next best thing, I begged for money from home.

Papa Chuck came through like a champ. For six months I lived off his generosity. I found a cheap loft. Yes, that was still possible then. I quit my job. I painted in a desperate fury, knowing that Papa Chuck's support would not last forever.

Oh, painting can be an evil mistress. The thrill of it can be like good sex. When you finish a painting and you know you've done it right, and you stand back and look at it, you shout, "Yass, by jingo! Yass! I done done it right." But it can also be like pulling teeth or yanking hair out by the roots or rolling in the gutter in a drunken stupor or beating yourself over the head with a hickory stick, because you've got to reach deep inside and wrench it out of your guts. And the loneliness! Oh Sweet Jesus Christ! You are all alone in a drafty old loft and you sling paint with a concentration tuned so fine it hurts, and then you set your paint bucket down and you look around, and there is not a living soul to share that moment with, be that moment ecstasy or be it loathing. The battle is just between you and that goddamn stoic canvas. And suddenly you get this flash of memory from art school where the professors ripped everything to shreds with their caustic criticism, and you begin to wonder if you could even recognize a real painting if it kicked you in the chops. That's when you want to crawl into your mama's lap and cry until the fear goes away. But you're a big boy now and you don't really need your mama; you need a sweet woman's caress. When I became so full of hurt and loss that I couldn't stand it anymore, I sought solace in the only place I could get it with ease, in the bars on Christopher Street.

When I finally got in touch with Cassie, she was a lifesaver for me. I finally worked up the courage to ring her bell, and she invited me in as if she had been waiting for me. In a way she had. She said, "I was wondering if you were going to ever come by."

"I know. I guess I was ashamed of what I have become. I'm not too proud of myself these days."

But she loved me and never judged me. She kept me from going completely out of my mind.

I finally hit on what I was after in my painting with my Hungry Frederick series. Hungry Frederick was a tall, stooped, taciturn Negro who showed up on the soup line on 13th Street every day. I created a single, abstract shape to symbolize Hungry Frederick, a sloppy, angular wedge in dull, raw colors, with previous layers of paint showing through as on peeled billboards. Hungry Frederick was beaten by life, but huge and defiant and angry as hell. That was what I tried to convey in my paintings. The paintings were abstract and minimalist in form, but not so clean and bright as minimalist paintings should be; they were harsh, sloppy, scratched, battered, layered. They were the abstract equivalent of beaten people whose spirit refused to die, the people that I, at least, always envisioned when I thought of Faulkner's famous quote about the indomitable spirit of man.

* * *

Lord, there must be forty thousand artists in New York City. Maybe more. Eight million bodies in The Naked City. That's what they used to say on the TV. Now there's more like eleven million, and all but ten of them are painters, all scrambling for a gallery to peddle their work, with maybe half a hundred galleries that handle contemporary art and each one handling no more than eight or ten artists. Artists carry their work door to door. They send out slides. Seven thousand guys each fork over a twenty-dollar entry fee for a competitive show that chooses thirty painters. Talk about desperation! And they talk: What's going to be hot next season? What's going to be the next trend? Who do you know? Who do you blow? Scramble for connections. Get a hold of some grass, some coke; slip it to the right person. Hell, I was no different. If the right opportunity came up, I might have done anything, no matter how depraved or unethical. But I didn't have to. I made it on dumb luck.

 I walked into Leo Garner's Broome Street Gallery with half a dozen rolled-up canvasses under my arm. It was during a goddamn opening! There were people asshole to elbow, all sipping wine and puffing cigarettes and yack-yack-yacking. I'd bolstered myself with beer and some fine Colombian weed, and I brazened right in there, wearing my overalls and my patched shirt and my whole gol-durn Redneck Dean Moriarty persona. I flipped those paintings out on the floor right in front of Leo Garner and said, "I wanna see these right up there on the wall."

 Leo Garner looked at me with a bemused smile. He looked at the paintings. He looked at the people who had scrunched back to make room. He looked back at the paintings. He looked at the poor artist whose opening I was ruining. He looked back at me, and he said, "All right. I'll give you a show. Come back and see me Monday afternoon. We'll work it out. What's your name, anyway, kid?"

 "Thank you, sir. Thanks a heap. I can't goddamn believe it."

 I was in shock. That sort of thing simply didn't happen. In a daze I gathered up my canvases, folks staring at me gape-mouthed, and I walked out muttering, "I'll be a double-damn hornswoggled motherfucker."

When I talked to Leo the next week he said, "You've got talent, son, but talent is only half of what it takes to be a successful artist. An artist today has got to be a media star, audacious, unique and charismatic. When you busted into my opening and laid your paintings out . . . normally I would have thrown you out, but there was something about the way you did it, and there was something about those paintings. It's always that indefinable something. Anyway, son, I think you can be a star."

And I was. I became a star so fast I was reeling from it. People invited me places. I never had to buy anything; folks were more than willing to give me anything I wanted: meals, clothes, booze, and sex. Cameras flashed everywhere I went. My mug was in all the magazines. I read about love affairs between me and people I didn't even know. I was invited to lecture, to show, to appear all over the world. All expenses paid. My paintings were in museums, magazines and textbooks. The funny thing was, hardly anybody ever bought my paintings. Two museums in ten years bought one each. One collector from New Orleans (I never even knew his name) bought most of what I sold.

For almost ten years I was just about the most famous living artist in America, but I barely made enough money to live. Leo got tired of me, and the critics started cooling off. Cooling off? Hell, it looked like an ice age coming. My work began to change, and the critics didn't like the changes. They started calling me a has-been whose undisciplined excesses were embarrassing and juvenile. That pissed me off. Wait 'till they see what Red Warner does next!

Time now expands and contracts. My life is a latex Halloween mask of some gleeful ghoul, twisted in the hands of a malicious child—me. I'm sitting in a green aluminum boat on the bayou, recuperating, a dirty bandage, warm beer, the taste of bile in my mouth. Confused memories. Brother Barnes in his black suit with his collar pinching his puffy, red neck, shouting, "Oh you vile generation of fornicators and blasphemers!" And I'm racing around the loft, swinging a butcher knife, and blood is gushing like gooey cadmium red squeezed from a tube, and the ceiling beams are swelling as if pumped with helium and they're swirling and swirling in a slow motion pool of crimson and black. Now I'm flat on my back on the hardwood floor in Cassie's Bank Street apartment, feeling like I'm crashing from some hideously bad acid trip, and she's cradling me in her arms and she is saying, "I love you, Travis. I love you. Everything's going to be all right."

Cassie cradles me in her tender embrace and the healing sway of the fishing boat on the bayou cradles me in its rock-a-by-baby rhythm, and gradually I sort out the past and put it behind me. I'm beginning to think that happiness is possible.

* * *

My last show at Leo's gallery was a disaster. The first review to come out said:

> The most disheartening thing a critic has to do is witness the total disintegration of a once great artist. The sheer madness of Red Warner's latest work, now at the Broome Street Gallery, attests to both the greatness of Warner's talent and its misuse.
>
> With his well-known reputation for high living and unbridled debauchery, it is no wonder that Red Warner's art has degenerated. He has mastered his technique, but seemingly does not know what to do with it. Warner's latest paintings are incoherent and void of design or purpose.

The rest of the so-called critics followed suit. I was dead as an artist in New York, and I knew it.

After that I went berserk. I only remember snatches of it. I got drunk, and I stayed drunk, and I went raving around town with Cassie at my heels, trying valiantly to hold me back, hanging on like a cowboy on a wild bull. I stormed into the gallery and slung a bucket of white enamel at one of my paintings. Some woman howled like a hyena and I said to her, right before I dashed out the door, "Now ain't that just purty as a picture."

I was high and I was flying and I was mad as hell, and my comings and goings were like debris in a tornado, all whirling and blowing and converging like the eye of the storm in a single moment and a single place, my loft. And Redneck Red Warner was the "I" of the storm.

Some two hundred or so idiots had crowded into my loft. God alone knows how they got there (I must have invited them). There were whores and pimps off the avenue and leather boys from the West Side bars, and a slew of artsy hangers-on, and some dame named Dianna who wore black lace undies and spike heels and nothing else. Couples were groping each other. Smoke was dense and the smell of marijuana was pungent.

Something snapped in my mind. Suddenly I was standing on top of a table in the kitchen area, shouting, preaching. Paragraphs from the Book of Job in the *Bible*—words that I never remember reading—spumed from my mouth. I was standing in the pulpit, calling them sinners to repentance, shouting with a righteous rhythm and providing the A-mens my own self.

"If in bed I say,"
"A-men!"
"When shall I arise?"
"When indeed, brother? When indeed? A-men."
"Then the night drags on."

"I am filled with restlessness . . ."

"Filled with it, filled with it!"

"Bless the Lord! Sweet baby Jesus."

"I am filled with restlessness until the dawn."

"Until the dawn. 'Till that mammy lovin' sun come peeking through."

"A-men, brother Ben. 'Taint much of a rooster but he loves his hen."

"Take me home, sweet Jesus!"

"My flesh is clothed with worms and scabs; my skin crawls and festers."

"Lawd have mercy!"

"My days are swifter than a weaver's shuttle; they come to an end without hope. Remember that my life—My life, sweet Jesus—it is like the wind; I shall not see happiness again."

I jumped off the table and grabbed a butcher knife from the counter and started weaving through the crowd, swinging the blade like a sword and screaming, "Scabs on humanity! Your days are numbered. Fornicators and liars, sucking off my fame and my talent."

They were laughing uneasily. Who was this madman? Was this an act? Hell-fire, Jack, how could they know? I didn't know.

I ripped my shirt off and flung it away. The idiots applauded. Some of them started ripping their shirts. Tattered garments in the air. I screamed, "I rend my garments! I'm a weird, wacko, washed up fool who can't even put his queer shoulder to the wheel (borrowing from Ginsberg). I used to be a simple country boy from Mississippi, but my pecker got me in a mess of trouble."

I whipped out my old tallywhacker right there in front of God and everybody, and commenced to prance around with it hanging loose like a sausage. Everybody laughed. I was a star once again. Still.

I said, "Looka dis muthuh! Looka heah! Look at dat old

floppy thang. Oh, my brothers and sisters, you ain't got no idea how much trouble a old floppy thang like that can cause."

I was crazier than ever. I plopped my meat on the table and raised the knife high over my head and shouted, "If thy eye offend thee, pluck it out! If thy hand offend thee, cut it off!"

I stood still as a statue and smiled like a leering ghoul and waited while the tension built. Then I brought the knife down with a horrible crash.

Epilogue
A Final Word From Johnny Lewis

I haven't seen Travis since I left him on the Mary Walker Bayou. Spending that time with Travis and Cassie was good. It was good to see the life they were living. And it was a relief to find out that his body was still intact—except for the missing fingers.

"Hell no, I didn't cut my thing off," he said to me, after I read his journal. "I ain't that crazy. It was my stupid fingers got in the way. That's what I cut off. I had no intention of hurting myself. It was all an act, but I was too stoned to pull it off. What'd I tell you happened to my fingers? That a gator got 'em? Yass! Thass what I always tell the tourists."